WHAT
HE
DID

BOOKS BY J.G. ROBERTS

THE DETECTIVE RACHEL HART SERIES
1. Little Girl Missing
2. What He Did

As Julia Roberts
THE LIBERTY SANDS TRILOGY
Life's a Beach and Then…
If He Really Loved Me…
It's Never Too Late to Say…

Christmas at Carol's
Carol's Singing

Alice in Theatreland
Time for a Short Story

One Hundred Lengths of the Pool

WHAT
HE
DID

J.G. ROBERTS

bookouture

Published by Bookouture in 2019

An imprint of StoryFire Ltd.
Carmelite House
50 Victoria Embankment
London EC4Y 0DZ

www.bookouture.com

ISBN: 978-1-78681-920-8
eBook ISBN: 978-1-78681-919-2

PROLOGUE

Neil plunged his hands into the warm, pungent earth, savouring the feel of soil and compost between his fingers. It was his choice not to wear gloves, although he knew he should to protect himself. Glimpses of sunlight filtered through the dense canopy of palm fronds as he dug away at the hole, the oppressive heat and humidity already creating damp patches beneath the arms of his polo shirt. This was the bit he liked the best: burying something gnarled and ugly, hiding it away from the world. He patted the soil until it felt firm to the touch, a satisfied smile spreading across his face, all traces of what lay beneath concealed in its shallow grave. Slowly, he struggled to his feet, arching his back and shaking the numbness from his left leg, which was always more troublesome in the colder months of the year.

The azure skies visible through the glass ceiling panels overhead belied the arctic conditions outside the Palm House of the world-famous botanical gardens in south-west London. Earlier that morning, Neil had woken to ice on the inside of the single-glazed windows of his bedsit in the attic of a Victorian terrace. It was a regular occurrence throughout the winter months if the overnight temperature dropped below freezing, but it was not so usual in early March. That morning, as his eyes traced the intricate icy patterns left by Jack Frost, which bore a remarkable resemblance to some of the exotic plants he worked with on a daily basis, he allowed himself to think about how different his life would have been if he hadn't sustained the injury that had crushed not only his leg but his dreams. He knew Elsa, his therapist, would not approve.

Neil had started seeing Elsa three years previously after he had tried to commit suicide, following a particularly big loss on the horses. It had seemed pointless carrying on living. He had no wife or children to miss him, and he had always felt like a burden to his parents since his injury. Over time, Elsa had helped him to realise that he had plenty to be thankful for. He was still only in his early forties, and he had a well-paid job that he loved. The only thing he was missing was someone to share his life with, which she believed was part of the reason he gambled. Because he had told her he was shy around women, she had suggested that he set himself up with a profile on a dating website. At the time, he hadn't felt sufficiently confident, but when Lydia, one of his female colleagues, had confided that she was on a dating website because she found it difficult to introduce herself to strangers in real life, Neil had taken the plunge and asked her to help him set up a profile. There had been a few matches in the early days, but no one he particularly liked the look of until, last month, Rose had come into his life. They were yet to meet because she travelled a lot with her work, but they chatted endlessly online and seemed to have a lot in common, not least a love of plants and flowers.

Smiling, Neil moved along to the next planting position and squatted down. *How funny that someone who loved flowers should be called Rose*, he thought. As he took the next hairy lily bulb in his hand and dropped it into the hole he had dug, a movement caught his eye.

He'd seen the woman before. She'd been in the Palm House every day that week with her sketch pad and pens. He assumed she must be a student. She glanced over in his direction and started to walk towards him. Neil dropped his head and concentrated on placing fresh earth over the bulb and firming it down.

'Excuse me,' she said, taking him by surprise. 'Do you work here?'

Her English was perfect but there was a hint of a European accent, maybe Spanish or Italian.

'Yes,' he said, indicating the logo on his polo shirt and feeling the blood rush to his cheeks.

'I wonder if you would take a look at these and tell me if they are any good,' she said, thrusting her sketch pad towards him.

'I'm no expert when it comes drawing. I just look after the plants,' he replied, flustered.

'But you know what they are supposed to look like,' she persisted.

Neil struggled to his feet, avoiding eye contact, and took the pad from her to look at the drawing she had been working on. The likeness was so good, it could have been a photograph.

'It looks pretty good to me, but like I said, I'm no expert,' he said, handing the pad back to her. 'Are you doing illustrations for a book?'

'No, it's just a hobby. I studied art and botany at school and I like to be precise with details,' she said, pushing her long dark hair behind her ear. 'I noticed you have a limp. What happened to your leg?'

She's definitely foreign, Neil thought, *English people are far too reserved to be that direct.*

'An old injury. A broken bone in my thigh that refused to heal properly. I'm lucky they didn't have to amputate.'

'You are lucky. It could have ruined your life.'

'In a way it did, although I prefer to think of it as changing the course of my life.'

'Oh?'

'You wouldn't think it to look at me now, but I was a professional footballer in my youth. The injury ended my career. My life would have been very different if I'd signed for Manchester United as I was supposed to,' Neil said, surprising himself at speaking so freely to a complete stranger, and a female one at that.

'I've heard of them. Their former manager is Portuguese, like me.'

'Ah yes, Jose, "the chosen one". I thought I detected an accent, although your English is very good,' Neil added quickly. 'Do you live here?'

'No, I'm just visiting. Have you ever been to Portugal?'

A shadow momentarily crossed Neil's face. 'Only once, a long time ago. Probably before you were born.'

'You didn't like it?'

'No, I did like it, but it was around the time of my injury and it brings back a lot of unhappy memories.'

'I'm sorry. I didn't mean to pry.'

'You're not. Like I said, it was all a long time ago.'

'It's good that you were able to build yourself a new life. Not everyone is that fortunate after bad things happen to them.'

'It took me a while. At first I had no idea what I wanted to do once it became apparent that I would never play football again,' Neil said, shaking his head as if trying to erase all memories of the months he had spent lying in his bed, in the darkened bedroom of his family home, wishing he was dead. 'Then one day I came here for a walk because my physiotherapist said I wasn't exercising my damaged leg enough, and I found it completely fascinating. When I got home, I looked into what qualifications I would need to get a job in horticulture and here I am, over twenty years later,' he said, moving along to his next planting position.

'Quite a change of direction. You must miss the lifestyle you had as a footballer.'

'You can't miss what you never really had. I was only eighteen when I got injured, and still living at home. I hadn't even passed my driving test, so there was no flashy Ferrari sitting on the drive. The big time was just about to start for me.'

'But the club you were at must have looked after you?'

'I'm very grateful to them. They paid for the best possible medical care, or I would probably have lost my leg. But once it was clear that I'd never play again, I was no use to them.'

'That's so sad. I hope your teammates rallied round.'

Neil finished patting earth over the latest lily corm and looked up at the woman. Until last month, he would never have felt comfortable having such an in-depth conversation with a female, but that was before he had started chatting to Rose online. She was easy to talk to, just like this woman, and it had boosted his confidence.

'At first, they used to visit me in hospital, but they had their own lives to get on with. And to be fair, it was probably my fault we lost touch. I wasn't very nice to be around.'

'Still, I'd have thought your friends would have stuck by you.'

Neil shrugged. 'I don't know if I would call them friends, really. They were people I worked with, and once I wasn't in football any more, we didn't have anything in common.'

'Didn't you have any other friends? People you grew up with?'

'I was always too busy playing football to have friends.'

'That's a shame. In the village where I come from, you stay friends for life. My best friend and I would do anything for each other. I'll probably give her some of these drawings. I particularly like this one,' she said, turning the pages of her pad until she arrived at a sketch of *Atropa belladonna*. 'Belladonna means beautiful woman in Italian, which suits her perfectly.'

Neil looked at the drawing. It was a perfect representation of the plant, with its shiny black berries not dissimilar to blackcurrants.

'It also goes under the name deadly nightshade,' he said. 'I hope you didn't get too close when you were drawing it. Even the slightest touch on the skin can cause a toxic reaction, and eating the berries can kill you.'

'You forget, I studied botany. I know all about the most toxic plants in nature. Most people would have no idea that ricin, one of the deadliest poisons, is produced from the innocent-sounding castor oil plant,' she said, flipping the page to show him a drawing of its flaming-red, sea-urchin-like flowers, and in doing so catching the back of Neil's hand with the nib of one of her drawing pens. 'Oh, I'm so sorry. Did that scratch you?'

*

Hours later, when Neil was writhing around in his bed in agony, sweating profusely and struggling to breathe, he began to wonder whether the encounter with the girl was as coincidental as it had seemed. Maybe the innocuous questions about his leg and whether he had ever visited Portugal were to confirm that she had the right person; she had even told him that she liked to be precise with details. His dying thought was: *this is no more than I deserve.*

CHAPTER ONE

8.10 p.m. – Saturday

DCI Rachel Hart checked her watch; it was ten past eight. They'd arranged to meet at eight at Trattoria Angelo, where they'd had their first date almost five months previously. On that occasion, Tim had been ten minutes late and she had been on the point of leaving when he had hurried in, out of breath and apologising profusely. She hated poor timekeeping, both in the workplace and socially, and had decided moments before he arrived that she wouldn't go on another date with him. Even if she really liked him, she felt his lateness showed a lack of respect. Within half an hour she had overturned that decision. He had been completely attentive, making sure her glass was topped up with wine and that she wasn't sitting in a draught created by the air conditioning. He was also very funny. *Who knew there could be so many amusing anecdotes in the world of a defence lawyer?*

They had been on several dates since, but this was the first time they'd been back to Angelo's, and for some reason she couldn't really justify, she had made a point of being late. She was regretting it now as she watched him get to his feet and stride across the restaurant towards her. It had been pretty childish, she realised, accepting his kiss on both cheeks before allowing him to take her coat and hand it to the waiter.

'I'm sorry I'm late.'

'No, you're not. You did it on purpose, and I don't blame you. You were just reminding me that I had the nerve to keep a beautiful lady waiting on our first date. I'm very lucky you forgave me sufficiently to agree to a second date.'

'Guilty as charged. I'm surprised you waited.'

'Was it a test?'

'Not really, but if it had been you would have passed with flying colours. Not that it matters, but were you early?'

'I've been here since the restaurant opened at half past seven. Only joking,' he said, reacting to Rachel's surprised expression, 'but I did get here before eight, just to be on the safe side. Do you want to get straight into the red wine, or do you fancy a glass of Prosecco first while we have a look at the menu?'

'Prosecco sounds good. I may stick with it, actually, I've got an early start in the morning.'

'Are you in the middle of a case?'

'No, work is a bit on the quiet side at the moment. It's all pretty mundane stuff, which means time to catch up with paperwork.' She pulled a face. 'Not my favourite pastime.'

'Be careful what you wish for. Before you know it, some dastardly criminal will be up to no good and you'll be rushed off your feet. I'm being purely selfish, of course. When that happens, you won't have any time to come out with me. So, if you're not working in the morning, what's with the early start?'

Although Rachel had been seeing Tim for almost five months, she hadn't told him about her sister Ruth. She never told any of her boyfriends about her sister. There didn't really seem much point in allowing them that amount of access into her personal life when she had no intention of pursuing a lasting relationship. The moment lust started to feel like love, and it moved from a purely physical relationship to something more meaningful, she would pull the plug. Looking at Tim now, with his intense green eyes and sandy hair just showing the first signs of grey at the temples, she knew the moment was fast approaching.

'I've been promising myself for weeks to have a proper spring clean, and tomorrow is the allocated day,' she said, the lie tripping easily off her tongue.

'Does that mean you're not coming back to mine tonight?' he asked, unable to hide his disappointment.

'Did I say that?' she said, looking at him from beneath her eyelashes. 'It just means I won't be staying for breakfast.'

'I make fantastic smashed avocado on toast with poached eggs.'

'Tempting, but the answer is still no. Shall we order? All this talk of food is making me hungry,' she said, trying to change the subject.

'I could always come to yours,' he said, unwilling to give it up as a lost cause. 'I'm a dab hand with a pair of Marigolds and a scouring pad.'

Why can't I just be honest with him? Rachel thought, as she watched the waiter approach with their bottle of Prosecco in an ice bucket. *Why can't I tell him that I love spending time with him and that sex with him is the best I've ever had, but that I can't allow myself to love him? Because*, she reflected, *he wants a relationship, maybe even a wife, and if you tell him that, you'll probably never see him again.*

'Another time, maybe. Cheers,' she said instead, holding up her glass to chink against his before taking a sip. She could read the disappointment in his eyes, but it wasn't the first time she'd seen that reaction from a boyfriend, and she was pretty sure it wouldn't be the last.

CHAPTER TWO

11.50 p.m. – Saturday

Maddy Shaw could feel the trickle of sweat running down her spine. Within moments she knew she would be engulfed by a hot flush or, as she preferred to call it, 'a personal tropical moment'. It was very distracting, making it difficult to follow the words on the autocue that her fellow news presenter, Callum Baines, was currently delivering.

The story was about yet another victim of a stabbing, bringing the number of deaths in London to thirty for the year so far. *We're not even at the end of March*, Maddy thought, fanning her hand in front of her face in the hope that her floor manager Laura might realise she was overheating and turn the air conditioning up. *Not that it will make much difference; by the time it's kicked in I'll have finished for the night and be halfway home.* Out of the corner of her eye she could see Laura in conversation with Jordana and Blake, the presenters who were taking over at midnight for the graveyard shift.

Clearly Maddy's fanning action had gone unnoticed not only by her floor manager, but apparently by her producer and director in the gallery, too. She tried to refocus her attention on the stabbing report. The boy had been on his way home from his job as a barista in a well-known chain. He had been attacked less than a hundred yards from his front door, where he had bled to death in his mother's arms. *He was only twenty-two, the same age as my Siena*, Maddy thought, a shiver running through her body despite the heat she was experiencing. *What is wrong with the youth of today? Is it their inability to make the distinction between real life and virtual reality?* In the stupid games they played, people got shot or stabbed and came back to life, but in the real world, death meant death: the end. She was relieved that her daughter had never been interested in computer games. Mind you, real life had been something of a drama for her of late. *Who am I kidding?* she thought. The drama hadn't only been Siena's, it had affected the whole family.

Maddy was suddenly aware that Callum had stopped speaking. She stumbled slightly as she led into the final story of the bulletin.

'And finally, following its closure to the public for the past fortnight after the unexplained death of one of its employees, Neil Edison, the botanical gardens will be reopening its world-famous Palm House on Monday. In a statement issued earlier today, a spokesperson said, "Extensive tests have been carried out on all the potentially harmful plants on exhibition and there is no evidence to suggest that they were a contributing factor in the death of Mr Edison. As a precautionary measure, the most toxic plants have been removed from display while further testing is carried out, and there will be more warning signs alerting the general public to the potential hazards of touching and ingesting the plants".

'Edison, who had worked at the gardens for eighteen years, would have been well aware of the dangerous nature of some of the plants in his care, according to the spokesperson. The forty-two-year-old was found dead at his home in North Sheen a week after failing to report for work. While expressing their sadness at his death, colleagues have said that he was a loner and prone to episodes of depression. It is believed Mr Edison took his own life. Now to find out what the weather has in store for us over the coming week, here's Shavani.'

*

'Are you okay?' Callum asked as he and Maddy unclipped their lapel microphones and headed out of the studio. 'You seemed a bit distracted.'

'Just tired, I guess. My shifts have been hellish lately.'

'Are you in tomorrow?'

'No, I've got a day off, thank God. But I'm back on air at midday on Monday. I hate that slot on a weekday, particularly Mondays. The traffic on the M4 is a nightmare when I'm trying to get in for make-up by nine.'

'It does seem a bit of a quick turnaround from lates to earlies. I'm not in until Wednesday. What have you done to upset Byron Farley?'

'Got old.'

'You're not old, and anyway, you look fantastic for your age.'

'I hate those three little words.'

'Which three little words?'

'Well, obviously not "you look fantastic", or "you're not old". "For your age" is what people start saying when you are old, but you just wear it well. I think I'm actually more than the combined age of those two,' Maddy said, indicating the monitor showing Jordana Starr and Blake Clarkson, two of the more recent presenters to join *News 24/7*, who were now live on air delivering the same news stories that she and Callum had been presenting for the past four hours. There had been a lot of new faces lately, which had made Maddy and others who had been at the channel a long time nervous about their position. Farley had made it clear that he was looking for budget cuts, and the most effective way of achieving that was to replace the more experienced presenters, who commanded high salaries, with those who were younger and cheaper. *Cheaper in every respect*, Maddy thought. She hadn't got to where she was by sleeping with the boss, but Byron Farley had made it abundantly clear that he was looking for a prime-time slot for his latest conquest, the twenty-three-year-old brunette currently reading the news.

'Well, neither of them is a patch on you when it comes to presentation,' Callum said protectively, 'and Jordana's face will probably cave in by the time she's forty with the amount of Botox and fillers she's already injecting.'

'Crazy, isn't it? I don't understand why someone as young and pretty as her would do that.'

'I blame the need to always be "selfie-ready".'

'My arms aren't long enough to take a decent selfie,' Maddy said, reaching her arm out as though holding a phone and pouting. 'Or maybe Farley is right, and I need a bit of help from that sort of stuff. I've been digging my heels in because I don't like the idea of injecting poison into my face. It hasn't been around long enough for anyone to be completely sure of the long-term effects. A bit like Victorian ladies using arsenic to whiten their skin. They had no idea they were slowly poisoning themselves.'

'Unlike that gardener in our final story. It sounds as though he knew exactly what he was doing.'

'Well, he certainly had access to all the ingredients to make himself a deadly cocktail. And his work colleagues did say he was suffering from depression.'

'It's tragic what people will do when they think there's no point in carrying on living. Shit. Sorry, Maddy, I wasn't thinking. Me and my big mouth.'

'It's all right, Cal, I think we're over the worst of it now. I'd rather you were able to speak to me normally than constantly worrying that you're going to say something to upset me.'

'Give Siena a hug from me.'

'Will do. And you and Josh must come round for dinner again soon, then you can give her a hug yourself.'

'Let's get it in the diary. Are you off home now?'

'Where else would I be going?' Maddy asked, a hint of amusement in her voice.

'You could come clubbing with me. It's only midnight, early for a Saturday night out.'

'One of these days I'll shock you and take you up on your offer,' Maddy said, reaching up to kiss him on the cheek. 'Have a great night out, and I'll see you at some point next week.'

'Safe journey home,' Callum said, disappearing into his dressing room.

As Maddy was taking her make-up off she found herself thinking about the death of the gardener. She wondered what the final straw had been that had prompted Neil Edison to take his own life. *What a dreadful waste of the gift of life suicide is*, she thought. If only he had reached out for help. But, if he was a bit of a loner as his work colleagues had suggested, maybe he had no one to reach out to. *It's funny*, she thought, creating raccoon eyes with her creamy make-up remover before gently wiping away all traces of mascara, liner and eyeshadow with a cloth, *that name has a familiar ring to it*. But try as she might, she couldn't think where she recognised it from.

CHAPTER THREE

8.45 a.m. – Sunday

The aroma of freshly baked bread welcomed Maddy as she pushed open the kitchen door on Sunday morning. Before she had headed upstairs to bed the previous evening, it had only taken three minutes to put all the ingredients in the machine and set the timer to start making a loaf while they were sleeping. As she had brushed her teeth, she had been forced to admit that the machine was one of the best Christmas presents her husband, Simon, had ever bought her, even if at the time she had been less than enthusiastic.

Maddy had been dropping hints about a diamond-encrusted angel-wing pendant that she really wanted for several weeks in the run-up to Christmas three years previously, and she'd been convinced that Simon had picked up on them. That was until he handed over a huge box wrapped in purple metallic paper. But she hadn't given up hope completely, because the gift tag read: *For a woman with great taste*. Right up to the last minute when she started to tear the paper off, she had wondered if it was a Russian-doll-type parcel where she would eventually find the jewellery hidden in the middle. Maddy could still remember his childlike expression when he said, 'You see, I do listen to you. You're always going on about how much you like freshly baked bread, and now you can have it whenever you want. Did you get the clue on the tag? A woman of great *taste*?' She had managed to hide her disappointment and had treated herself to the pendant with her next pay packet; the pendant that now hung around her daughter's neck as a symbol of hope and protection.

There's no denying that I love bread, she thought, lifting the pan out of the machine and tipping the golden-crusted loaf onto the wire cooling tray, *but as for having it whenever I want, no chance if I want to stay a size 12.* It was a treat reserved for Sunday mornings along with fried eggs and grilled bacon and tomatoes, and whatever was left was usually finished off as toast on Monday and Tuesday mornings before another carb-free week. *At least Byron Farley can't have a go at me about my weight*, she thought, heaping ground coffee into the machine and flicking the switch. *I could still fit into the first-ever suit I wore on air at News 24/7, although I doubt it would sit well with the new image the channel is going for.* Hemlines were up and necklines down in an attempt to win back viewers from *News Today*, the latest twenty-four-hour news channel to hit satellite TV. Ironically, they had tried to headhunt Maddy to launch *News Today* until they found out from her agent the salary she commanded. It seemed to Maddy that Farley had been on her case since around the same time, which could be coincidental, but was more likely a result of one CEO expressing to another that he thought they were overpaying some of their more seasoned presenters.

'Mmm, something smells good,' Simon said, walking across the room and planting a kiss on his wife's lips.

'Coffee and freshly baked bread, soon to be joined by bacon. We'd probably sell the house instantly if it was on the market.'

'We don't need homely aromas to sell this place. People would be falling over themselves the moment we put a For Sale board outside.'

'True, but we'd struggle to find anywhere that comes even close in terms of the perfect home, so let's hope we never have to,' Maddy said, returning her attention to slicing beef tomatoes and therefore missing the shadow that flitted briefly across her husband's face.

'What time did you get in last night?' she asked as she pushed the pan, now laden with back bacon and tomatoes, under the grill.

'Just after you, I think, but you were already snoring.'

'I don't snore,' she said, throwing a tea towel at her grinning husband.

'You think? I'll record you one of these days.'

'Were you drowning your sorrows? I heard you lost again.'

'Did you really have to add "again"?'

'Sorry, but they're not on a great run at the moment.'

'It's hardly surprising. They're a bunch of overpaid, talentless nobodies who all seem to think they're the next Lionel Messi or Cristiano Ronaldo. They all earn more than me, even the kids coming through from the academy and signing their first contract, which does nothing for respect and discipline. It wasn't like that in my day. We were expected to clean the first team players' boots, even if we'd been called up to play alongside them the previous week. I can't wait to get them on the training pitch first thing in the morning and give them a piece of my mind.'

'Won't that just antagonise them? You want them on your side, don't you?'

'Well, what do you suggest? If I tell them they were unlucky with the result yesterday, they'll just carry on doing their own thing and that doesn't help them improve, and certainly doesn't help my position. The trouble is, if the players decide they don't want to put in a shift for you, you lose the dressing room and if that happens, you're history. It's always the manager's fault.'

'Are you genuinely worried about losing your job?' Maddy asked, trying to keep the anxiety she felt from her voice. She hadn't mentioned anything to Simon about the meeting she'd been summoned to with Byron Farley because she hadn't wanted to distract him from his preparations for the game yesterday. Farley had accused her of bullying Jade, one of the make-up girls, and warned her that that type of behaviour was not acceptable and could result in suspension or even dismissal if it happened again. *A warning because I questioned a make-up girl about why she'd applied emerald-green eyeshadow when she knows full well I normally wear shades of brown…* She'd had to promise to be more considerate in the way she spoke to junior members of staff in the future. *Talk about the snowflake generation*, she'd thought as she'd left his office, making a great effort to close the door quietly behind her rather than slamming it as she had felt like doing.

'It goes with the territory,' Simon said. 'Seven defeats and a draw from the last eight league games, and we're out of the FA Cup. I'm not going to lie – the pressure's on.'

As he finished speaking, the kitchen door opened. They both went silent as Siena entered the room. Neither of them wanted to talk about the possibility of Simon losing his job in front of her when she had enough to deal with already.

'Were you talking about me?'

'No, of course not, love. What do you fancy for breakfast?'

'I'm not hungry,' she said, slumping into one of the pale grey dining chairs.

'Come on, you have to eat something. I've made fresh bread. I can do you toast if you don't fancy eggs and bacon.'

'I said I'm not hungry.'

'Or cereal?' Maddy persisted.

'What's the point? If I don't eat, I'll just fade away and die, which suits me. I've got nothing to live for now, anyway.'

'Don't talk like that, Siena. You know it upsets your mother.'

'Why does it always have to be about her? I'm the one whose life is over.'

Maddy turned back to the cooker. She could feel tears welling at the backs of her eyes, but she was determined not to let them fall. She had wept bucketloads in the days immediately following the phone call that had changed her happy, outgoing daughter into a suicidal wreck.

'You're being ridiculous,' Simon said. 'You've got your whole life ahead of you. You were too good for him, anyway.'

'You would say that. Rob knew you didn't like him. He always used to say, "nobody's ever going to be good enough for you in your dad's eyes", and he was right.'

'So it's my fault, is it?'

Maddy spun round and shot a warning look at her husband. 'It's nobody's fault,' she said in an attempt to smooth things over. 'Things like this happen. We just need to try and help you through this difficult period.'

'I thought you understood, Mum,' Siena said, pushing her chair back from the table. 'He is the love of my life. I'll love him to the day I die, and hopefully that won't be too far away.'

Maddy tried to reach out for her daughter, but Siena pushed past and ran out of the room. She rounded on Simon. 'Why did you do that?'

'Do what? I was trying to protect you. She's put you through hell this past month.'

'She isn't doing it on purpose,' Maddy hissed. 'Her heart is broken. She honestly believes she'll never love anyone ever again.'

'You're as bad as she is. By pandering to her you're making her believe the things she's saying are true. He was her first proper boyfriend, and they were totally unsuited. Why can't you just be honest and tell her that?'

'And then what? Have to deal with her taking another overdose of headache pills? Have you forgotten that we nearly lost her? If I hadn't got her to hospital as quickly as I did, we wouldn't even be having this discussion – she'd be dead.'

'You're so bloody dramatic. She's not the first young woman to have her heart broken by a bloke and, let's be honest, she won't be the last. It was a cry for help, nothing more.'

'You weren't here, so how can you be so sure?'

A shrill, piercing sound interrupted the angry exchange. Maddy turned round to see smoke billowing from the cooker and promptly burst into tears.

'I'll deal with it,' Simon said, squeezing his wife's shoulder as he rushed across the kitchen and pulled the charred remains of their breakfast out from under the grill.

CHAPTER FOUR

9.45 a.m. – Sunday

Bella ran her hands down her pale blue uniform to smooth out the creases that had started to form during her train and bus journey from Staines to Mountview Private Hospital. She hadn't intended to go into work until Monday, which would have allowed her a bit more time to unpack her things and run a couple of loads through the washing machine after getting back from visiting her elderly grandmother in Portugal last night, but the nursing agency had rung her just over an hour ago in a bit of a panic. The nurse who was supposed to be covering holiday leave had called in sick and some of the agency girls wouldn't work on Sundays because of family commitments, which didn't apply to Bella.

She pushed the revolving door and stepped out on the other side onto a teal-coloured carpet with a small paisley design on it. The walls of the reception area were painted ivory and were adorned with framed modern prints, and the chairs were upholstered wood rather than plastic. There was no mistaking the fact that this hospital was private rather than NHS, despite the huge efforts to make government-run hospitals less institutional. Bella walked up to the main reception desk, behind which sat two women tapping computers, neither of whom looked familiar from her previous shifts there.

'Can I help you, dear?' the older of the two women asked, looking up at her.

'I'm Isabella Viegas, but everyone calls me Bella,' she said. 'Melrose Nursing Agency sent me.'

'You've made good time. We only got the confirmation thirty minutes ago to say you were on your way. I'm sorry you've had to come in on a Sunday, but we were already very short-staffed before Nadia called in sick.'

'I'm glad I could help, but I hope the agency told you I need to finish at 5 p.m.'

'Yes, they did,' the woman said, consulting her notepad. 'Is this your first time here?'

'No, I've covered a few shifts previously.'

'You're up on the second floor today, in the residential wing.'

'I haven't worked in that section before.'

'Okay, then I'll take you up and introduce you to the team,' the woman replied, rising from her desk before leading Bella out of the reception area. 'It can get quite busy at the weekends with family visits, so we like to get the rounds done early. I'm Maureen, by the way,' she said, swiping a card to gain them access through a door which said STAFF ONLY.

Less than ten minutes later, introductions complete, Maureen left Bella with the charge nurse, Rita, who brought her up to speed with what was required of her.

'Most of the patients in this wing have been with us for some time. They all have their own rooms, but they have a communal area for group activities and their own cafeteria for lunch and dinner, although they can have meals in their rooms if they are having a particularly difficult day. One of the most crucial things when dealing with our residents is making sure they get their medication on time, as they can get agitated or even turn violent, but I'm sure you remember that from when you were last here. When did you say that was?'

'About three or four weeks ago. I was looking after a woman around my age who was recovering after taking an overdose of headache tablets.'

'That would have been Siena Shaw. Everyone was talking about it because she's the daughter of the newsreader Maddy Shaw. It just goes to show that money can't buy you happiness.'

But at least she had the support of her family, Bella thought, remembering seeing Siena's anxious parents sitting either side of their daughter's bed, each holding one of her hands in their own, *something else money can't buy*. 'Is she still here? She seemed to like me, and I could pop in to see how she's doing.'

'No, she was discharged, and anyway, I'm not sure you'll have that much spare time on your hands as we're still one person down on preferred patient–nurse staffing levels. Quite a few of the residents gather in the day room on a Sunday morning before their visitors arrive, so I'll take you along there in a minute and introduce you. Some of the patients can get unsettled by new faces, so let them approach you rather than the other way around.'

The first four hours of Bella's shift had gone very smoothly. No one had reacted badly to her introduction into their world. The facility was teeming with visitors, and she couldn't help thinking how lucky the residents were. Not only did they live in surroundings more akin to a five-star hotel or an apartment building than a hospital, but most of them had people who cared enough about them to spend their Sunday visiting them.

The majority of residents were elderly and were suffering from dementia or Alzheimer's, but there was also an area that housed younger people. It made Bella sad to see men and women of a similar age to her living in a place that kept them safe but away from the outside world. *Mind you*, she thought, *if it wasn't for their families coming up with the money to keep them here, some of them might well be living on the streets, or even worse if the drugs or equipment they used were contaminated.* She knew from the medication chart she had studied that most of the younger patients were trying to beat addictions to drugs or alcohol, but there were also a couple of inmates whose medication suggested that they were simply unable to cope with normal everyday life outside the confines of the hospital. One of them was Ruth Hart, who hadn't been in the day room earlier, and as she tapped lightly on her door, she wondered what kind of reception she would get.

'Come in.'

Bella pushed the door open. An attractive, well-dressed woman in her mid-thirties with a neat shoulder-length bob was sitting in one of the two chairs by the window. *She looks so normal*, Bella thought. *Out in the world, no one would ever guess there was anything wrong with her at all, but sometimes the people you suspect the least are the ones to be feared the most.*

'Hello, I'm Bella,' she said, smiling. 'How are you doing today?'

'I haven't seen you here before.'

She sounds pretty balanced too, Bella thought. 'No. This is my first time in the residential wing. I've brought your medication.'

There was the sound of a toilet flushing and the door to the en suite bathroom opened. A woman who was very similar in appearance, but slightly more dishevelled and with an altogether wilder look in her eyes stopped in her tracks.

'Ruthie,' said the woman sitting by the window, 'this is Bella. She's new.'

'I don't want her in my room. Make her go away.'

'That's not very friendly of you. She's only bringing your tablets.'

'I'm not having them from her. She might be trying to poison me.'

'Why would she do that? She's a nurse, like all the other nurses who look after you. I'm Rachel, by the way,' the woman by the window said, getting up from the chair and crossing the room to shake Bella's hand. 'You've probably realised by now that Ruth and I are twins.'

'I thought as much. You're very alike. I'm supposed to watch Ruth take her medication, but I can leave the tablets with you if my being here is upsetting her.'

Rachel turned to her sister. 'That's kind of Bella, but we wouldn't want to get her into trouble, would we? She could lose her job if someone found out that she didn't supervise you having your tablets.'

Ruth's head tilted to one side. She looked as though she was considering what her sister had said, until she spoke.

'Where are you from? You're not English.'

'No, I'm not. I'm from Portugal.'

'Then why are you here?'

Bella caught her breath. The question was very direct.

'Don't they have sick people for you to care for in Portugal?' Ruth continued, oblivious to the momentary discomfort she had caused.

'Of course they do,' Bella said, releasing her breath, 'but there are plenty of nurses in Portugal and not enough here, so I came where I was needed.'

The answer seemed to satisfy Ruth. She smiled and walked across the room towards Bella, holding her hand out for the tablets before swallowing them down with a glass of water from her bedside table.

'You're nice. I like you. Will you come here again?'

'I hope so.'

'I hope so too, then you can teach me to speak Portuguese.'

'That might take a while. It's not the easiest of languages, but I can teach you your first word right now. "*Obrigada*" – it means thank you.'

'I always thought it was *obrigado*,' Rachel said, relieved that Ruth had taken a liking to the nurse.

'If you're a man, it is. For us girls it's *obrigada*, but lots of people get it wrong, even Portuguese people.'

'Well, I won't. I like to get things right,' Ruth said.

'Me too,' Bella said, ticking the medication chart at the foot of Ruth's bed and heading towards the door. 'Enjoy the rest of your day.'

CHAPTER FIVE

'Can I do anything to help?' Siena asked.

'Well, you could set the table, if you wouldn't mind,' Maddy replied, lifting the roasting tin out of the oven and placing it on a glass chopping board to allow the joint of beef to rest for fifteen minutes.

Following her outburst that morning, Siena had spent the rest of the day in her bedroom. At lunchtime, Maddy had taken up a cheese sandwich and a glass of summer fruits squash, but when she had knocked on her daughter's door there was no reply. She had to exercise enormous restraint not to go into Siena's room uninvited. 'I'll leave this out here for you, then,' she had called out, before retreating downstairs to the kitchen. When she had checked an hour later, the glass of squash had gone but the plate with the sandwich was still there – the edges of the bread were starting to curl upward as they dried out.

'And maybe you could give your dad a call in a few minutes, to carve the meat.'

'Okay. Where is he?' Siena said, opening the wide drawer that housed the cutlery and selecting three lots of knives and forks, before picking up three placemats and carrying everything over to the dining table.

'He's in the den, watching football. You'd think he'd get enough of it all week, but he insists that watching the Premier League teams reminds him why he still loves the game so much. I'm sorry if he upset you this morning, he didn't mean to.'

'I know, but he doesn't understand how I'm feeling, and sometimes I wonder if you really do either, or if you're just saying things to make me feel better.'

'I think it's harder for men to understand stuff like this. They see everything in black and white, with no shades of grey. He doesn't understand that while Rob's feelings for you may have changed, you still love him as much as you ever have and you're hoping that he'll realise he's made a big mistake.'

*

It seemed so much longer than four weeks ago that Siena's perfect world had come tumbling down. The two of them had been chatting in the kitchen, catching up on each other's day at work, while Maddy was making the cheese sauce to pour over steamed cauliflower and broccoli for their dinner. Siena's phone had started ringing and her face had lit up when she'd seen Rob's name on the screen.

'Don't be long, this will be ready in ten minutes,' Maddy had said as her daughter headed upstairs to her bedroom to take the call in private.

'Okay, Mum,' she'd said, 'he can always ring me back later if we haven't finished.'

It was the last time she had seen her daughter's face happy and smiling. A few minutes later, as she was whisking the skimmed milk into the butter and flour mixture bubbling in the saucepan, there was a scream and an almighty crash from Siena's room, directly above the kitchen. Instantly, Maddy had turned off the gas rings on the cooker, run upstairs and flung the bedroom door open, terrified of what she might find. Her daughter's computer was lying on the floor, hence the loud crash, and Siena was sitting on her bed, as white as a sheet, with tears spilling down her cheeks.

'Whatever's the matter?' Maddy had said, rushing across the room and flinging her arms around her distraught daughter.

'He's dumped me,' Siena had cried.

Maddy had felt a tiny flutter of relief that it wasn't anything more serious before reality kicked in.

'My life's over, Mum. Without Rob there's no point carrying on.'

'Shush, darling,' she had said, rocking Siena to and fro as she had done so many times throughout her life when she had needed comforting. 'Maybe he wasn't the right one for you.'

'No, Mum, you're wrong. I love him. I'll never love anyone else,' she'd said, pulling away from her mother and flinging herself onto her pillows, sobbing hysterically.

Maddy had felt helpless. Nothing she said or did could calm her devastated daughter. When Simon had got home from an evening match more than four hours later, he had found his wife sitting propped up against Siena's headboard, embracing their daughter, who had fallen into an exhausted sleep.

'What's going on?' he had mouthed at his wife.

'Rob,' she had mouthed back, slowly drawing her finger across her neck in a cut-throat action.

'Dead?'

Maddy had shaken her head at him, and the penny had dropped.

'Good riddance,' he'd whispered, 'I never could stand the bloke.'

They had both thought Siena would quickly get over the shock and that her life would return to normal, but they were terribly wrong. A few days later, Siena had tried to take her own life by swallowing several packets of headache pills washed down with a bottle of vodka. If it hadn't been for Maddy coming home unexpectedly early from work, they would have lost her.

*

Much to Simon's relief, dinner went surprisingly smoothly. Siena ate the small amount of food Maddy served her and even asked for more broccoli. *It's not enough to sustain a small child for long, let alone a fully-grown adult*, Simon thought, *but at least she's eaten something.* She had also helped clear the dishes from the table and stack them in the dishwasher before going through to the lounge to join her parents. They were all settled in front of the television watching an episode of *Vera* when the phone rang. Simon picked it up.

'Hello?' he said.

'Can I speak to Siena?'

'Hold on a minute,' he said, putting his hand over the mouth-piece, and getting up off the sofa. 'You girls carry on, I need to take this in the den.' He closed the lounge door behind him and crossed the hallway to his den, closing that door behind him too. 'What the hell do you think you're doing ringing this number?'

'I'm ringing to see if Siena's okay. I thought if I rang her mobile, she might not answer.'

'Well, why would you think that?' Simon asked, his voice laced with sarcasm.

'Because last time we spoke she was crying and upset. Look, whatever you may think of me, we were going out together for two years and I care about her,' Rob said.

'You've got a funny way of showing it. Two days after getting back from a fortnight in the Dominican Republic together, you dump her, out of the blue, because you couldn't see a future with her. Bullshit. Besotted as Siena was with you, even she saw through your pitiful lie about no one else being involved in the break-up. She did some checking up on you.'

'What do you mean?'

'Social media, Rob. You'd be surprised what you can discover when you're friends with someone on Facebook. Siena knows about Izzy, including when you first added her as a friend,' Simon said, pausing slightly to allow the information to sink in. 'For an intelligent man, that was a pretty stupid thing to do, unless, of course, you wanted Siena to find out. Maybe that was it,' he continued, as though the thought had just occurred to him. 'Despite acting the big hero, with three tours of duty in Afghanistan behind you, you couldn't tell a girl ten years your junior that you'd found someone you liked better than her. You're pathetic!'

'Look, I can understand why you're angry. Trust me, I didn't mean for it to happen like this. I would never willingly have hurt Siena. I'd been having doubts about us for a while and then Izzy came into my life and I knew she was my "one". There was no easy way to tell Siena without breaking her heart.'

'Oh, man up! If this other girl was "the one" in your eyes, you should have told my daughter that it was over between the two of you before you started seeing her. That's what any decent bloke would do. If Siena had known you'd been seeing someone else behind her back, she might not have taken an overdose and tried to kill herself.'

'It wasn't like that. Izzy knew I had a girlfriend, so we were just friends to start with. In fact, it was Izzy who told me earlier this evening that she'd seen something on Facebook about Siena taking an overdose. I had no idea the break-up had affected her so deeply. That's why I'm ringing. I wanted to check that she's doing all right.'

'Yes, she is, no thanks to you,' Simon said, not wanting to reveal that his daughter was still struggling to come to terms with being dumped and that she continued to believe Rob was the love of her life. 'You might be a hero on the battlefield, but in real life you're nothing but a coward.'

'Is there anything I can do to try and make amends?'

'Stay out of our lives,' Simon said. *The last thing I need right now is anything else to worry about*, he thought. 'I'm warning you, if you ever ring this number again or try to contact Siena in any way, you'll be sorry. I know plenty of people who would happily wring the neck of a cheating, cowardly arsehole like you.'

'You should remember who you're talking to, Simon. Soldiers are trained to kill and aren't afraid to when they are under attack,' Rob said, his voice low and menacing.

'Are you threatening me?'

'I'm just reminding you that I'm better placed than most to defend myself.'

'You don't scare me. Now piss off out of our lives,' Simon said, disconnecting the call.

His hands were shaking as he walked over to his bar area and poured himself a large glass of brandy before slumping down on the sofa. *Arrogant prick, who the hell does he think he is?* Simon thought, feeling the familiar burn at the back of his throat as he took a sip. He swirled the amber liquid around in the glass, wondering how he would have made it through the past few months without his friend, Rémy Martin. He massaged his forehead with his free hand. *It's no good, I can't go on like this,* he thought, *I'm going to have to tell Maddy the truth, whatever the consequences.*

Right on cue, there was a knock at the door and Maddy popped her head around it.

'Everything okay? I thought I heard raised voices.'

'Come in and shut the door,' Simon said.

'What is it? Who was that on the phone?'

'Rob.'

'You're kidding. What was he ringing for?'

'Probably to try and assuage his guilty conscience. I've never liked that bloke. Rude, sullen and with table manners like a pig. I don't know what Siena ever saw in him.'

'None of us can really explain what attracts us to another person,' Maddy said, 'but I take your point. We went out of our way to make him feel welcome in this house, even though we could both see he wasn't right for her. I guess I just hoped she would grow out of her infatuation.'

'Well, hopefully she's starting to now. I'm glad she found out he'd been cheating on her. His shiny suit of armour must be looking a little tarnished now, even through her rose-tinted spectacles.'

'I wouldn't be so sure of that, if I were you. When she came downstairs earlier, she showed me a letter she spent the afternoon writing to him. After everything he's said and done, she still loves him and would still take him back. She'd poured her heart out on the page, it was so sad to read.'

'Chrissakes! What's she planning on doing with the letter?'

'She asked me if I thought she should send it. I wanted to say no, but she had such a look of hope in her eyes, I didn't have the heart to. I said she should sleep on it for a few nights before deciding whether or not to send it.'

'He's moved on, Maddy. We shouldn't encourage her with false hope,' Simon said, going over to his wife and enveloping her in a hug.

'I know you're right, but I'm just so scared that if we try and move her on too quickly, she'll do something stupid again.'

'Then we'll take things slowly. Hopefully we've heard the last from Rob. I told him never to ring this number again or I'd contact some mates who'd happily wring his cowardly neck.'

'You didn't!' Maddy said, pulling out of the embrace, a look of horror on her face.

'I bloody did, and can you believe he had the nerve to threaten me back?'

'Be careful, Simon. Whatever else soldiers are, they're trained killers. Don't pick a fight with him, because you could easily end up on the losing side.'

'Thanks for the vote of confidence. Look, I don't think Siena needs to know it was him on the phone, so when we go back into the lounge, I'll say it was Kenny from work. All right?'

'There's no need to say anything, she's gone up to bed. She wasn't enjoying the programme because she said *Vera* reminded her of

Rob's mum. It was probably the Geordie accent. I think I'll go up too, if you don't mind. I hate the switch from late to early shift.'

'All right, I'll just be a few minutes while I finish my nightcap,' he said, raising his brandy glass in her direction. 'We'll get through this, love, as long as we stick together,' he added, as she pulled the door closed behind her.

Poor choice of words, he thought, knocking back the rest of his brandy. *If I hadn't agreed to do that, I wouldn't be in the mess I'm in now.* He went over to his desk, opened up his leather-bound diary and read the note again before tucking it back into a pocket in the front cover. *I'll talk to her after work tomorrow*, he thought. *This has got to stop*.

CHAPTER SIX

6.30 a.m. – Monday

Maddy tilted her head backward, allowing water from the overhead drench shower to cascade over her face in an attempt to wash away sleep. It really was the worst time slot to have on a Monday, and she was pretty sure Byron Farley had arranged it on purpose. Not content with reprimanding her over the alleged bullying incident, he was clearly trying everything in his power to force her to quit so that *News 24/7* wouldn't have to give her a golden handshake to get rid of her.

It was all so different from Byron's early days with the company, when a mutual friend had introduced them because she knew that Maddy would help him find his feet. *It's amazing what short memories some people have*, she thought, working the shampoo into a lather more aggressively than was good for her scalp. *Without my help he probably wouldn't have made it beyond his six-month probation period. Now he's got his feet firmly under the table, he's a 'yes man' to the CEO, whose main priority is coming in under budget at the end of the financial year.*

Their once-good professional relationship had been steadily in decline for a couple of years, but since Jordana had appeared on the scene in early January, it had positively nosedived, and Maddy found herself tiptoeing over broken glass every time they were in the building together. She rinsed the shampoo and applied conditioner, leaving it on while she speedily washed her body. It wouldn't do to give him more ammunition by being late. *I hope the traffic won't be too bad*, she thought, stepping out of the shower and towelling herself dry.

Fifteen minutes after stepping into the shower and with her shoulder-length hair still damp, she tapped on Siena's door.

'I'm off now, darling. I should be home around seven.'

There was no reply. Siena had been signed off sick from work since her failed attempt to kill herself. The certificate was due to run out at the end of the week, and Maddy hoped her daughter would feel able to return to her job at *What's New in Beauty* before the company, who had thus far been very understanding, lost patience with her.

She picked up her car keys from the console table in the hallway and headed out into a bright but cold March morning.

The traffic was surprisingly light as Maddy approached the junction for the M25, and she was just thinking that she might be so early to work, she'd have time to get herself a cappuccino and maybe even some poached eggs from the canteen, when she noticed that the vehicles ahead of her were applying their brakes in a sea of red lights. Some drivers were giving a few flashes of their amber hazard warning lights to alert other drivers that they needed to slow down. Within twenty seconds Maddy's speed had reduced from 50 to 15 mph, and shortly after that she was at a total standstill. *Great*, she thought, checking the clock on her dashboard. *It's nearly eight and if it's back-to-back traffic all the way from here, I haven't got a hope of getting in for nine. Why didn't I just get up when Simon did and leave early?*

Despite going to bed later than her, Simon had been up and showering shortly after 6 a.m., his usual routine. He thought it was worth having less time in bed as a trade-off for the journey into work being quicker, and he was happy to get his full English breakfast in the canteen before he started his working day. He had thoughtfully brought Maddy a cup of black coffee in bed before he left.

'I shouldn't be too late back tonight,' he had said, dropping a kiss on the top of her head. 'How about you?'

Taking a sip of the strong, dark liquid in attempt to galvanise her reluctant body into action, she had replied, 'I don't get off air until four, but I should be able to get out by five unless I have to go to a meeting. More delightful rush hour traffic on the way home,' she had added, turning the corners of her mouth down.

'Just keep reminding yourself that we're lucky to have the jobs we do. They're what pays for all this,' Simon had said, indicating their opulent bedroom. 'Remember, watch your back and be nice to everyone.' He had blown her a kiss from the bedroom doorway. Then he was gone.

Maddy tapped the fingers of her right hand in agitation on the steering wheel, while switching on the local talk radio channel with her left just as the news bulletin was coming to a close. She knew it would be followed by a travel update. *Please don't let this be the queue all the way into London*, she prayed silently.

Following earlier reports of a major accident on the M4 between Junction 3 and the A4 elevated section, we can now confirm the motorway has been closed to allow the air ambulance to land. Stay tuned to this station for updates and we'll let you know when the road reopens. Motorists are being advised to use alternative routes, but if you're already in the resulting traffic jam, take direction from the police who are permitting use of the hard shoulder to bring traffic off the motorway at Junction 3. If you're beyond Junction 3, the delays are expected to be in excess of two hours. The surrounding area is also very busy, so public transport is recommended if you haven't yet embarked on your journey.

So much for my prayers, Maddy thought. *What the hell am I supposed to do now? Do I notify work that I'm caught up in this and I'm going to be late, or do I just wait until I get there and hope it's one of the speedier girls in make-up?* Some members of the team could talk and work at the same time while others kept stopping to chat, and as she was already on a warning there was no way Maddy would be able to try and hurry one of the slower girls without being accused of bullying. Most of the cars in front of her were indicating left and Maddy followed suit, easing forward slowly as three lanes reduced to two. She tapped the traffic app on her phone for guidance as to the best route to take, once she had managed to get off at Junction 3, and it was giving an expected arrival time of 10.45 a.m. *It's no good, I'm going to have to let the channel know, even if the shit does hit the fan. At least they can have someone on standby if I don't make it on air for midday.*

While she was waiting for the call to connect, she wondered if Simon had managed to get in to work before the accident happened. *I'll try him once I've spoken to Gary.*

'Production office, Sasha speaking.'

Sasha was the director's PA.

'Hi Sasha, it's Maddy. Is Gary there?'

'Hi Maddy. He's a bit busy at the moment. Everything okay? Please tell me you're not calling in sick. Gary's already in a shitty mood.'

Great, that's all I need, Maddy thought. 'Not sick, but I'm having a bit of trouble getting in. Presumably we're running the story about the big accident on the M4?'

'Yes. That's why he's in a mood. He's trying to organise a crew to get out there and cover the story but there's no one in who can ride a motorbike and the roads are gridlocked.'

'Tell me about it. I'm being directed off the motorway and my app says I won't be in until around eleven. Nothing I can do about it, I'm afraid, but I thought I should give you a heads-up.'

'No problem, Maddy. I'll let Gary know and I'll warn the make-up team that you're on your way but likely to be very late.'

'Thanks, Sasha, I'll get there as soon as is humanly possible.'

'Don't take any unnecessary risks. It's only television, not a matter of life or death.'

Maddy smiled as she disconnected the call. She had a lot of time for Sasha. The South African was very down to earth but also extremely good at her job. *If only we had a few more people with her work ethic and morals at the channel,* she thought, pressing Simon's name on her phone. It rang out a few times before going to voicemail.

'Hi,' she said, 'I was checking whether you managed to get into work okay. I'm stuck in horrendous traffic because of a big smash on the M4. I should have left when you did. Catch you later.'

Maddy guessed the reason he hadn't answered was because he was halfway through his breakfast. He wasn't a fan of phones at the dining table, either at home or when they were out. She could almost picture him dipping fried bread into his fried egg, the rest of his plate overflowing with baked beans, fried bacon, sausage and hash browns. It was a wonder he stayed so slim. Considering the canteen were feeding elite sportspeople, she had never quite understood why there wasn't healthier stuff on the menu, although Simon said the majority of the players didn't have breakfast there; it was usually only the coaching and office staff. Merely thinking of the breakfast he was most likely enjoying made her stomach rumble. *Too bad, I definitely won't have time to eat before we go live. In fact, I'll be lucky to get a coffee.*

Eventually, after crawling along at a snail's pace for the best part of three hours, Maddy swung into her allocated parking space at the *News 24/7* studios and hurried into the building carrying the outfit she had selected for her shift. The royal blue dress was

a neat fit, chosen to show off her figure without revealing any
flesh. She changed into it quickly and ran along the corridor to
the make-up room in her stockinged feet rather than attempting
it in the high-heeled shoes she was holding. It was already twenty
past eleven when she slid into the make-up chair, but fortunately
it was Tricia doing her make-up and she was one of the girls who
could multitask.

'Let's get your rollers in first, Maddy, so they've got a chance
to cool down while we're doing your face. Ben left you a script
to have a quick read through,' she said, indicating the sheaf of
coloured papers on the countertop, 'and a cappuccino.'

'Bless him,' Maddy said. 'I know I've been late before, but this
really is cutting it fine. Do you think I'll make it?'

'You just sit back and relax and leave everything to me. None
of the viewers will have any idea what a close call we had.'

True to her word, Tricia had Maddy on set by three minutes to
twelve and was giving her nose a final powder when the morning
team signed off after their four-hour stint.

Maddy and Ben took their seats as the music started and
alternated delivering the headlines before Ben started on the first
big news story about a bank worker defrauding his company of
£2 million. While Ben was reading, Gary was talking to Maddy
through her earpiece.

'So glad you could join us,' he said. Maddy wasn't sure if she
detected sarcasm, annoyance or relief in his voice. 'We're just
getting some pictures in from the crash scene on the M4. Can
you read what the crawl says on your monitor?'

Is he having a dig at my eyesight? Maddy wondered. The writing
was small, but she could just make it out. *BREAKING NEWS –
eyewitness footage from this morning's crash on the M4 coming up.*
She nodded her head slightly to acknowledge she had read it.

'When Ben's finished boring the pants off everyone with the
dishonest banker, hardly news is it, it's just this guy got caught, I

want you to lead in with the breaking news that we've got exclusive footage from this morning's accident on the M4 – then we'll roll the footage in. Jesus, what a mess, I can't believe the driver got out of it alive. Okay, Ben's wrapping, coming to you on camera two in 3 – 2 – 1.'

'Following up on the news we've been reporting this morning about the accident on the M4, one of the main arteries feeding into London, we have just received exclusive footage from the scene.'

'Okay, pause for effect, Maddy,' Gary said. 'Roll the footage. And carry on, Maddy.'

'The motorway had to be closed for almost three hours in rush hour traffic to allow an air ambulance to land and for police to examine the scene and remove the debris. The cause of the accident is unclear at this stage, but it appears there was only one vehicle involved, although other vehicles sustained minor damage as a result of the initial incident. The driver of the car had to be cut from his vehicle before being airlifted to Charing Cross Hospital, where he is believed to be receiving treatment for life-threatening injuries.'

As she read, Maddy could feel her mouth going dry and an uncontrollable shiver ran through her body. Her attention was on the autocue, so she wasn't able to look at the pictures from the scene for fear of losing her place. As she paused for a quick breath, she stole a glance at the monitor. The car was smashed in at both the front and the back where it had cartwheeled along the carriageway before coming to a halt on its roof, across the central reservation. Maddy's world started spinning and the ice-cold shiver from moments before turned into heat.

'Carry on with the story, Maddy…' Gary instructed. 'Link to the eyewitness… Speak, Maddy… God damn it, can you hear me?'

Gary was shouting in her ear now, but, to Maddy, his voice seemed to be coming from the end of a very long tunnel.

'What's wrong with her? Is her talkback down? Ben… pick up the story and throw to the eyewitness. What the fuck, Maddy?

You've seen worse stuff than this. Pull yourself together.' That's when he became aware of the tears streaming down Maddy's cheeks. 'Get her off set,' he said to Hanif, the floor manager. 'You're flying solo, Ben.'

CHAPTER SEVEN

1.35 p.m. – Monday

Bella's rubber-soled shoes made a squeaking noise underfoot as she strode purposefully along the corridor towards the nurse's station. Her shift at Charing Cross Hospital had been due to start at 2 p.m., but for the second day running she had received an emergency call on her mobile phone from the nursing agency. 'There's been a major accident on the M4, and some members of staff have had difficulty getting in – is there a chance you could get in any earlier?' Although it had been a rush, Bella had reached the hospital shortly after midday. It had been very busy for the first hour or so, but as the affected members of staff began to trickle in, she had become a spare pair of hands until the shift handover at 2 p.m.

What a difference a day makes, she thought, comparing the calm hotel-like atmosphere of the private hospital from the previous day to the hustle and bustle of one of the busiest NHS hospitals in London. As she walked through the reception area for people waiting to have MRI scans, she estimated there must have been at least a dozen people sitting around on orange plastic chairs. Most were idly thumbing through magazines they had little interest in or on their mobile phones as the illuminated noticeboard informed them of a wait time of fifty-five minutes.

'Ah, Bella,' the ward manager said, 'there you are. Would you mind taking a cup of tea along to the relatives' room for me, please? The catering staff are still busy collecting lunch trays from the wards, and we've got the wife of the driver whose car crashed this morning waiting for the outcome of his brain scan. As you can imagine, she's in a bit of a state, so if you wouldn't mind staying with her for a short while now that things have calmed down a bit on the wards, it would be much appreciated.'

'Of course,' Bella replied. 'Do we know how she takes her tea?'

'I don't suppose she'll care, to be honest. I just think having someone fussing around her for a few minutes, rather than her sitting there on her own, might benefit her. She was understandably in a state of shock when she arrived. I'm surprised the television station didn't send someone with her, but hopefully she's got a friend or family member meeting her here.'

'Television station?'

'Yes, she's a newsreader on *News 24/7*. Apparently, she was live on air when the first pictures came in and she realised it was her husband in the accident.'

'How awful. Is there any news about him?'

'He was rushed straight into theatre on arrival and they were able to stabilise his condition, although he's still critical. They're planning on inducing a coma after the MRI. Maybe you could ask her if she's got anyone meeting her here when you take her tea in.'

'Yes, sister,' Bella replied.

Rather than going to the machine for a cup of watery tea in a plastic cup, she went into the nurse's kitchen and got out a proper cup and saucer, then proceeded to make quite a strong brew to which she added two spoons of sugar and a little milk. Cup and saucer in hand, she made her way along the corridor and tapped lightly on the door of the relatives' room. There was no reply, but she pushed the door open anyway. In the far corner of the room, Maddy was sitting on a low-slung olive-green chair hugging her arms around herself as though in an attempt to stay warm. Her head was dropped forward and she was rocking gently.

'Mrs Shaw?'

Maddy looked up slowly, a confused expression on her face.

'I've brought you a cup of tea.'

'I didn't ask for one,' she said, 'or did I? I'm sorry, I can't remember. This is all a bit surreal.'

'Sister thought you might like one,' Bella said, crossing the room and offering the hot drink to Maddy.

She reached out for it, but her hands were shaking so much that the tea slopped over the lip of the cup and spilled into the saucer. Bella retrieved the cup and placed it on the low wooden table next to her chair. Using a tissue from her pocket, she mopped up the liquid in the saucer.

'I'm Bella. You probably don't remember me, Mrs Shaw, but we met briefly before when I was nursing your daughter in Mountview Hospital.'

Maddy shook her head. 'I'm sorry, I'm afraid I don't remember, but please, call me Maddy.'

'I wouldn't expect you to, you must have seen a lot of different nurses while Siena was in hospital, and I only had a couple of shifts there. How's she doing?' Bella said, perching on the chair at Maddy's side and placing a hand on her forearm.

It was the first physical contact Maddy had had since Hanif ushered her into the back of a taxi almost two hours previously, telling her not to worry, they would get someone to sit in for her. *Had he really thought she was going to just nip to the hospital for an hour or so, then come back and continue to read the news as though nothing had happened?* They'd all seen the pictures of the wrecked Jaguar. It was a miracle Simon had survived at all, but she could only imagine what kind of state he was in. In the back of the black cab, with tears silently spilling down her cheeks, she had kept reliving the horrific moment when she had realised that it was her husband's car in the eyewitness footage. She had been struck dumb. Gary, the director, had been shouting instructions at her through her earpiece but she hadn't been able to act on them. She had just sat there, as though paralysed, in a state of total shock. When Ben had started to speak and the camera was on him rather than her, Hanif had crept onto the set, put his arm around her shoulders and ushered her out of the studio through the heavy double doors.

'What's wrong, Maddy?' he had asked. 'You look like you've seen a ghost.'

It had taken several moments before she had been able to explain that it was her husband's car in the footage. That was when she had begun to shake uncontrollably and her legs had given way beneath her. She had heard Hanif relay the information to the production gallery, and moments later he had said, 'We've ordered you a cab. You need to get to the hospital. Don't worry, we'll cover the rest of your shift.'

'Well, she had been making progress slowly, but now this…' Maddy said, her voice trailing off. 'God knows how it's going to affect her,' she continued, her voice heavy with defeat.

'Has she got someone with her or is she on her way here?'

'I haven't told her yet. I'm worried about how she'll react when she hears the news. She shouldn't be on her own, but obviously I can't leave here.'

The look on Bella's face was one of incredulity. 'The story's been all over the news all morning, Maddy, not to mention social media. Siena could hear about it any minute. Is she at home?'

Maddy nodded.

'Do you have a friend or neighbour you could contact to be with her, if you were to call? It would be better if she heard about the accident from you.'

'Sonning isn't that kind of a place. Everyone keeps themselves to themselves. The houses all have electric gates closing them off from their neighbours. As for friends, I don't really have many. I'm always too busy working, and when I'm not, Simon and I do things together. He's my best friend,' Maddy said, a sob catching in her throat. 'I don't know what I'll do if he doesn't make it.'

'Try to think positively,' Bella said. 'There must be someone you could call.'

'I've got one friend I could ask, if she's not too busy at work.'

'I'm sure she would try to help if you explain the situation. Would she be able to bring Siena to the hospital, just in case?'

'In case what? Do you think Simon's going to die? Has someone said something to you?' Maddy said, a look of terror in her eyes.

'No, of course not. I was meaning if things improve. You would want Siena to be here for him, wouldn't you?'

'Yes, yes, of course I would. I'll call my friend now.'

'Will you be all right on your own for a while? The nurse's station is just along the corridor and there's always someone manning it. I'm going to try and find out how your husband is doing.'

'Thank you for looking after me, Bella,' Maddy said, reaching into her bag for her mobile phone.

'That's why I'm here,' Bella said, 'to take care of you and Simon.'

CHAPTER EIGHT

1.55 p.m. – Monday

The pile of paperwork on DCI Rachel Hart's desk finally seemed to be reducing in size. She had spent the whole of Monday morning and the early part of the afternoon making sure that all the reports filed by her team of officers had been filled out correctly. As a stickler for detail herself, she never wanted there to be loopholes for defence lawyers to take advantage of that could potentially lead to a guilty defendant walking free. Some of her officers were more thorough than others, in particular PC Eleanor Drake. *I doubt if she'll stay in the rank of constable for long*, Rachel thought, *at least, not if I have anything to do with it.* As she put her signature on the bottom of a document about a recent missing child case, her mobile phone started to ring. *How pertinent*, she thought, glancing at the screen and seeing Tim's number.

'Hi,' she said. 'Were your ears burning?'

'Have you been talking about me again?'

'Not exactly talking about you. I was just signing off on the Cassie Bailey abduction.'

'Oh, yes. What a delightful character my client was, but without her, we may never have met, so in some ways we owe her a debt of gratitude. Anyway, I didn't call you to talk shop. I wondered if you'd managed to get all your spring cleaning done and if you fancied going out to dinner tonight? Or we could get a takeaway and stay in and watch a film, maybe at your place if it's all neat and tidy now?'

It wasn't the first time Tim had dropped a hint that he would like to be invited inside Rachel's home. The closest he had got so far was the front doorstep, when he was either picking her up or dropping her off from their meals out together. Rachel knew that she was fast approaching the point in their relationship where she would either have to call it a day or allow things to move on from just the dating stage, something she had so far failed to do with any prospective long-term partner. The moment she started to become emotionally involved with anyone, she would send a text message starting with the words *I'm sorry*, and ending with the words *It's not you, it's me*. This course of action was usually prompted by an intense conversation, with her boyfriend at the time asking when things were going to progress to the next level. Occasionally she would receive a response asking her to reconsider, or a one-word reply such as *bitch*, but usually the recipient just accepted it as a fait accompli and moved on without question.

The situation with Tim was different, though. For one thing she hadn't met him through online dating. In Rachel's line of work, she didn't often come across suitable men. She had an unwritten rule not to date another police officer, and most of her other male contacts on a day-to-day basis were criminals. She had never made the effort to foster female friendships and didn't like the idea of socialising with female colleagues because she felt it wouldn't do for them to see their superior officer slightly the worse for wear due to an overindulgence of alcohol. With virtually no social life, so very little opportunity to meet men, she had turned to a dating website and, so far, it had worked out just fine. She got what she wanted without strings for a few months before moving on to the next eligible bachelor. Tim was the first man since her uni days that she had actually met in the flesh first before going on a date. She liked him because he was less demanding than most of her boyfriends in terms of time. Naturally, he understood more about her job as he was also involved in law enforcement, but it was more than that. If they were out for dinner and she wasn't very talkative, he didn't keep saying, 'Are you okay? Have I done something wrong?' The silences were comfortable rather than awkward. And if she fell asleep on his shoulder while watching a film at his house, he didn't get defensive and question whether she found him boring; he just seemed pleased that she could relax so totally in his company. *When I'm working on a big case he knows there's precious little time to eat and sleep, let alone socialise. That's why he's exerting a bit of pressure now because I told him I'm not working on anything in particular.*

'Are you still there?' he asked.

'Oh yes, sorry. I was just checking my diary to see if I had anything on tonight.' She cringed at her pathetic excuse. *He's not stupid. He knows I was stalling for time.*

'And have you?'

'No. A completely blank page.'

'Good. So, what's your preference? Dinner out, or a cosy night in?'

'Actually, I quite fancy a curry. We could get a takeaway, but I didn't get quite as much tidying up done as I would have liked yesterday. There's a new restaurant opened near you called India Dining that I'd quite like to try.'

It wasn't far from the truth. She had spent most of her day at Mountview Hospital with Ruth, as she did every Sunday, but there was very little out of place in her two-bedroom Victorian cottage as she had a cleaner who came in two mornings a week while she was at work.

'Of course. Do you want me to pick you up, or will you drive over and meet me there?'

'I'll drive. Criminals are no respecters of office hours and I might be needed in a hurry.'

'Shall we say 7.30 p.m.?'

'Perfect,' Rachel said. 'See you later.'

Before she had even opened the next file from the much-reduced pile to the left of her desk, her phone rang again. She was smiling as she reached for it, thinking it was probably Tim asking for the actual address of the restaurant. She pressed the green button without checking caller ID.

'Hi. Not having second thoughts, are you?' she teased.

'Rachel?' the quivering voice on the other end of the line said. 'It's Maddy… Maddy Shaw. I need your help,' she added, before dissolving into floods of tears.

'Maddy? Hey, what's wrong? Is it Siena? Has she tried to hurt herself again?'

The two women had met after Siena had been admitted to Mountview Hospital following her suicide attempt. Maddy had been sitting alone in the cafeteria of the residential wing, nursing a cup of coffee, when Rachel had gone in there to buy a bottle of water for her journey home. She knew she recognised the face but had initially thought it must be from a case she had worked on. As she was paying the cashier for the water, she had noticed that the woman was crying and had decided to go over and ask if she could be of any help. The moment Maddy had spoken, Rachel had realised she was the television newsreader. She had sat down at the table and asked her if it would help to talk about things. Maddy had opened up, and the story of Siena's devastation and attempted suicide after her cheating boyfriend had dumped her had come spilling out. Although Siena's reasons for trying to take her own life were different from Ruth's, Rachel had been able to empathise. In her mind, there could be nothing worse than witnessing someone you love so entirely struggling to survive a suicide attempt, whatever the reason for it. She just couldn't comprehend why neither Ruth nor Siena would reach out for help to the people who loved them. In some ways it was selfish that their only thoughts were to relieve themselves of pain while giving no thought to the devastation that their death would cause to others. She and Maddy had seen each other at the hospital a few times over the following couple of weeks, and when Siena was discharged they had exchanged numbers, with Rachel telling Maddy to call if she ever needed her help.

'Talk to me, Maddy. Is Siena okay?'

'It… it's not Siena,' she stammered through the tears, 'but I didn't know who else to turn to.'

'What's happened? How can I help?'

'Have you seen the news today?'

'No,' Rachel said, reaching for the remote control and pointing it at the television on her office wall that was always tuned in to the twenty-four-hour news channel that Maddy worked for. 'I've been wading my way through a mountain of paperwork.' She caught her breath as she read the words scrolling across the bottom of the screen while listening to a pretty newsreader with the slightest of foreign accents deliver the latest update.

'Oh my God, Maddy. Is that your Simon?'

'Yes,' she answered in a barely audible whisper.

'Are you at the hospital? Is Siena with you? Do you need me to come?'

'I… I haven't spoken to her yet.'

'What? Why not?'

'She's on her own, Rachel. I'm frightened to tell her while she's on her own in case she does something stupid again.'

'You need to get someone to go to your house as soon as possible, Maddy. What if she turns the television on? It would be a dreadful way to find out about her dad.'

'I wondered if you could go? I know it's a lot to ask, but she really connected with you at the hospital. You're one of the few people she trusts at the moment.'

'I'm on my way,' Rachel said, turning the television off and reaching for her jacket and her handbag. 'I should be there in about twenty minutes. I'll text you when I'm outside, and then you have to ring straight away. She'll probably suspect something is wrong the minute she sees me, and she needs to hear this from you.'

'I know, but I have no idea what I'm going to say.'

'You'll just have to tell her the truth as gently as you can. Once you've told her, I'll bring her up to Charing Cross. She ought to be with you and her dad,' Rachel said, only too aware of the trauma families faced when something devastating threatened to destroy their lives.

'I don't know how to thank you, Rachel.'

'There's no need,' Rachel said. A flashback flooded her mind of the hospital waiting room she had sat in, huddled next to her mum while her dad paced the corridor outside, desperate for news of her twin sister. *Maddy and Siena will need each other*, she thought, *whatever the outcome*.

CHAPTER NINE

2.35 p.m. – Monday

Rachel swung her car off the road into the entrance of Maddy and Simon Shaw's home and stopped in front of the imposing wrought iron gates. Beyond them was a gravel driveway flanked by high laurel hedges with their glossy leaves hiding all but the roof of their house from view. Despite meeting up on several occasions at Mountview Hospital, Rachel hadn't previously visited Maddy's home. It had been a surprise to discover that they both lived in the same village, during one of their heart-to-hearts, but perhaps less surprising that their paths had never crossed. Rachel lived in the centre of Sonning in an end-of-terrace cottage, whereas Maddy had a five-bedroom detached house, with views over the River Thames, on a road leading out of the village. *I guess that's one of the perks of being married to a former footballer*, Rachel thought, opening her driver's window and reaching out to press the intercom button. *Mind you, I don't suppose a newsreader's salary is exactly peanuts.* While she was waiting for Siena to answer, she texted Maddy to say that she had arrived.

There was a crackling sound from the intercom. 'Hello?'

'Hi, is that Siena? It's Rachel here, your mum's friend from the hospital.'

'Oh, hi Rachel. My friend too, I hope?'

'Of course.'

'Mum's not here, she's working.'

'Yes, I know. She asked me to pop by and see you.'

'Really? She never mentioned it. Not that I mind. I get fed up being here on my own all day. Come in and I'll put the kettle on.'

The intercom went dead as the gates began to swing slowly open. Rachel tapped her fingers impatiently on the steering wheel until there was enough of a gap to guide her car through. She moved forward, her tyres crunching on the gravel, and gasped as she came to the end of the hedges and the Shaws' home was revealed in all its glory. *I don't know what I was expecting*, she thought, *but it certainly wasn't this.* The house was of typical Jacobean construction, with wooden struts and leaded windows, and it was as wide as the whole row of four cottages that Rachel's home was part of. As she pulled up in front of the dark oak front door, it opened and Siena appeared, wearing jeans, a bright orange sweater and a pair of fluffy slippers.

'How are you doing?' Rachel asked, getting out of her car.

'A bit better today, actually. Oh, would you believe it, that's my phone ringing now. Typical. I've been sat around all day doing nothing much, and then I get a visitor and a phone call in the space of five minutes. Can you close the front door behind you, please, while I get that?' she said, disappearing back inside.

Rachel hurried up the steps and into the hallway, following the sound of Siena's voice for guidance. She opened the door on to a huge open-plan kitchen–dining room with spectacular views over the swimming pool and the manicured lawn to the river beyond.

'Yes, she just got here,' Siena was saying. 'I'm about to make us a cup of tea. Are you okay? You sound a bit weird. Sure. She wants me to put it on speakerphone,' she told Rachel, shrugging her shoulders and pressing the button so that they could both hear Maddy.

'There's no easy way to tell you this, Siena. I'm at Charing Cross Hospital with your dad. He's been involved in an accident.'

'What? Is he okay? Can I speak to him?'

'N-not at the moment, darling. He's... well, he's... having an MRI scan done.'

'On which bit of him?'

There was a pause.

'Mum? What aren't you telling me? Is this why you asked Rachel to drop by? What's happened?'

'It was an accident on the motorway... a bad one.'

Rachel watched as Siena's expression turned instantly from concern to panic.

'How bad?'

There was no answer from the other end of the line.

'Mum? Are you still there? What isn't she telling me, Rachel?'

Rachel waited for a moment to see if Maddy was going to respond before she said, 'Your dad was badly injured, Siena.'

'Nooo,' she wailed. 'No, no, no, this can't be happening!'

'I've come to take you to the hospital,' Rachel said, crossing the kitchen to where Siena was leaning heavily on the granite work surface, seemingly for support. She placed her arm around the young woman's shoulders. 'You need to put some shoes on and then we can get going,' Rachel explained gently. 'Your mum and dad need you.'

'Is it my fault, Mum?'

Between sniffs, Maddy said, 'Why would it be your fault?'

'Do you think Dad was worrying about all the stuff that's been going on with me, and not paying proper attention to the road?'

'No. I don't think that. It could have been a puncture, or him swerving to avoid an animal or something else in the road. There are any number of things that could have caused the accident, but you're not one of them and I don't want you thinking that way.'

'Mum, I'm scared. I don't want him to die.'

'He's not going to die. We won't let him.'

'Promise?' Siena said, her voice trembling.

'I promise. Look after her for me, Rachel,' Maddy said, abruptly ending the call.

Siena was very quiet for the first part of the drive into London. Whenever Rachel glanced sideways at her, she was staring straight ahead with tears trickling silently down her cheeks. She wanted to utter some words of comfort, but everything she tried to formulate in her head seemed crass and inadequate. Eventually, it was Siena who spoke first.

'Is he going to make it, do you think?'

Rachel had never been one for making false promises. 'Let's just say he's in the best possible hands at Charing Cross. Their medical staff are among the most highly qualified in the country.'

Siena nodded, letting the reassuring words sink in before she spoke again. 'Do you know what happened?'

Rachel hadn't told Maddy, but she had asked her DI, Graham Wilson, who had formerly been with the traffic division, to make a few enquiries about the accident. First and foremost Rachel was a police officer and, as such, she wanted to know if anything external had caused the catastrophic crash, or whether it was just a lapse of concentration on Simon Shaw's part. Graham had phoned her while she was on the way to the Shaws' house. She chose her words carefully.

'According to witnesses at the scene, it seems like your dad lost control while he was in the outside lane, causing him to crash into the central reservation. Maybe your mum was right when she suggested it could have been a tyre blowout. At the sort of speed your dad would have been doing in the outside lane it would be very difficult to control the steering if that's what happened.'

She omitted to mention that one eyewitness had been fairly sure he'd seen a motorbike driving erratically moments before the crash. She had tasked Graham with trying to get hold of the witness's details and make a few enquiries of his own. Traffic accidents didn't come under their jurisdiction, but she knew she could trust Graham not to tread on anyone's toes while pulling in a few favours. If the accident had been caused by a third party's dangerous driving, Rachel wanted to know about it.

'Dad's a good driver. He's just about the last person on the planet I would ever have expected to have a crash. I can't believe it. I don't know what Mum will do if anything happens to him. He's her world.'

'Try not to worry too much, Siena. We'll know more when we get to the hospital.'

After dropping Siena at the hospital entrance, Rachel was parking her car when Graham's call came through.

'Okay, Guv?'

'Talk to me, Graham. Did you manage to speak to the witness?'

'Yes, his name is Adam Jarvis. I just got off the phone with him now.'

'And?'

'He confirmed the statement he gave earlier. He said that a motorbike overtook him at speed and was flashing his lights at Simon Shaw's car, presumably trying to get him to move over so he could get past.'

'That's odd. In my experience motorbikes just weave in and out rather than trying to get cars to move.'

'Mine too. Pretty much a law unto themselves, usually. But apparently this guy kept flashing his lights and when the Jag didn't move over, the motorbike cut in front of our witness and pulled alongside Simon Shaw's car. Next thing Adam remembers was trying to avoid the Jag after it struck the central reservation while trying not to get hit by cars from behind.'

'Have you asked him if he'd be willing to go into his local police station to give a full statement?'

'He's happy to and, as luck would have it, we're his local nick. Adam's a commuter, so he drives that stretch of road every day, just like Simon Shaw.'

'Good work, Graham. I know that technically this isn't our case, but this is personal. My friend's husband is in a critical condition and if it turns out that the driver of this motorbike was responsible for the crash, we should be able to trace him with the help of the traffic cameras.'

'We may not need them, Guv.'

'How come?'

'Adam Jarvis had a passenger – his girlfriend, Sarah. She captured some of the incident on her mobile phone. Apparently they didn't mention it earlier because they thought they may have said on the recording that they were speeding and they didn't want to get into trouble. He said they'll both come into the station on their way back from work.'

'Are you all right to stay late and deal with it? I've just got to Charing Cross Hospital with Siena, the Shaws' daughter, and I've got a feeling it's going to be a long night.'

'No problem. Are we keeping this video footage to ourselves?'

'Let's take a look at it first before we get anyone else involved. Jarvis may not have remembered things accurately, particularly after the trauma of witnessing the crash, but if the footage shows he's right, this motorcyclist needs to be found and held accountable.'

CHAPTER TEN

7.57 p.m. – Monday

Tim checked his phone again. *Nothing.* It was almost 8 p.m. and there was still no sign of Rachel and no message to say that she was running late. *Surely she's not doing it deliberately to underline the point she made the other night?* he thought, breaking off another piece of poppadom and dipping it first in lime chutney followed by a cooling cucumber raita. The lentil crackers were crisp rather than soft, always a good indication of the quality of food to come, and the aromas wafting around the restaurant from the other diners' food was mouth-watering. The owners had done an excellent job with the interior decoration, too. Instead of flocked wallpaper in a dark red or burnt orange, the walls were painted a very pale grey and they displayed original art rather than a giant-sized print of Mount Everest or the Taj Mahal. It was classy, modern and understated, a bit like the woman he was there to meet.

He drained his glass of beer and signalled for the waiter to bring him another. Never a fan of eating out in restaurants on his own, it was beginning to look as though he would have no choice if Rachel was a no-show. He hadn't bothered to get anything in for dinner and the supermarket would be shut now, even if he could have been bothered to cook for one. *I suppose I could get a takeaway from here*, Tim thought, *but what's the point? It will only draw the attention of the other customers if I leave with my dinner in a paper carrier bag, having sat here at a table for the past forty minutes. I'll just give the waiter some excuse for my friend not turning up, to save face, and no one needs to know I've been stood up.* The waiter was approaching with his glass of Cobra, so Tim made a point of looking at his phone as though he was reading a text message.

'Your beer, sir.'

'Thanks. I'd like to order now, please. My friend has had to work late, so won't be able to join me.'

'Very good, sir.'

'I'll have a prawn *puri* to start and a chicken *shashlik* with plain rice.'

'More poppadoms?' the waiter asked, lifting up the silver basket, which was now empty barring a few crumbs.

'I think I've had enough already, thanks. I won't have room for my dinner if I have any more,' Tim answered, patting his stomach.

'Thank you, sir.'

As soon as the waiter had returned to his position behind the bar and was tapping the order into the computer, Tim texted a row of question marks to Rachel's phone. Less than a minute later he received a message:

OMG, Tim, I'm so sorry. Something came up which made me completely forget we had made plans for this evening. Not work – a friend needed me. I'll explain next time I see you – assuming there is a next time? I hope you can forgive me.

Tim read the message twice. He needed to be sure that Rachel wasn't just making an excuse because she'd changed her mind about meeting up. It sounded genuine enough. He had to trust his instincts, which in turn meant trusting her. He tapped a quick reply:

Already forgiven. Call me tomorrow. Xx

As an afterthought, he sent a second text:

Good call on the restaurant, btw, food is delicious.

Even though the only food he had tasted was the poppadoms, he didn't want Rachel to think he had been sitting waiting for her to show up for half an hour. *What kind of a saddo would that make me seem?* he thought, deliberately turning his phone off to end any further communication with her that evening. He couldn't deny he was hurt that she had forgotten their date. With most women he wouldn't have entertained seeing them again, but Rachel was different. It had taken a while for her to come into his life, but now that she had, he was determined to keep her in it.

CHAPTER ELEVEN

10.55 p.m. – Monday

It was almost 11 p.m. by the time Bella let herself into her one-bedroom flat in Staines, a formerly posh suburb of London which, having been in decline for a number of years, was on the rise again. She knew she had been incredibly lucky to find a flat within a five-minute walk of the railway station for a rent she could afford. A lot of the rental properties in the area had been snapped up by buy-to-let investors and then modernised sufficiently to charge high rents from young professionals. Fortunately for Bella, that wasn't the case with her flat. The decor was dated, and the furniture best described as lived-in, but it was perfect for someone who relied on public transport to get around and couldn't afford central London prices.

Most of the jobs Melrose Nursing Agency booked Bella for were in London, but living where she did, she was well placed to travel west to any of the places along the train line to Reading as well as to the private hospitals and nursing homes in the Windsor area. It was also extremely handy for getting to Heathrow airport for her ever more frequent trips back to Portugal to see her ailing grandmother.

Dumping her handbag and keys on the breakfast bar that divided her tiny kitchen from the living room, Bella headed towards the bathroom, hanging her coat on a hook in the hall as she passed. She pulled the shower curtain back and reached her hand in to turn the water on. From past experience, she knew she had at least two minutes to undress in her bedroom before the water, travelling along pipes from the combination boiler in the kitchen, would have heated sufficiently. It had been a long and tiring day, despite being allowed to leave thirty minutes before the end of her shift, and she couldn't wait to wash the grime of the city off her skin and out of her hair. She was looking forward to getting into bed with a mug of hot milk.

Bella stepped under the gentle stream of water, more akin to a garden sprinkler system than a power shower, and moved around until her skin was wet enough to apply shower gel. Just like the patient she had met at the private hospital the previous day, people often asked why she put herself through the ordeal of living a solitary existence in a country where she knew very few people when she could easily have found work in a hospital back home in Portugal. Her mother Rosa's face swam before her eyes as she tilted her head back, allowing the gentle stream of water to pour down her face and mix with the flowing tears that she could never control whenever she thought of her.

Her grandmother, Vovo, had told Bella that following her birth, she had cried relentlessly every single day for the first nine months of her life. It had earned her the undesirable nickname *chora bebe* – cry baby. The people in their small village near Tavira, in southern Portugal, believed she was unlucky, the devil's child, because she had been conceived out of wedlock. They had verbally abused Rosa, even spitting at her in the street, and by the time her baby was nine months old, she was spending most of her days lying in bed in a drunken stupor, unable to face the outward displays of hatred towards her. Out of desperation, Bella's grandmother had told her daughter that she would take over the responsibility of raising the baby if she returned to her job as a waitress in Porto. Rosa had refused point-blank to go back to Porto, but she had accepted a job in Lisbon, and handed the child over to her mother.

For more than ten years, Rosa had stayed away, despite her promises to visit, until she showed up unexpectedly after hearing about her mother's small win on the lottery. Eleven-year-old Bella could still remember how shocked she had been by her mother's appearance. Rosa was thin and haggard, and looked at least twenty years older than her actual age, bearing no resemblance to Bella's impression of her from the photographs her grandmother had shown her. Those had been taken when Rosa was a happy, smiling teenager welcoming her best friend, Beatriz, to the hotel in Porto where she had managed to get her a job working alongside her in the bar.

Rosa had only stayed with Vovo and Bella for a couple of days, just long enough to persuade her mother to give her some money to keep her off the streets, and that was the last they had seen of her until she appeared uninvited on Bella's eighteenth birthday.

Bella could still vividly remember the vitriol in her mother's voice when she had revealed that she had cirrhosis of the liver, a condition caused by heavy drinking. 'Beatriz and I should have got rid of you when we had the chance, even though it was against our Catholic upbringing. We never wanted you after what those bastards did,' she had said, her voice low and laced with ice. 'You ruined our lives. I wouldn't care if I never laid eyes on you again.' Although Bella had never had a normal relationship with her mother, the words had devastated her.

It had been Vovo's idea that Bella should train to be a nurse, maybe hoping that one day she would be able to encourage her alcoholic mother to give up drinking before it killed her, but on the few occasions Rosa had visited since, she refused to listen to any advice Bella had offered.

'You know why I drink. I have nothing else in my life,' was all Rosa would say before taking another defiant swig from a bottle.

After warming some bedtime milk, as her grandmother had always done for her when she was growing up, Bella carried her mug through to the bedroom. It was almost midnight, so nearly 1 a.m. in Tavira, but she decided to email anyway to check on her grandmother.

Hi Beca,
    I know you're away for a few days but I wondered if you had heard from Rosa today about how Vovo is?

Bella x

She hit send, wondering where Beca's travels had taken her to this time. 'Work,' she had said vaguely when the two friends had sat talking late into the night in Vovo's living room the previous Friday, with the old lady sleeping overhead. Idly, she scrolled through the rest of her emails, most of them from mailing lists, while she sipped her hot milk. Ten minutes later she refreshed her emails and smiled when she saw a response from Beca.

Hi Bella,
    Rosa emailed me earlier and everything is still the same with your vovo. The doctor is calling in each morning to give her pain relief and your mother is at her bedside most of the time. I'm back on Wednesday morning so I'll pop in and see her then. I'll let you know if anything changes before I get back to Tavira.

Love you,
Beca x

Bella wanted to believe that Rosa spending time with her dying mother was her way of showing remorse for all the things that had brought shame and heartache to her family, but she wasn't convinced that was the truth. *Sadly*, she reflected, *it's far more likely that Rosa is after any money left over from the lottery win to spend on drink. She's welcome to it,* Bella thought, closing the lid of her computer, her mind drifting back to the very different mother-and-daughter relationship she had witnessed earlier in the day. After his MRI scan, Simon Shaw had been moved to a private room where the consultant had induced a coma to give him the best chance of recovery. She had gone to check on him, but had found the door to his room ajar. Maddy and Siena Shaw were clinging onto each other for several minutes before Maddy had gently pushed her daughter away and begun to explain to her, in a voice faltering with emotion, that it was better they were both there as they would be able to support each other whatever the outcome. Bella had experienced a sharp stab of jealousy as she had crept away, not wanting to disturb them. Her mother had never held her or spoken to her in that way. There was an unbreakable bond between Maddy and Siena, while her relationship with Rosa had been fractured from the start.

CHAPTER TWELVE

12.15 a.m. – Tuesday

'Are you going to be all right?' Rachel said, holding Maddy's hands in hers as the two of them stood on her front doorstep watching Siena make her way wearily up the stairs. It was past midnight, and Rachel knew she needed to get at least a few hours of sleep if she was going to function properly the next day. Earlier in the evening, her DI had rung her following his interview with the two eyewitnesses. He had also viewed the mobile phone footage and seemed fairly sure that the motorbike was the cause of the accident on the M4. Although she trusted Graham implicitly, she wanted to watch the captured images for herself before approaching the DVLA for details of the driver. She hadn't mentioned the motorbike to Maddy. There seemed little point in upsetting her friend further until she had proof that the driver of the motorbike had caused the crash. 'I can stay over if you want me to?'

'No,' Maddy said, shaking her head, 'you've done enough already.'

'Are you sure? I can just as easily pop home in the morning for a shower before work if you'd rather not be in the house on your own.'

'We'll be fine; I just want today to end. It's honestly been the worst day of my life. Seeing Simon hooked up to that machine with its constant beeps was frightening. He looked so peaceful and unaware of everything going on around him. I found myself wondering where he is inside his mind. Is he reliving happy times in his life to trick his body into not feeling the pain and trauma? Or is it all just white and sterile and nothing? I guess those are the questions we all ask ourselves about what happens after we die.'

'But he's not dead, Maddy,' Rachel replied, sad to see her friend so distressed. 'Try not to worry too much – the consultant sounded very positive once they had the results of the MRI scan. He said the brain activity was fairly normal, and that suggests Simon won't have any lasting brain damage when he wakes up. We have to have trust in the experts.'

'*If* he wakes up. They don't even know for sure that he will.'

'I got the feeling they were confident he would, and I promise you, I'm not one for giving false hope when I don't believe there is any,' she said, squeezing Maddy's hand.

'Thank you for that. I keep thinking this is all a horrible dream and I'm going to wake up in a moment, but then I look at your concerned face and I know it all really happened. Just hearing you say that you think he'll pull through gives me the strength to keep believing. I don't know how we would have got through today without you,' Maddy said, her bottom lip trembling.

'I told you to call me if you ever needed help, and I'm glad that you felt you could.'

'But that was for help with Siena. None of us could ever have imagined that something like this would happen.'

'Speaking of Siena, I think you should keep a very close eye on her. She's actually taken this better than I would have expected, but she might just be hiding her true feelings until she's on her own. You should get her to talk about how she's feeling if you can,' Rachel said. An image filled her mind of the exasperated expression on her dad's face as she'd clung onto her mother, with tears rolling down her cheeks, the day they dropped her off at university. 'For goodness' sake, Rachel,' her dad had said, 'anyone would think you were the one that pervert meddled with. Ruth was much more grown-up about moving away from home. You should take a leaf out of her book.' Her mother had come to her defence, saying, 'Leave her alone, John. People deal with things differently.' How right her mother had been. Ruth's attempts to deny what had happened to her in childhood by never talking about it had eventually led to her suicide attempt and her mental frailty.

'You're right. I'll go up and see if she wants to talk things through. Thanks again for today.'

'I'll let you know if I get any more details on the cause of the crash,' Rachel said, giving Maddy a quick hug before heading down the steps and climbing into her car for the short drive home.

Maddy pressed the button to close the gates after watching the red lights from the back of Rachel's Audi disappear into the inky darkness of the night, swallowed up like a pebble in quicksand. She shivered. There were thousands of times over the years when she had been in the house without Simon, but this was different. He wasn't away for a night or two in Preston or Grimsby because his team had a match the next day; he was clinging onto life in a hospital bed thirty-five miles away.

'Mum?'

The sound of Siena's voice caught her by surprise. She spun round to see her daughter sitting on the top step of the staircase in her pyjamas, exactly as she had done so many times as a young child when she had been awoken by a nightmare.

'He is going to be all right, isn't he?'

Her daughter needed reassurance. For a split second she wished she had asked Rachel to stay. It was hard to force herself to feel positive, but she knew she had to keep Siena's spirits up.

'Rachel seems to think so,' was the best she could manage in response. 'You go and get into bed and I'll be in to say good night when I've turned everything off down here.'

'Can you sleep in with me tonight, Mum?'

'Of course. I'll be up in a few minutes.'

Maddy watched as her daughter hauled herself to her feet and stumbled towards her bedroom, head down and shoulders slumped. She was reminded of the days directly after Rob's devastating phone call. 'Please don't leave me on my own, Mum. I don't want to be alone,' Siena had begged. Simon had protested, 'For Christ sake, she's twenty-two, not twelve. She's a grown woman, she should be able to deal with stuff like this at her age.' But Maddy had given in to her daughter's pleas. 'I'm her mother, and she will always be my little girl whatever her age. She needs me, Simon, surely you can see that?' Night after night she had lain at the side of her distraught daughter, waiting until Siena's sobs had quietened and she had fallen into a fitful sleep in the early hours of the morning. Once she had been sure her daughter was asleep, Maddy would ease herself out of her bed and creep across the room, careful not to wake her grieving child, before sliding between the cool sheets of her own bed. She would lie there in the dark, tears streaming silently down her cheeks, with little hope of sleeping herself, trying to work out how she was going to help their only child recover from the trauma of losing the love of her life. In her waking hours, Siena had kept on saying, 'my life is over, I've got nothing to live for', and every time it had been like a dagger twisting in Maddy's heart. 'She'll get over it,' Simon had said, 'a pretty girl like her will have another boyfriend by the end of the week'. He couldn't have been more wrong. By the end of the week she was in Mountview Hospital having her stomach pumped after taking an overdose of headache pills. Maddy had been forced to leave Siena on her own while she went into work, or she risked losing her job. The guilt of choosing her job over her daughter's well-being had consumed her, and that was why she'd been crying in the hospital cafeteria the night Rachel had approached her.

It's funny, she thought, flicking the kitchen lights off, *I've only known Rachel a few weeks and yet she is the closest thing to a friend I have. What does that say about me? I have lots of acquaintances, but no real friends, with the possible exception of Cal.* He'd left several messages throughout the day, asking if she was all right, but she hadn't felt up to replying. *I'll do it tomorrow*, she thought, putting her clothes in the dirty linen bin and replacing them with an oversized T-shirt that she only wore in bed when Simon was away. She quickly cleansed her face, removing the lingering traces of make-up that had survived the tears throughout the day, and brushed her teeth.

'Here I am,' Maddy said, climbing into bed beside her daughter.

'What took you so long?'

'This old face of mine needs a bit more attention than yours to stay looking half decent.'

'You're talking rubbish. You've got better skin than people half your age. No wonder Dad fell in love with you. You're so lucky to have each other. Most of my friends' parents are on their second or third marriage,' Siena said, turning off the bedside lamp so that they were both lying in the dark with only the merest hint of moonlight filtering into the room from around the curtains.

'It was love at first sight for me,' Maddy said, reaching for her daughter's hand under the covers. 'I knew within a week that he was the person I wanted to spend the rest of my life with.'

'It must have been the same for Dad.'

'I don't know. I think he was on the rebound when we met. For the first six months we were together he never once said "I love you", instead he made up the word "loke". He said it was a combination of like and love, and that's what he felt for me.'

'Did it bother you that he never said "I love you"?'

'Not really. Words are just words. I think I was secretly pleased that he'd invented a special one for me.'

'Rob used to say "I love you" all the time, but obviously he didn't really mean it.'

Maddy could hardly believe what she was hearing. Until that moment, Siena hadn't uttered a single criticism of Rob's behaviour towards her, even when she had found out that he had started seeing his new girlfriend before he had finished with her. What she really wanted to say was that Rob was a lying, cheating bastard, but she didn't think her daughter was ready to hear that yet.

'Maybe Rob meant it when he said it,' she said, gently squeezing Siena's hand. 'I don't think he deliberately set out to hurt you, he just came to the conclusion that you weren't right for each other, whereas your dad never says anything unless he means it. His world is all black and white, with no shades of grey.'

'Did he mean what he said to Rob on the phone on Sunday night?'

'You were listening to his conversation?'

'Only a bit of it. I was going to go in on my way up to bed and apologise for being rude earlier, but I could hear he was still on the phone and I knew straight away who he was talking to. I heard him threaten Rob. I don't think that was a good idea, Mum.'

'What do you mean?'

'Rob has a kind of superiority complex. He wouldn't have liked being spoken to like that. And he has a bad temper, too.'

'You're not suggesting he would actually have done anything to harm your dad, like tampering with his brakes or something, are you?' Maddy said, feeling a prickle of fear. *They had all assumed the crash was an accident, but what if it wasn't?* 'Didn't you tell us he'd been doing a mechanics course?'

'That was just so he could keep his old motorbike on the road without constantly paying out to have it repaired. No, I was meaning I wonder if Rob threatened Dad back and Dad was preoccupied by it when he lost control of the Jag.'

Maddy could hear the worry in her daughter's voice. Even if there was a possibility that Rob had something to do with the accident, either physically or psychologically, there was nothing to be gained by letting her fret about it.

'I think we're both exhausted and probably overthinking things. Let's get some sleep and talk about it in the morning,' Maddy said, making a mental note to have a word with Rachel about Rob's possible involvement.

'You're not going to creep off to your own bed in the night, are you Mum?' Siena said, turning onto her side away from Maddy.

'You knew I did that?'

'Of course. Your side of the bed was never warm when I woke up.'

'No, I won't creep off, I promise,' she said, turning so that she could see the rounded outline of her daughter beneath the duvet. Without the warmth of her husband and the sound of his breathing punctuated by the occasional snore, there was little point in retreating to the marital bed. Her final thought before drifting into an uneasy sleep was, *if he pulls through, I'll never moan about his snoring again.*

CHAPTER THIRTEEN

8 a.m. – Tuesday

When Rachel pulled into the police station car park at 8 a.m. on Tuesday morning, DI Graham Wilson's car was already parked in his allocated bay. She took the two flights of stairs rather than the lift up to her second-floor office, planning on stopping by the kitchenette to make herself another cup of coffee. The first one of the day had failed to cut through the tiredness she was feeling following her late night. Graham had beaten her to that, too.

'Morning, Guv. Coffee? The kettle's just boiled.'

'A nice strong one, please,' she said, watching him heap two spoons of granules into her mug, labelled THE BOSS. 'I can't seem to get going this morning.'

'What time did you get back to Sonning from the hospital?'

'I'm not sure, but it must have been after midnight cos I wasn't in bed until 1 a.m. and I only live a few minutes away from the Shaws' house. It felt like I had only just closed my eyes when the alarm went off at half past six.'

'Any more news on Simon Shaw's condition?'

'Thankfully, he's stable now, although still critical and still in a coma. The MRI scan didn't show any major brain damage as far as they can tell, but it's early days yet.'

'He was lucky to get out of that wreck alive.'

'I know. It's also pretty amazing that there were no other major casualties.'

'Agreed, but when you see the phone footage, it's fairly obvious why. Vehicles were keeping their distance from the lunatic on the motorbike, and that's what gave them time to stop with just a few minor prangs even though they were all doing around sixty.'

Rachel took a sip of her strong black coffee and grimaced at the bitter taste. 'If that doesn't do the trick of cutting through my brain fug, I don't know what will,' she said, leading the way through to her office.

'I've sent the footage to you in an email, so we can view it on the bigger screen in here. I think it's pretty clear that the road rage incident caused the crash. The witnesses said they'd noticed the motorbike way before the crash happened, but it didn't seem to be behaving oddly until the traffic picked up speed after the M25 exit. See what you think.'

Rachel hit the arrow on the touchscreen of her computer and the film appeared on the TV on her office wall. It was quite unsteady as it was being shot from a moving vehicle and she could hear the voices of the two witnesses as the drama unfolded.

'What does that idiot think he's doing?' a man's voice said.

'He's still flashing his lights at that Jag in the outside lane,' a woman replied.

'Why doesn't he just undertake if he's in such a flaming hurry? We're already doing over the reduced speed limit. It would serve him right if he got nicked by the speed cameras.'

Graham interjected. 'Like I told you on the phone last night, they were a bit worried about playing me the footage as they didn't want to get done for speeding.'

'Is that why they didn't play it to anyone at the scene?'

'Yes. I just told them to be more speed-aware in future. This is the bit, Guv.'

Rachel's eyes hadn't left the screen while she and Graham had been talking.

'Watch the bike cut in front of our witnesses.'

There was a jolt to the filming, as though the brakes of their car had been applied suddenly, along with several expletives. 'That was a bit bloody close,' the woman's voice said.

'See if you can get a close-up of the number plate. What the hell is the passenger doing now?' the man asked.

In the footage, Rachel could see the pillion passenger wafting his right arm up and down.

'You don't think the Jag's got a puncture, do you, and these guys are just trying to be good citizens?' the woman said.

Before the man could answer, the motorbike suddenly sped up and cut in front of the Jag and there was a scream on the audio as the Jag flew up into the air, then nothing.

'That's where she dropped her phone, Guv,' Graham explained. 'She was too upset to carry on filming after her boyfriend had narrowly missed going into the car in front. As it was, the car behind couldn't stop in time and crunched the rear of their car. She was really shaken up by it all, as you can imagine.'

'Have you done a screen grab of the number plate?' Rachel said, scribbling the words *number plate* on the pad on her desk.

'I've tried to, but it's blurred. It almost looks as though it has something smeared across it, but the techie boys may be able to clean it up a bit.'

'I just want to watch the last few seconds again,' Rachel said, touching the on-screen dot on the timeline of the filming and moving it to the left. 'What do you think the arm signal was about?'

'At first I thought it was to try and get the Jag to slow down, but then I thought that didn't make sense, as he was flashing his lights because he wasn't going fast enough. I wondered if maybe he was trying to get them to wind the window down.'

'That's what I was thinking, but why? If he wanted to shout abuse at Simon Shaw it would never be heard if they were both driving above the speed limit. This is the bit,' Rachel said. 'I thought I saw something. Yes, there,' she said, freezing the picture as best she could.

'What is it, Guv?'

'It looks like it's a flash of some sort.'

'It could be sunlight catching on a piece of jewellery.'

'Maybe, but it could also be something more sinister.'

Graham turned to look at his boss. 'You're not suggesting a gunshot, are you, Guv?'

'I don't think we should rule it out. Have the footage sent to the tech team marked high-priority. I want to have a look at this section frame by frame.'

'On it, Guv.'

'Where is the wreckage now?'

'It was taken to the compound yesterday afternoon. The forensics team have already started examining it, but they hadn't found anything when I called my friend, Martin, last night after our witnesses left. I'm having to tread a bit carefully on this. This isn't really our case, and you know how tetchy other divisions get if we muscle in on their patch.'

'I appreciate it, Graham, and don't worry, I'll take the flack if we get any, although we do have justification for investigating as the driver of the Jag lives in our area. I know they like to be sure of the facts before sharing them, but it does sometimes feel as though they would benefit from having a rocket stuck up their arses.'

Graham suppressed a smile.

'Having watched the footage,' Rachel continued, 'it's pretty obvious that whatever the flash turns out to be, the motorbike caused the crash. Once we get the number plate, we can track the rider and his passenger down and ask them a few questions.'

Rachel's phone started ringing as Graham got up to leave. It was Maddy. Rachel swallowed. It was early for her friend to be ringing. *Why would she be calling unless she had some bad news from the hospital?* She steeled herself to be met with a near-hysterical

Maddy, and was relieved when she sounded quite calm, although it was difficult to hear her, as she appeared to be whispering into the phone.

'Hi Rachel, I'm sorry to ring you so early.'

'Is everything okay? Did you manage to get some sleep?'

'Sleep would be overstating it, but I did doze off a few times.'

'And Siena? How is she this morning?'

'She's not up yet, which is why I'm keeping my voice down. Before she fell asleep last night, something she said worried me.'

Rachel waited for Maddy to continue, but there was silence from the other end of the phone so in the end she had to prompt her.

'Go on.'

'I'm not going to lie. I never really liked Siena's ex-boyfriend, and neither did Simon. We did everything to try and make him feel welcome in our family, but he never reciprocated. I had to put up with him because Siena was so besotted, and I thought if I said anything to try and come between them, she would choose him over us. I was terrified that she might walk out of our lives and I couldn't bear the thought of losing her. It was never going to work between them. He's ten years older than her, and they really had very little in common. He made her feel as though the job she does is completely worthless, just because she isn't a nurse or a teacher or something. Not everyone is cut out to be a nurse, and anyway, nurses and teachers wear make-up and like beauty products, too. In a way she's providing them with a service by helping them to find the best products at the cheapest prices…'

Rachel was wondering where Maddy's rambling was leading.

'I should probably have told you about this before, but I didn't think it was relevant until Siena was talking about it last night. She said she didn't think her dad should have threatened Rob because he's got a bad temper and might retaliate.'

'Hold on a minute, Maddy. Are you saying that Simon threatened Siena's ex? When was this?'

'On Sunday night. Rob rang the house wanting to speak to Siena, but fortunately Simon answered the phone. He took the call in his den, but Siena told me last night that she overheard some of the conversation on her way up to bed. Simon warned Rob off trying to contact her again, telling him he knew people who would gladly wring his neck. Siena seems to think that Rob would most likely have threatened him back, and that it might have been playing on her dad's mind when he crashed. When I was lying in bed last night trying to sleep, I couldn't help wondering if Rob took it one step further. It probably sounds silly, but you don't think he could have tampered with Simon's car, do you? You know, the brakes or something?'

'It's one thing to threaten someone, Maddy,' Rachel said, finding it hard to believe that Siena's ex-boyfriend would have either the ability or the desire to tamper with Simon's car, 'but to actually do something to cause them harm is something else entirely. Something like brake failure could potentially have caused a multiple pile-up with lots of people being killed or injured, and most people wouldn't want that on their conscience. Not only that, but you'd need to know a thing or two about cars, or it would flag up as a fault on the dashboard.'

'But he does know about stuff like that. I think I told you he's in the army?'

'Yes, you mentioned it. Is he something to do with vehicle maintenance?'

'No, but he's just been on a mechanic's course. He told them it was so that he could get army vehicles going if they were out on patrol and one broke down, but it was really because the repair bills on his motorbike have been totting up and he can't afford them on his army pay.'

Rachel's interest was piqued. What she had been prepared to dismiss as a far-fetched idea from her friend, who was clutching at straws in her attempt to try and prove that her husband wasn't a bad driver, suddenly became a credible cause of the crash from someone with a clear motive.

'He's got a motorbike?'

'Yes. I was always terrified when Siena was out on it with him. He was always driving too fast, even though I know she asked him not to. He thinks he's invincible because he survived Afghanistan, but it only takes a minor concentration lapse on the roads to become another traffic accident statistic.' Maddy went silent for a moment, obviously realising what she had said. 'Do you think I'm being irrational?'

'I think it would be a massive overreaction on Rob's part to tamper with Simon's car, knowing that the likely outcome would be death or serious injury,' Rachel said, aware of the sharp intake of breath from the other end of the phone line. 'But I don't think it would do any harm to go and see him and ask him a few questions about his whereabouts on Monday morning.'

'Or more likely Sunday night, when it was dark.'

'Yes, of course,' Rachel said. She had been thinking about the footage she had viewed a few minutes ago, rather than Rob having the opportunity to tinker with Simon's Jag, but of course Maddy knew nothing about that. 'What's Rob's surname? And where is he based?'

'It's Turnbull, although I've always added the letter "y" to the end because he bullies people. He's based at the barracks in Windsor.'

'Do you know what regiment he's in?'

'I can't remember, but I know I've seen photographs of him wearing a red jacket at ceremonial events.'

'I'm not up on my army regiments, but I'll get one of my officers to check it,' Rachel said, immediately thinking that it was a job for PC Eleanor Drake.

'Do you think it's the right thing to do, Rachel? I mean, if he doesn't have anything to do with what happened, will he come after us in revenge?'

'Let me deal with it, Maddy. I'll go over to Windsor myself, and I promise he will have no clue as to why I'm there unless he incriminates himself. Okay?'

'Okay.'

'Let me know when you've had an update from the hospital on Simon's condition, and I'll get back to you when I've spoken to Mr Turnbull.'

'Sergeant Turnbull.'

'Whatever. I'll speak to you later.'

The moment Rachel disconnected the call on her mobile, she picked up her desk phone and dialled the extension for the video viewing room. 'How are we doing with the footage?' she asked.

'Larry's isolated the last few frames from the point you asked, Guv, and we've just run them forward frame by frame a few times. It's inconclusive because of the angle and the quality of the footage, but Larry's going to keep working on it to try and enhance it. I think you should probably take a look at it, though.'

'I'm on my way,' she said, virtually throwing the phone back in its cradle and rushing out of the room. If it did turn out to be a gunshot, fired at Simon Shaw from the back of a motorbike, Rachel now had a prime suspect.

CHAPTER FOURTEEN

10.20 a.m. – Tuesday

The drive to the barracks in the centre of Windsor had only taken thirty minutes and with DS Errol Green at the wheel, Rachel had been able to liaise with PC Eleanor Drake, who had discovered that Sergeant Rob Turnbull was in the Grenadier Guards. She had phoned ahead to make sure that access to the barracks would be granted without divulging the reason for her visit or who she was there to see. She would request to speak to Sergeant Turnbull on arrival and would be ambiguous with her questions about his whereabouts the previous morning, keeping the Shaws' name out of things.

Her decision to take Errol rather than Graham had been deliberate. If, as Maddy Shaw had implied, Rob Turnbull was a bully, her DS had a bigger physical presence and would prevent her from feeling intimidated by him. At five foot four and with a slight build, despite all the junk food she ate when she was tied up on a case and couldn't be bothered to cook for one, Rachel's exterior belied the steel within. *To have survived what I did as a six-year-old and go on to lead a normal life, I've had to be made of stern stuff. Normal life: who am I kidding?* she thought, as the car came to a halt at the barrier next to the gatehouse. *I'm thirty-five and I've never been able to maintain a relationship with a man for more than three months, until now*, she had to concede.

Things were different with Tim. There had been an instant attraction on both sides the day he had walked into the interview room as the defence lawyer for a particularly unpleasant client. Although he had asked her out within twenty-four hours of meeting, he had understood her need for space. Their dates were sporadic, never more than twice a week, and there had been no pressure from him to spend Christmas together or to meet his family, if in fact he had one. Rachel realised she really knew very little about him apart from where he lived, what he did as a job and the fact that he was great in bed. A shudder of pleasure ran through her. Because she was so loath to allow anyone to get too close emotionally, she set a huge store on the physical side of her relationships with men, and there was no denying that she had never felt so well-suited to someone as she did to Tim. It was as though they were two pieces of an intricate jigsaw that fitted together perfectly. To date, she hadn't uttered those three little words, 'I love you', although at times she had felt close, but neither had he. *Maybe that's why I'm still seeing him five months on. But the moment can't be far away for us to decide what happens next.* Rachel didn't want it to end. It was the closest thing to love she had ever felt for anyone apart from her twin sister, but she also had to admit that the thought of moving on to the next stage was terrifying.

'We're here, Guv,' Errol said, pulling the car to a halt in a space marked 'visitor'.

'Right,' she said, getting back into a work frame of mind, 'let's go and lock horns with Sergeant Turnbull.'

Twenty minutes later, they were driving past the gatehouse and back out of the barracks having achieved nothing. Sergeant Turnbull wasn't there. Apparently he and the rest of his troop had been transported to Wales on Sunday morning for a training exercise in the Brecon Beacons. The phone call to the Shaw household must have been made from there. According to the officer Rachel had spoken to, he would be out of contact with base camp until

Wednesday evening, as the soldiers were not permitted to have their personal mobile phones with them when out on manoeuvres. She had already contacted the local Welsh police to check at the barracks that Rob Turnbull was definitely in the group that had gone out on field manoeuvres on Sunday night. It was highly unlikely that there was an error on the part of the army, but it wouldn't hurt to check.

As she fastened her seat belt in the back of the car, Graham rang with a second piece of bad news. Larry's best efforts at deciphering the number plate on the motorbike had so far drawn a blank.

'Someone has smeared what looks like engine grease all over it, making it virtually impossible to read,' he said. 'It's obviously been done deliberately, which points to someone trying to hide their identity and would suggest that maybe this wasn't such a random act of road rage. I've left Larry working on it while I head over to forensics. Is it worth asking Maddy Shaw if there was anyone in Simon's life, apart from Sergeant Turnbull, who might wish him harm?'

'I'll call her now. Let me know if you get anything from forensics.' Rachel hung up and then dialled Maddy's number as the barrier rose to let them out of the barracks, and Errol swung the car back onto the road. 'Hello Maddy, it's Rachel. Any news from the hospital?'

'I spoke to them shortly after I called you this morning. There's no change, but they seem to think that's a good thing. Siena's just in the shower, and then we're heading back there to sit with Simon. Any joy with Rob?'

'It looks as though it's a non-starter, Maddy. I'm on my way back from Windsor now. His troop travelled down to Wales on Sunday morning for manoeuvres, so he couldn't have been in the Sonning area on Sunday night or Monday morning.'

'In a way that's a relief, although I'm sorry I wasted your time with my crazy suspicion that the crash wasn't down to Simon's driving.'

'Actually, Maddy, we have reason to believe that Simon might not have been at fault.'

'Oh?'

Rachel could picture the tense expression on her friend's face. 'I didn't mention it to you earlier, but there is some eyewitness footage, shot on a mobile phone, showing a motorbike acting very suspiciously just before Simon's car hit the central reservation.'

'So that's why you didn't think my idea of Rob being involved was crazy. But now you're saying it wasn't him?'

'It can't have been him, but that's why I'm ringing you. Can you think of anyone that Simon has argued with lately who might want to hurt him, or worse?'

'No. He's not the arguing type. He's actually a bit of a pussycat, really, apart from when he gets mad at the players in the dressing room at half-time.'

'Have any of them got a violent past, do you know? Has Simon mentioned facing up to an individual player?'

'He certainly hasn't said anything to me. Some of the younger ones don't like him. They think his training methods are old-fashioned, and I remember him saying that his captain told him his tactics are from the 1990s. That said, I don't think any of them would resort to any kind of violence. They don't need to. All they have to do is carry on ignoring what they've been working on when they play on a Saturday and it will get him fired. He was talking about "player power" over breakfast on Sunday morning, after Town's latest defeat.'

'And you can't think of anyone else he's crossed swords with?'

'No. Obviously he doesn't tell me everything, and we're not together 24/7, but I'm sure I would have noticed if something was bothering him.'

'Does he have a diary?'

'Yes, it's on his desk in the den.'

'Maybe you could have a look through it for names you don't recognise.'

'Will it be all right to do it tonight? Siena's just come downstairs, so I'd really like to get off to the hospital now.'

'Of course. It's only a tentative line of investigation. It may well turn out to be a random case of road rage. There are some very angry people in the world today. Call me later to let me know if there's any change in Simon's condition.'

Rachel ended her call with Maddy, and before she could slip her phone back into her bag, it rang again. 'What have you got for me, Graham?' she asked.

'I'm with the forensics team, Guv, after you suggested I should drop by.'

Rachel smiled at Graham's tact, following what she had actually said back at the station earlier that morning.

'And?'

'They'd already been investigating the fragments of glass from the windscreen. Apparently, they can tell by the size of the glass pieces that the windscreen had already shattered before the impact of the crash. Initially they thought a stone might have struck it and Shaw had lost control of his vehicle while he was punching the glass outward. But then they found the piece where impact occurred, and it wasn't just a chip with a tiny hole, it was a bigger hole made by a missile travelling at speed.'

'By missile, do you mean bullet?' she said, exchanging a look with Errol.

'Exactly. Looks like you were right, Guv. The flash on the mobile phone footage must have been the pillion passenger shooting at Simon Shaw before the motorbike sped off. This is starting to look less like road rage and more like attempted murder.'

'Simon doesn't have a gunshot wound among his long list of injuries, so the bullet must be embedded in the interior of the car somewhere. Once forensics find that, we'll know what type of gun was used. It will be interesting if it's army issue.'

'Are you back to thinking that Rob Turnbull is involved?'

'I think it's a strong possibility. With Turnbull miles away in the Brecon Beacons, he has a perfect alibi. But there are a couple of options here. Either he managed to slip away from the training camp, maybe getting one of his mates to cover for him, cause Simon Shaw's crash and then drive back to Wales on his motorbike before he was missed. After all, we're only talking about three hours or so each way on the M4.'

'Or?'

'Or he got somebody to do his dirty work for him. Either way, I think a trip to Wales is on the cards, and you may need an overnight bag if he can't be tracked down straight away.'

'Would it be all right to pass on that, Guv? It's my daughter's birthday tomorrow, and we've booked to go to Legoland after school.'

Although Rachel didn't have children of her own, she wasn't completely heartless. She knew the importance of family celebrations, even though her parents had never taken them to crowded places after the abduction, just to be on the safe side. She could have insisted, but why spoil a good working relationship when there were other options? 'How are you fixed, Errol?'

There was an awkward pause.

'Um, actually Guv, Graham invited me and my missus and our two little ones to go to Legoland with them. I could cancel, though.'

Rachel hadn't expected that. She hadn't given a thought to the possibility that two of her subordinates could be friends out of work. *Just because I don't mix business with pleasure, it doesn't mean they shouldn't*, she thought.

'No, of course not. I wouldn't hear of it. I'll head down there myself, and I'm sure PC Drake will be only too happy to get out from behind her desk,' she said, turning her attention back to the phone. 'Maybe you could organise that for me, Graham. I think it might be better to go tomorrow anyway. If they're due back from manoeuvres late tomorrow night, it will mean they don't have to track Turnbull down and bring him in. I don't want him doing a disappearing act in the Welsh mountains before we've had a chance to question him.'

'Good point, Guv. I'll keep you posted if I hear anything more from forensics,' he said, ending the call.

If I'm going to be away for a couple of nights, I should probably let Tim know, Rachel thought. *I don't want him to think I'm avoiding him after standing him up last night.* She tapped a quick message out on her phone:

Hi Tim, I really am sorry about last night. I've got to go to Wales tomorrow, maybe for a couple of days, so I wondered if you fancied coming over to mine for dinner tonight? Nothing fancy. Spag bol sound okay? Xx

A couple of minutes later, she received his response:

Spag bol sounds fine. I'll bring a bottle of red. 7.30 p.m. okay? X

Rachel responded with a smiley face emoji before slipping her phone back in her bag.

*

At his office in Reading, Tim wanted to punch the air. At last there was a chink in Rachel's armour. With most women, he wouldn't have been as patient or persistent, but Rachel wasn't most women, she was special. He'd waited five months to be invited into her home, and hopefully her life, and now his patience had paid off.

CHAPTER FIFTEEN

It was after six by the time Maddy and Siena got home from the hospital. They had sat at Simon's bedside for more than five hours, taking it in turns to fetch coffee or water to keep them going, but neither of them had felt like eating. As a consequence, Maddy's stomach was rumbling as she unlocked the front door and let the two of them into the hallway.

'I think I'll make an early dinner, if that's okay with you?'

'I'm not really hungry, Mum,' Siena said, heading towards the foot of the stairs. 'I think I'll just go up to my room and have a lie-down. I had no idea how exhausting it could be sitting at the bedside of someone you love, silently praying that they're going to pull through.'

Maddy swallowed hard. She knew that as well as talking about her dad, Siena was acknowledging the pain she must have put her parents through with her recent suicide attempt. In her own way, she was trying to say she was sorry.

'You know, I don't really fancy a proper dinner either. Why don't I just make us some tea and toast and then we can both get an early night? What do you say?'

'Okay,' Siena said, following her mum into the kitchen and sitting down at the dining table. 'It just doesn't seem possible that we were all sitting here on Sunday evening with not the slightest hint of how our lives were about to be ripped apart.'

'I know. These past two days have seemed like an eternity, watching and hoping for your dad's eyes to open and for him to crack one of his dreadful jokes. The sight of him just lying there when he usually can't sit still for five minutes is surreal.'

Between the shock of finding out about Simon's accident and then the worry of how Siena would react to the news, Maddy hadn't really had much time to consider who might want to harm her husband or why. While Siena was at the cafeteria getting them both a cup of tea, she had tried to recall any telltale signs that all was not well. Simon had been a bit short-tempered and snappy at times since Christmas, but that was when Beechwood Town's run of bad form had started and she had just assumed he was under pressure from work. *What if there was something else bothering him, something he hadn't shared with her?* She had looked at her husband lying peacefully in his hospital bed as though in a deep sleep and had rested her head next to his on the pillow, whispering, 'Is there something you're not telling me, Simon?' She had hastily brushed the tears away from her eyes as Siena had come back into the room holding two paper cups full of tea.

'Do you think he knew we were there today, Mum? Could he hear us when we talked to him?'

'Truthfully, I don't know, but the nurse said they advise talking to coma patients. Research suggests that the sound of a familiar voice can help them.'

'I think I might take a book in tomorrow and read to him. I found it difficult putting into words all the things I wanted to say.'

'From what I heard, you did pretty well.'

'This happening to Dad has put the whole business with Rob into perspective. I feel such an idiot, Mum. Seeing Dad lying there, hooked up to a machine to help him breathe, made me realise what a gift life is, and how throwing it away would have been such a waste. I'm so sorry for what I've put you both through these past few weeks,' Siena said, tears streaming down her cheeks.

Maddy abandoned the bread she was cutting and rushed over to wrap her arms around her daughter. 'It's okay, it's okay,' she said, stroking Siena's long dark hair back off her face.

'No, it's not okay, Mum. It's all my fault. Things hadn't been right between Rob and me for a while. I knew he didn't love me as much as I loved him, but I hoped that my love would be enough for both of us. Sitting at Dad's bedside today gave me time to think about all the chances Rob gave me to finish with him, but I'm so damn stubborn I didn't want to admit to myself that I wasn't the person Rob wanted to spend the rest of his life with. Looking back, him forgetting to bring the tickets for our holiday must have been because he didn't want to go. Little did he realise how persuasive I could be in getting the travel agent to email me new documents. I wish I hadn't,' Siena said, pulling away from Maddy's embrace and looking her mother in the eye. 'The holiday wasn't great. Rob kept leaving me alone on the beach while he went off surfing. I didn't think too much of it at the time, because I know how much he loves to surf, and I knew how hard he'd worked to earn the extra money to go. But since he... since he dumped me,' Siena said, swallowing to try and control her tears, 'I realise that it was a way of not having to spend time with me unless he absolutely had to. At dinner on the last night, he said he had something to tell me, but before he could speak, I interrupted him and told him that I loved him more than life itself. Maybe in my heart I knew what he was going to say, but I couldn't bear to hear the words, and when I asked him what he had been about to say, he said it didn't matter.'

Maddy waited, not wanting to interrupt her daughter's flow now that she was finally opening up to her. Although Siena had had one-to-one sessions with a therapist at the hospital where she had been treated, she had refused to speak to either of her parents about taking the drug overdose and her reasons for wanting to die. It was now becoming clearer to Maddy that Siena had seen the warning signs of the imminent break-up but had refused to acknowledge them. She was so heavily invested in her first proper relationship, believing Rob to be the person she would create a family with, and grow old with, that she had refused to accept that he didn't want her any more. *The feeling of rejection must have completely overwhelmed her*, Maddy thought, *and I couldn't really help because I'd never experienced it. I married my first true love.*

Simon had tried to encourage his wife to let the experts deal with the situation. 'You need to take a step back from this,' he had said. 'You're not helping her by being so understanding, and you're not helping yourself either. It's her pain, not yours.' Little did Simon know the agony she had been going through. How could he? He wasn't her mother. The special relationship Maddy and Siena shared, that was more like sisters than mother and daughter, had been the envy of all Siena's friends throughout school and university, but now it was having its weakness exposed. A sister's role was unity and unwavering support; a parent's role was guidance, but ultimately allowing their child to learn from their own mistakes. *Maybe Simon was right after all*, Maddy thought, resisting the urge to say something to comfort her daughter. *Perhaps I allowed myself to get too emotionally involved.*

'If only I hadn't stuck my head in the sand, refusing to accept that I wasn't Rob's "one", Dad's accident wouldn't have happened. When Rob rang here on Sunday, I genuinely think he'd only just heard about my attempted suicide and was ringing to see if I was okay. If I'd been more honest with you two, Dad might not have threatened Rob in the way he did. Regardless of his bravado, Dad was probably a bit concerned that maybe he had misjudged Rob and overstepped the mark, and if he was worried about it, he wouldn't have been paying full attention to the road. You see, it *is* my fault.'

Maddy hadn't told her daughter about her conversation with Rachel Hart earlier that morning that had led the police officer to open a line of enquiry on Rob Turnbull. In light of what she had just heard, maybe he wasn't the villain both she and her husband had believed him to be, although there was still the issue of the motorbike at the scene of the crash.

'Actually, Siena,' she said, 'the police do now have reason to believe that maybe it wasn't an accident after all.'

'What?'

'They have footage of a motorbike behaving suspiciously just before your dad crashed.'

'Do they think it was Rob?' Siena asked, a look of horror on her face.

'Not necessarily. They do want to interview him to exclude him from their enquiries, but there's a strong possibility that it was a random road rage incident.'

'Oh my God. Please don't let it be Rob—'

'Rachel also asked me if your dad had any enemies who might do him harm.'

'Dad? Enemies? He's Mr Nice Guy to everyone.'

'That's what I said, but I did promise Rachel I'd have a look through your dad's diary for any unfamiliar names, just in case. I'll do it after we've had a bite to eat.'

'I'll help you. We could take our toast through to the den.'

'And risk getting crumbs and greasy fingermarks all over Dad's desk? I don't think so. He wouldn't be very pleased with us when he gets home.'

'He is coming home, isn't he, Mum? You're not just saying that?'

'Your dad's a fighter. If anyone can bounce back from something like this, he can. Now, do you want Marmite on your toast, or just butter?'

'Just butter. And I'll make the tea while you're doing the toast. Things are going to be different from now on, Mum. I'm twenty-two. I have to start standing on my own two feet instead of needing someone to lean on. You were always my crutch until

I met Rob, and for the past two years it's been him. From now on I'm going to walk unaided, a bit like that scene in *Forrest Gump*.'

Maddy depressed the lever on the toaster, suppressing the slightest of smiles. *I've got my daughter back – but I just hope the price wasn't too high.*

CHAPTER SIXTEEN

7.05 p.m. – Tuesday

Before heading into the den to go through the things on her husband's desk, Maddy decided to give Rachel a quick call and update her on Simon's progress, not that there was much.

'Hi, Maddy, how did it go today at the hospital?'

'Not much to report, really. Simon is stable, but still breathing with the aid of the ventilator. The nursing staff seem satisfied that he's doing all right.'

'Well, that's good. Call me tomorrow if there's any change.'

Am I imagining it, or does Rachel seem anxious to get rid of me? Maddy thought.

'I just rang to say that Siena and I are about to go through Simon's diary and the papers on his desk. Do you want me to get back to you tonight if we find anything?'

'Tomorrow morning will be fine.'

Maddy couldn't be sure, but it sounded as though Rachel was crying. 'I don't want to pry, but are you okay? You sound as though you're in tears.'

'I am, but don't panic, I'm chopping onions. I'm expecting company this evening, and I've promised a spag bol but I'm not the greatest cook in the world. I've got a feeling he'll be the one crying when he tastes it.'

Maddy realised that she knew nothing about Rachel's private life, apart from the fact that she had a twin sister with mental health issues who was a resident at Mountview Hospital. She hadn't given any thought to whether or not she might be married or dating.

'Oh, I'm sure it won't be that bad. There's not a lot you can get wrong with a spag bol sauce. Just don't overcook the pasta. I'll let you get on,' she said. 'I shouldn't have bothered you out of office hours, particularly after you had such a late finish with us last night.'

'Don't be silly, I asked you to keep me updated. And obviously it goes without saying that you can call if the situation changes dramatically.'

Maddy was fully aware of what the comment alluded to, but she chose to ignore it.

'Have a nice evening,' she said before disconnecting the call. Glancing at the screen, she could see another two missed calls from Cal. *I'll ring him later when Siena's gone to bed*, she thought, going into the den to join her daughter.

'Hasn't Dad heard that there's a global environmental crisis and we need to stop cutting down trees to produce paper?' Siena said. 'What is all this lot?'

'Bills, most likely. Your dad insists on taking care of stuff like that even though I'm perfectly capable of doing it,' Maddy replied, checking through them to ensure none of them was due for payment.

'Why can't he do it online like most normal people?'

'Replace the word "normal" with "young",' she said. 'Young people do everything online, but our generation and people older than us like to have actual paper statements sent out in the post. He doesn't trust paperless. He thinks it's easier for mistakes to go unnoticed.'

Siena rolled her eyes in exasperation.

'He's the same with his diary. Instead of entering appointments on his phone, which even I do, and I'm a bit of a technophobe, he writes everything down in his desk diary. Then he has to ring me from work to check his diary because it's too big and heavy to carry around. Figure that one out,' Maddy added.

'And if you're not at home? What does he do then?'

'Misses stuff? Speaking of which, pass it over and I'll go through it while you check his desk and drawers.'

For the next thirty minutes, the two of them continued their search, only occasionally commenting if either of them found anything out of the ordinary. Most of Simon's diary entries were to do with away matches and details of the hotels they would be staying in overnight, but there was one entry in early February that didn't seem to be related to the football club, so she went back to it.

'What do you make of this?' she said, carrying the diary over to the desk and indicating a scribbled entry.

'It looks like *Check with Raj?* And after the dash, *has he had one?* Had one of what, I wonder?'

'I've no idea. I haven't heard him mention anyone called Raj at the club, and there's no one by that name in our circle of friends. And then there's this bit, *Contact details for others?* I wonder who he's talking about?'

For some reason that Maddy couldn't quite put her finger on she felt uneasy. She had always assumed that she and her husband knew everything about each other's lives, but this diary entry suggested otherwise.

'Sorry, Mum,' Siena said, 'I know it's only eight o' clock, but I'm going to have to call it a day. I'm shattered. I've done the top of Dad's desk and this middle drawer, but the side drawers will have to wait until tomorrow.'

'You're right. I think I'll turn in, too. We're likely to miss something, if there is anything to find, if we're too tired. You go and get ready for bed and I'll be up in a few minutes. I'm just going to try and call Cal. He's left loads of messages since the accident, and I haven't got back to him yet.'

'He's such a good friend to you, Mum, well, all of us, really. When Dad's home you should invite him and Joel over for dinner.'

'We were only saying that we should get something in the diary when we finished our shift the other night. I can't believe that was only Saturday – it feels like a lifetime ago,' Maddy said with a slight wobble in her voice.

Siena reached her arms around her mum, pulling her into a hug. 'I'm so lucky to have a mum like you. You'll make everything all right. You always have. Don't chat to Cal for too long,' she said, crossing the room towards the door, 'and remember to come in and say good night.'

'Will do,' Maddy replied, slightly surprised that Siena wasn't expecting her to sleep in with her again. *Maybe these two dramas in her life are helping her to grow up*, Maddy thought as she dialled Cal's number. It went straight to voicemail, so she flicked the television on to see if he was covering a shift on *News 24/7*. Blake Clarkson was just rounding up a story, but instead of Jordana at his side, it was Kristina Gruber, another of the recent young female additions to the channel. *Strange*, Maddy thought, switching the television off and heading towards the door, *I wouldn't have thought Jordana would want to miss the opportunity to present the prime-time slot. She must be ill.*

CHAPTER SEVENTEEN

7.15 p.m. – Tuesday

The evenings were much lighter now the clocks had gone forward an hour for British Summer Time, meaning that Father Ray's coaching session could go on until 7 p.m. rather than finishing at 6 p.m. in near darkness. The church had been happy to allow the priest to convert a field adjacent to the church into a football pitch, and had even funded the mobile goalposts and nets, but their pockets didn't go as deep as to provide lighting for evening training sessions.

Since Father Raymond Kiernan had come up with the idea of a church football team as a way to try and keep teenagers in the community away from underage drinking, smoking and drug-taking, there had been a marked reduction in petty crime in the area and the team itself had gone from strength to strength. It had been a shaky start, though. Only four youngsters had turned up to the first training session five years ago, and three of them had been girls. That had been part of the problem. The priest had said everyone was welcome, and that hadn't gone down well with the boys, who were his primary target. The only boy at the first session was thirteen-year-old Jason Leeming, regarded as a leader in his peer group. He loved football, and had been captain of every year-group team he had played in at school. He had been annoyed that a clergyman thought he could just start coaching football without any experience, so his intention had been to make a fool of Father Ray by showing off his footballing skills. Within fifteen minutes of the start of the first session, Jason realised that he had underestimated the priest's ability, and at the end he shook him by the hand, promising to bring some of his friends along the following week. 'Where did you learn to play like that?' he had asked, to which Father Ray had replied, 'I used to play professionally, but that was a long time ago.'

Jason, who had turned eighteen the previous week, now helped to coach, and, at Father Ray's suggestion, was in the process of training to be a referee. He raised the whistle to his lips and blew, the shrill sound marking the end of the seven-a-side game they had played for the final thirty minutes of the session, causing it to overrun by fifteen minutes.

'Well played, everyone,' Father Ray said, making a clapping motion with his hands as he encouraged them all to gather around him at the centre of the pitch. 'There's no practice Friday evening because we've got an early kick-off on Saturday morning. Anyone not here by 8 a.m. won't be picked for the starting eleven, so please make sure you tell your parents to get you here on time,' he said, looking across to the handful of spectators gathered next to the small parking area. 'Tom and Ashley, it's your turn to collect up the balls, bibs and cones, and the rest of you can go.'

Jason and Father Ray watched as the youngsters stripped off their bibs, leaving them in an untidy pile, before running in the direction of their waiting parents.

When Tom and Ashley were out of earshot, Jason said, 'Frankie had a good game tonight. Were you thinking of starting him up front at the weekend alongside Tom?'

'Provided he's here on time. That's why I made a point about being here by 8 a.m. He has a lot of talent but not much self-discipline. There's no doubt the team will suffer if he doesn't play, but he needs to start obeying the rules or he'll never get anywhere in life.'

'I'll have a word with him, if you like. I know from personal experience that it can be tricky growing up without a dad.'

'That might make all the difference. Thanks, Jay. Are you all right to lock the equipment shed when the boys have finished collecting the stuff? I need to have a quick shower before confession. That's the trouble with these lighter evenings. The temptation is to play until the light fades, but I need to get back to the day job.'

'No problem. I'll lock up and leave the key in the collection plate by the entrance. See you Saturday, Father,' he said as the priest hurried up the path to the church, outlined against a pink and orange sunset.

It was a little after 7.30 p.m. when Father Ray pulled aside the curtain and sat down on his side of the confession box. He heard confessions on Tuesdays and Thursdays between 7.30 p.m. and 9 p.m., but he made it clear to his congregation that he was always available if something urgent came up. Sometimes he would sit for the entire hour and a half without a single person coming to confess their sins, but he didn't mind. He used the peace and solitude for contemplation without interruption. He had just closed his eyes when he thought he heard a sound from the other side of the wooden screen. He hadn't heard the metallic scraping sound of the brass rings on the curtain pole to signify the arrival of someone wanting to confess their sins. *Maybe they arrived before me*, he thought, acknowledging that he had been a few minutes late. He pulled the velvet curtain back on his side of the screen.

'Is there someone there?' he asked.

There was a rustling sound and then a very quiet female voice spoke. Despite being only a few inches away from him, he couldn't make out what she was saying.

'I'm so sorry, I can't hear you very well. Could you speak up a bit, please?'

'I've got laryngitis,' she whispered, 'I'm afraid I can't talk any louder.'

'Well, if I lean in close on my side and you do the same on yours, we might just be able to make this work,' he said, virtually resting his head on the open fretwork of the wooden screen that divided them.

He could feel her warm breath against his cheek as he kept his head facing straight in front of him, his eyes closed to enable him to concentrate better on what she was about to say.

'Forgive you father, for you have sinned,' she whispered.

For a split second, Father Ray thought he had misheard her until his brain registered the excruciating pain of the ten-inch blade the woman had plunged into his neck, severing his carotid artery. He tried to cry out, but no sound came except for a kind of gurgling as he fell forward, blood spurting from the wound and spewing from his mouth.

CHAPTER EIGHTEEN

7.40 p.m. – Tuesday

Rachel wasn't sure that Maddy's confidence in her cooking ability was justified as she ladled the thick tomato and meat sauce on top of the strands of pasta. It smelled all right, but when she'd risked a taste off the back of the wooden spoon, moments before the doorbell had rung at precisely 7.30 p.m., she couldn't help thinking it lacked flavour. Already sipping her second glass of wine to steady her nerves, she picked up the bottle and added a generous slug, giving it a quick stir before she answered the door to Tim.

He was standing there with a bottle of red wine in one hand and a bunch of freesias in the other. Rachel wasn't a particular fan of plants and flowers, but freesias had been her mum Denise's favourites, and she'd felt an uncharacteristic lump of emotion in her throat that made it difficult to thank Tim and invite him into her home. Her mum had grown them in every possible colour in the garden of her childhood home, close to the back door so that the aroma would waft into the kitchen while she was going about her chores. Denise had been a stay-at-home mum. Her priority was to look after her twins, which had made things so much worse when they had gone missing from under her nose. At her mother's funeral, Rachel had opted for a simple arrangement of fragrant colourful freesias from Ruth and herself in preference to an ostentatious display of blooms. The sweet, peppery aroma would always remind her of her mum.

Rachel picked up the laden pasta bowls and carried them across to the small round table where Tim was pouring them each a glass of wine from the bottle he had uncorked the moment he had arrived. 'It needs to breathe,' he had said, 'to allow the flavour to develop.' She had been only slightly offended that he thought she wouldn't know that.

'I'll get the parmesan,' she said, returning to the kitchen area, aware that the flowers he had thoughtfully brought her were stuck unceremoniously in a measuring jug, alongside the colander she'd used to drain the pasta in the kitchen sink. 'And I'll pop those in a vase after we've eaten,' Rachel added, 'if I can find one, that is. I don't often get given flowers.'

'I'll change that, if you'll let me,' Tim replied, raising his glass to chink against hers. 'Cheers to us,' he said, causing a tingle to run down Rachel's spine.

'To us,' she agreed, holding his gaze while she took a sip of the ruby-red liquid. 'Delicious. Hopefully it will mask the taste of the spag bol.'

'Don't put yourself down. This is really good, and I wouldn't say it if I didn't mean it.'

Rachel had to agree as she tasted her first forkful. *The addition of wine certainly did the trick*, she thought, watching him twizzle the spaghetti deftly around his fork as he took another mouthful. *He really is very handsome. I wonder why he hasn't been snapped up? Or maybe he has been and now he's divorced?*

As though he was reading her mind, Tim said, 'Maybe tonight we can start getting to know each other a bit better, and I don't just mean in bed.'

'I'd like that,' she said. 'Let's start with you.'

By the time they had finished their dinner and a second bottle of wine, Rachel had learnt quite a lot about Tim. He'd been brought up by foster parents from his early teens; his mother had left home when he was a toddler and eventually his father hadn't been able to cope. Feeling rejected, he'd taken comfort in food and had piled on the pounds, until at the age of eighteen he weighed almost twenty stone. His weight had ruled him out of taking part in sport at school, but he hadn't wasted his leisure time on computer games. Instead, he had studied hard and won a scholarship to Durham University to study law.

'While I was at uni, I started to take an interest in girls,' he said, lifting his arm so that Rachel could nestle into his chest while she curled her legs up under her on the sofa. 'The trouble was, the ones I liked weren't interested in me, looking the way I did, so I decided to change. I joined the gym, stopped eating junk food and got myself in shape.'

'They must have been falling at your feet,' Rachel said, feeling mellow from the wine.

'I guess they were, but I didn't know how to behave around them because I had no experience at all during my teens, and no dad to turn to for advice.'

'What about your foster dad? Couldn't you talk to him?'

'When I said foster parents, I meant lots of different ones. I never stayed anywhere for more than a year. Maybe they thought they weren't getting paid enough money to cover all the food I was eating,' he said, a smile twitching at the corner of his mouth. 'I was probably costing them money rather than them earning money from me.'

Rachel punched his arm gently. 'You're joking, right? Foster parents don't take kids on to earn money. It's because they want to look after them, surely?'

'Most of them, maybe, but I was pretty unlucky in the homes I was put in. This is turning into a right old sob story. Can we start talking about you now?'

'Not yet. You haven't told me how you learnt to chat up girls.'

'I'm not sure I did, which is why I'm still single at forty.'

'But you've had lots of girlfriends before me?'

'A few, but no one special… until now,' he said, tilting her chin up towards him and kissing her tenderly on the mouth.

Rachel was relaxing into Tim's kiss and starting to kiss him back when her mobile phone started to ring.

'Leave it,' he said, as she pulled away from him.

'I can't. My friend's husband is in a coma. If anything has happened to him, she's going to need me.'

She swung her legs down and reached for her phone from the coffee table. She could see straight away that it wasn't Maddy calling, but she answered it anyway.

'Talk to me, Graham.'

'The night crew have just rung me about a stabbing incident in Little Waterton.'

'Really? We don't usually get much trouble around there. Is it another teenager?'

'Not this time, Guv. He's a priest, or should I say, he was a priest. He's dead.'

'What is the world coming to? Motive? Money, I'm guessing.'

'You're off the money on this one. Nothing was taken at all. He was found in the confession box with a knife wound in his neck. It would appear he bled to death. Do you want to meet me there?'

Rachel hesitated. She looked across at Tim, who was studiously avoiding eye contact with her.

'I can't drive. I'm over the limit.'

'Oh, right. Well, I can deal with it, or I can swing by and pick you up. It's your call, Guv.'

'What time?'

'I can be at yours in fifteen minutes.'

'Okay, I'll see you then,' Rachel said, ending the call. 'I'm so sorry, Tim, but something's come up.'

'Have you got to go? Isn't your DI capable of dealing with it?'

'He is, but this is a fatal stabbing, of a priest, I might add, and I'm the senior officer.'

'The senior officer who's been drinking throughout the evening.'

'What's that supposed to mean?'

'Just that your DI may have a clearer head than you for making judgement calls.'

Rachel couldn't decide if her overriding feeling was one of anger or disappointment. *I thought Tim, of all people, would understand, but clearly I was wrong.*

'This isn't open for discussion. I'm going.'

'But why? What's the urgency? The priest is dead, and he'll still be dead in the morning. Why do you need to go rushing over there?'

'That's a ridiculous thing to say. I think you should leave now, before we both say things we will regret.'

For a moment the two of them stood facing each other, eyes blazing, before Tim lowered his gaze. 'I'm sorry. You're right. It's your job, and you must do it in the way you see fit. I'll let myself out.'

The door closed behind him and Rachel sank down onto the sofa where, minutes before, they had been cuddling. *Is he right? Should I have just let Graham deal with this? The trouble is, I've had to work so hard to get to where I am, I don't always know when to let go*, she thought, brushing a tear from her eye. *But I'm damned if I'll let someone I've only known for a few months make professional decisions for me. Maybe I was wrong about Tim. Maybe there isn't any room for him in my life.*

Rachel got up off the sofa and hastily cleared away the pasta bowls from the table, not wanting Graham to see any visible evidence that she'd had company. She intended to put the bowls in the sink out of view, but it was already full with the colander and the jug containing her flowers. She lifted the jug onto the draining board, replacing it with the bowls, before tipping the water down the sink and dumping the freesias in the bin.

CHAPTER NINETEEN

8.25 a.m. – Wednesday

Maddy picked up her coffee mug and carried it through to the den to continue searching through the stuff on her husband's desk while her daughter was still sleeping. The only thing she and Siena had found the previous evening that was remotely out of the ordinary was the diary entry in early February. As she had lain in bed thinking about it, she had convinced herself that there was probably a perfectly innocent explanation. Raj must be a new member of the coaching staff at the football club, and the question 'has he had one?' was probably to do with a pass or some paperwork. Similarly, contact details for the others would most likely be to remind Simon to give him the mobile phone numbers and email addresses of other members of the coaching staff. *I must have been tired and overwrought with the whole situation to have been so suspicious last night*, she thought, sitting down at the desk and pulling the top right-hand drawer open. Siena was right about the amount of paper Simon squirrelled away. *It's a wonder he can ever find anything*, Maddy thought, closing the top drawer and opening the next one down. She immediately recognised the name of their mortgage company on the folder on top of the pile. *Why is that not in the filing cabinet?* Maddy wondered, opening it up to make sure it was their mortgage paperwork rather than an empty old file that should have been thrown away. Her breath caught in her throat. It was an application to remortgage their house. Her eyes quickly scanned the document.

Under the section headed, *Reason for Remortgage*, Simon had written: *to consolidate loans. What loans? We haven't got any now that the cars are both paid off,* Maddy thought. Even more worrying was the fact that the mortgage application was in both their names; but Simon had faked her signature, so he'd obviously wanted to keep it from her. *Why would he do something like this behind my back? What is he trying to hide from me?* A prickle of apprehension filtered through Maddy. *What if there was a whole secret side to Simon that she knew nothing about... Could it be another woman?* she wondered, a sick feeling starting in the pit of her stomach. *Maybe he needed money to set his new girlfriend up with a love nest? Raj could be a nickname for her or him – the jotting at the side of the name said 'has he had one?'.*

Maddy's mind was racing and the slow thud, thud, thud of her heart was deafening in her ears. Throughout their marriage, she had never previously considered that Simon would cheat on her, even when he was a professional footballer and girls flirted with him openly in the Players' Lounge after matches. But now, she wasn't so sure. She couldn't imagine why else he would need £100,000 that he clearly didn't want her to know about. *Their whole lives together were built on trust, but what if he had betrayed that trust?* She had always assumed that getting home late on match days was because he had stayed at the club drinking with the rest of the coaching staff, but what if he'd actually been with someone else? Her theory that there was nothing suspicious about the diary entry had now been turned on its head. Thinking about her husband's behaviour over the past few months, Maddy could recall times when he had seemed very short-tempered with her, and she was pretty sure she remembered an occasion when he'd ended a call on his phone very abruptly when she had gone into the den to tell him his dinner was ready. *What if he'd been having an affair and the road rage attack was to warn him off? Perhaps it wasn't so random after all.*

'Oh, God, Simon. What have you been up to?' she muttered, reaching for her coffee mug with a shaking hand and carrying it over to the sofa where she crumpled in a heap. 'I can't believe you'd do something like this.' She took a sip of her coffee but struggled to swallow it.

I need to talk to Cal. This can't be right. I'd know if Simon was having an affair, I'm sure I would. I'm probably overreacting because I'm so stressed out about the accident, but Cal will see things with clearer eyes, she thought, instinctively turning on the TV to see if he was on air.

Cal wasn't on the morning bulletin either, and Maddy was just about to turn the television off and try calling him when she spotted the *Breaking News* headline scrolling across the bottom of the screen: *Priest stabbed in motiveless attack.* The volume was low as she hadn't wanted to disturb Siena the previous evening, so she reached for the remote control to hear the details of the story, just as a photograph of the middle-aged priest filled the screen:

His body was found at around a quarter past nine by one of his parishioners, who noticed that the front door of the church was open when it was usually locked at 9 p.m. She went inside to investigate and found the priest lying in a pool of blood in the confession box. The police were on the scene within thirty minutes, but have yet to reveal details of the killing or a motive. Father Raymond Kiernan had been a priest since retiring from a career in professional football in 2008.

Maddy could feel the blood in her veins turn to ice. 'Oh my God,' she whispered, 'it's Ray Kiernan.' And then, as if in slow motion, the pieces started to slot together. There had been something nagging at the back of her mind ever since she had read the live news bulletin about the gardener who had been found dead at his home. The name had sounded oddly familiar, and now she knew why. Neil Edison had been a player in the Kings Park Rovers team when she had first met Simon, and so had Ray Kiernan. She was now fairly certain that the scribbled entry in Simon's diary had nothing to do with a secret lover. It was the name Ray, not Raj, and now Ray, just like Neil, was dead, and her husband was in a coma. *Forget Cal*, she thought, jumping up from the sofa and hurrying through to the kitchen to grab her mobile phone, *I need to speak to Rachel*. She punched in Rachel's number, tapping her fingers impatiently on the work surface and muttering under her breath, 'Come on, come on, answer the damn phone.'

But Rachel didn't answer; it went straight to voicemail.

CHAPTER TWENTY

8.28 a.m. – Wednesday

Rachel slung her hastily packed overnight bag onto the front seat of the Audi, seriously doubting whether she would now be using it, following the stabbing of the priest in Little Waterton the previous evening. As the senior officer, she would be expected to head up the murder investigation, rather than heading down to Wales to interview Sergeant Turnbull in connection with Maddy's husband's crash on the M4 motorway on Monday morning.

The initial enquiries she had instigated when she had believed the crash was a road traffic accident that she was just looking into as a favour for her friend, were unofficial. They had only been able to gain access to information and resources because DI Graham Wilson still had very good contacts within the traffic division, having moved from there three years previously. But the discovery by the forensics team that Simon Shaw's windscreen had been shattered by an object travelling at high speed had changed all that. Rachel was just pulling out of her parking space when her phone rang. It was Graham.

'Morning, Guv, are you on your way in?'

'I'm just leaving now. What have you got for me?'

'Nothing on the stabbing as yet. It's the Simon Shaw case. I've just had forensics on the phone, and you were right – he was definitely shot at.'

Normally Rachel would feel satisfaction that she had spotted something missed by others, but it was tempered with shock that her friend's husband had actually been targeted by a gunman. 'Go on,' she said.

'They've found a bullet embedded on the edge of the driver's seat. It could only have missed Shaw by millimetres. If he realised what was happening, it must have been terrifying. No wonder he lost control of his car.'

'Have they said what type of gun it was fired from?'

'Yes. It's a Glock 17 Gen4, and before you ask, it's been standard issue for UK troops since 2013.'

Rachel's grip on her steering wheel tightened.

'But before you get too excited, Guv, that type of weapon has been used by drug dealers in the States since the 1990s and would be readily available for anyone to buy if they knew where to look.'

'Even so, Graham, I think this means we have to interview Sergeant Turnbull as a suspect in an attempted murder inquiry. Simon Shaw is a Sonning resident, so it does fall under our jurisdiction, although I'll run it by the super first to put it on an official footing.'

'How do you want to play this? Should I take the lead on the stabbing, and you go down to Wales with PC Drake today as planned?'

'Again, I'll run it by the super. He might want me to head up the murder, but don't worry, I'll make sure you don't have to miss your daughter's birthday party. Can you organise a meeting for 9 a.m. in the incident room, and we'll bring everyone up to speed with what we have on the Simon Shaw case so far?'

'On it, Guv. And thanks.'

When Rachel arrived at the police station thirty minutes later, she was still undecided as to whether she should request to interview

Sergeant Turnbull in Wales, or begin to coordinate the evidence-gathering surrounding the death of Father Raymond Kiernan. Stabbings were an everyday occurrence in and around the capital city, but attacks were usually between warring groups of teenagers. This was altogether different and, at first glance, the motive did not appear to be robbery, as the collection box in the porch of the church was untouched. She dropped her bag and phone on the desk in her office while she nipped to the toilet prior to the 9 a.m. meeting getting under way; when Rachel returned, she noticed that she had a missed call and a voicemail from Maddy Shaw. Every time she had seen her friend's name on her phone over the past thirty-six hours, she had dreaded calling her back, fearing that her friend's husband, Simon, may have taken a turn for the worse. This morning was no exception, so she played the voicemail first:

'Rachel? Rachel, are you there? Please pick up. They're all linked. Neil, Ray, Simon, they all knew each other years ago. It can't just be a coincidence. Please call me as soon as you get this.'

What on earth was Maddy going on about? Rachel wondered, instantly returning her call.

'Thank God you got the message, Rachel. Like I said in my voicemail, it's all linked. Neil's dead, Ray's dead and Simon's in a coma. Someone's out to get them.'

'Calm down, Maddy, you're not making any sense.'

'Right, sorry, let me explain. On Saturday night I was at the studios reading the news and there was a story about the professional gardener who died about a fortnight ago. The police have been investigating his death as a probable suicide because he'd been suffering from depression. I kept thinking the name sounded vaguely familiar, but I was tired, and I couldn't think where I recognised it from. I forgot all about it on Sunday, and then with Simon's accident it went completely out of my mind until this morning. I turned on the news and they were reporting on the priest being stabbed and then they said his name: Raymond Kiernan. I could hardly believe it when I looked up at the television screen and saw his picture. He was in the Kings Park Rovers team at the same time as Simon.'

Rachel felt the hairs on the back of her neck stand up. 'Are you sure? That must have been a few years back, and people's appearance can change markedly.'

'I'm absolutely certain. I particularly remember him because Simon was so surprised when he joined the priesthood after retiring from football. A lot of ex-Premiership players get jobs in the media as pundits, or they take their coaching badges and go into management like Simon did, but it was the first time he'd heard of someone becoming a priest. You wouldn't really think of it as a natural choice after a career in professional football, would you?'

'No, I suppose not,' Rachel conceded.

'It was while I was thinking what a coincidence it was for two former teammates to be on the news within days of each other that I realised why I recognised the name of the dead gardener. Neil Edison was a young player in the same squad as Simon and Ray, although I think his career was somewhat short-lived. He had a terrible injury when he was a teenager and it stopped him playing, if I remember rightly.'

If Maddy wasn't a newsreader with a background in investigative journalism and a nose for a story, Rachel wouldn't have been so open to the possibility that the three incidents were somehow linked. It was also a pretty big coincidence that three former teammates should be on the news within weeks of each other and in such dramatic circumstances. Even so, she chose to tread carefully.

'I'm going to be honest: I think it's fairly unlikely. I'm not usually one to believe in coincidence, but in this case, it might be, and I really can't see how Neil Edison's suicide fits into it at all.'

'Just hear me out, Rachel. When I was going through Simon's diary last night I found a scribbled message about someone called

Raj, at least I thought it said Raj at the time, but I now realise it must be Ray. Simon has dreadful handwriting. If the Ray in Simon's diary was the priest and they had recently been in contact, surely you must agree that it's a bit odd that one of them has been stabbed to death and the other is currently in a coma? And what if Neil Edison's death wasn't a suicide? There's something going on here, I'm sure of it.'

Rachel looked out through her office window at the officers gathered in the incident room waiting to be brought up to speed on the latest developments in the Simon Shaw case. Maddy had her suspicions that the three incidents were linked without even knowing that her husband had been shot at while driving. Having become increasingly sure that Rob Turnbull was somehow involved in Simon Shaw's accident, doubts were now creeping into Rachel's mind.

'Look, Maddy, I'm already late for a meeting, so I'm going to have to go, but once I'm through with that I'll head over to yours and we can talk about your theory.'

'What time will you be here? Siena and I are planning on leaving for the hospital around eleven.'

'Don't worry, it will be well before that,' Rachel said, disconnecting the call.

In light of the information that Simon Shaw, Ray Kiernan and Neil Edison all knew each other, Rachel realised that she wouldn't be making the trip to Wales today. It might make her unpopular with some of her officers for a while, but she had to do what she believed to be best for the case. Errol had always been her preferred choice to be in attendance at any interview with Turnbull because of his physical presence. She had been soft yesterday in saying that she would go with PC Drake in his place because he had a social arrangement. He was needed to go to the army barracks in Brecon as the senior officer, and he would be taking a different constable as she couldn't spare Eleanor Drake. Her expertise was methodical research, so she was the obvious choice to do a bit of digging on the three former teammates. *How well had they known each other? How long were they all playing in the same team together? What may have happened to make someone attack the three of them all these years later?* There was also the question of whether or not Turnbull knew either of the other two. Rachel had assumed he only had a connection with the Shaw family, but assumption was a dangerous thing in her line of work. She headed out into the incident room, steeling herself for the reaction to the orders she was about to give.

CHAPTER TWENTY-ONE

It was quarter past ten by the time Rachel pulled her car to a halt outside the Shaws' house. Maddy had already opened the front door and seemed to be in an agitated state, moving from foot to foot as Rachel climbed out of the car.

'I know you must think I'm crazy,' Maddy said, before Rachel could utter any form of greeting, 'but I have a gut feeling about all of this. I can't imagine why anyone would want to stab a priest unless they wanted to rob him, but all the news reports I've been watching this morning have said nothing was taken.'

Rachel waved to Siena, who she could glimpse through the open kitchen door spooning cereal into her mouth. Siena wafted her spoon in response. *That's the trouble with the media these days*, she thought, following Maddy into the den and closing the door behind her. *One of my officers, or even the woman who found Father Raymond, may well have said that nothing 'appeared' to have been taken and before you know it, all the news channels are ruling out robbery as a possible motive.* Hopefully DI Wilson and his team would give them a bit more to work with when they'd finished questioning the Little Waterton residents.

'I've been having another look in Simon's desk,' Maddy said, 'but I haven't really found anything more than I did last night. I was about to go through his diary again when you pulled up. Can I get you a coffee?'

Rachel was already wired after her third coffee of the morning. 'No thanks, Maddy,' she said, 'let's go through the diary together. We haven't got much time if you and Siena need to leave for the hospital at eleven. Have you mentioned your theory to her?'

'No. I don't want her thinking that there's some crazy guy out there who's going around killing people. She might worry that he would go after the victim's families next, although I'm not sure Neil has ever been married and, of course, Ray was a priest, so wed to the church.'

'It's probably for the best at the moment, although I do have some slightly alarming information that I wanted to tell you in person.'

'What is it?'

'We've all been working on the assumption that Simon simply lost control of his car, possibly because of the erratic driving of the motorbike that I told you about, something we initially thought might be a road rage incident. What I didn't mention was that on the eyewitness footage there appeared to be some sort of flash a moment before the crash.'

'A flash?'

'Yes. We thought it might have been sunlight catching a piece of jewellery or even the windshield of the motorbike, either of which could have momentarily blinded Simon, but we've now had a chance to look at the footage in more detail,' Rachel said, wondering how Maddy was going to react to the information she was about to deliver.

'And?'

'It was a gunshot, Maddy. The pillion passenger fired at Simon before the motorbike sped off.'

Maddy gasped.

'When we examined the footage frame by frame, we could see the path the bullet took and this morning our forensics team found it embedded in the foam of the driver's seat. Simon was lucky it didn't catch him, although it was probably his instinctive reaction in trying to protect himself that made him jerk the steering wheel. Travelling at high speed, even the tiniest of movements can be catastrophic.'

Maddy sank down onto the sofa, her face as white as a sheet. 'I can't believe what I'm hearing. This is like something out of a movie, not something that happens to ordinary people on their way to work. Oh my God,' she said, 'do you think this means it could have been Rob after all? Not only has he got a motorbike, he's also got access to guns. I'd managed to convince myself that he had nothing to do with it, but now I'm not so sure.'

'Rob's potential involvement is one of our lines of enquiry. As we speak, two of my officers are on their way to Wales to interview him when he returns to barracks after the training exercise. But if, as you suspect, these incidents are linked, I can't see what possible connection Rob Turnbull might have to a priest and a gardener, can you?'

'Maybe I'm wrong. Maybe they're not linked. Oh, I don't know what to think any more,' Maddy said, running her fingers through her hair.

'I'm sorry, Maddy. It's bad enough that Simon's in a coma without all these questions about who may have put him there. I wonder if it might be better to take Simon's diary back to the station and have one of my officers go through it?'

'I think I'd rather go through it with you. A diary is so personal. I feel like I'm sticking my nose into his private business, but it would be even worse if it was strangers.'

'That's fine at this stage, but you do understand that if we find anything, I would have to take it as evidence.'

'If it provides clues as to what on earth is going on, then so be it. I thought I knew my husband, but now I'm not so sure. I wasn't going to mention it, because I don't think it's relevant to the case, but this morning I found out that Simon's remortgaged our house without telling me. Why would he do that, unless we're short of money?'

'You're not, are you?'

'Not as far as I know. We both have decent salaries that easily cover the mortgage, with money left over each month for our savings and holiday fund. My Jag's paid for and I don't have anything else on credit.'

'Hold on a minute, did you say *your* Jag? I thought it was Simon's?'

'We both drive it, but technically it's my car and I drive it more than Simon. He takes it if I've got a shift where I'm likely to be stuck in rush hour traffic both to and from work. I take the Yaris because it's a hybrid so it's lighter on petrol, better for the environment and also because it's easier to manoeuvre around some of my shortcuts. Is that important?'

'I'm not sure. Am I right in thinking the Jag's got tinted windows?'

'Yes. To be honest, they're slightly more tinted than they're supposed to be.'

Rachel raised her eyebrows. 'I'll pretend I didn't hear that.'

'It's because I hate pulling up to traffic lights and the person at the side of me recognising me as "that woman off the telly", particularly if I haven't got my make-up on.'

Rachel was only partly listening to Maddy's explanation. Suddenly the pillion passenger's arm action made perfect sense. They wanted the driver to drop the window to make sure that they were shooting at the right person. But the window hadn't been lowered, and there could only have been a split second to take a shot before the motorbike sped off. *Was it possible that the intended victim hadn't been Simon, but his wife?*

'What, Rachel? Why are you looking at me like that? You're scaring me.'

The last thing Rachel wanted to do was to panic her friend unnecessarily. It seemed even less likely that someone would want Maddy dead, but she couldn't rule it out completely.

'I was just wondering if it could have been a case of mistaken identity.'

'What do you mean?'

There was no easy way to say it. 'Maybe you were the target, not Simon.'

'You can't be serious?'

'I'm just trying to look at all possibilities. Have you ever had a stalker?'

'Never. Some of the girls have, but the closest I've ever come is lewd letters or filth on social media. I just block people who post abusive messages, so I don't have to look at their depraved comments.'

'Have you ever reported it?'

'Only to my bosses at the channel, not to the police. You don't seriously think that a keyboard warrior would plan to attack me, do you?'

'People do weird things to get noticed if they feel they are being ignored by the object of their desire. Just to be on the safe side, I'd feel happier if one of my PCs drove you and Siena to and from the hospital today.'

'How will I explain that to Siena without spooking her?'

'Maybe just pretend that your car won't start and that I offered a lift as a friendly gesture?'

'Do you really think it's necessary?'

'I'm just being cautious. There's no point in taking any chances. Look, time is pushing on. Would you mind if I take Simon's diary back to the station with me? I'll make it clear to PC Drake that if she finds anything suspicious, she reports it directly to me. How does that sound?'

'Okay, I suppose. I'll get you a carrier bag from the kitchen – the diary's too big to fit in your handbag.'

'Thanks. I'll organise a car for you,' Rachel said, selecting Eleanor Drake's number on her phone.

'Guv.'

'How's the football club research going?'

'Slowly, but I'm getting there. As far as I can see, Simon Shaw, Ray Kiernan and Neil Edison only played together in the same team for a matter of a few months, although Neil Edison was in the academy at the club prior to joining the first team in July 1994 for preseason training.'

'That's not bad for a little over an hour, Eleanor. Carry on with that for now, but I'm bringing Simon Shaw's diary back to the station with me and I'd like you to personally go through that as a top priority, reporting any findings only to me,' Rachel said, underlining her assurance to Maddy as her friend came back into the den holding a Waitrose bag for life.

'Will do, Guv.'

'One other thing: can you tell Sergeant Bradling to arrange a car to transport Mrs Shaw and her daughter to Charing Cross Hospital as soon as possible.'

'On it, Guv,' Eleanor said, as Rachel ended the call.

Maddy lifted the heavy leather-bound diary and carefully put it into the hessian bag. 'Be careful with it, won't you? I know it's only a diary, but if anything happens to Simon, things like this will become very precious,' she said, clearly struggling to control her emotions.

Gently squeezing Maddy's shoulder for reassurance, Rachel said, 'Don't you worry. Eleanor Drake is one of my most diligent officers. Not only will she look after the diary, if there's anything even vaguely suspicious in it she'll find it.'

CHAPTER TWENTY-TWO

11.50 a.m. – Wednesday

The traffic was light on the journey from Sonning to the centre of Reading, so Rachel was back behind her desk before midday, even after stopping to pick up a chicken salad wrap from her favourite deli for lunch.

'Close the door behind you, Eleanor,' Rachel said when the young constable appeared in her doorway. 'Right, before I hand over Simon Shaw's desk diary, have you made any further progress with the football club?'

'I've just got off the phone with a chap called Peter Kingsley in their press office who has been with the club for the past thirty years. I was wondering how I was going to phrase my questions to him, but he pre-empted me, as though he was expecting my call.'

'Really?'

'He asked me if I was ringing about the preseason training camp in Porto in 1994 which Neil Edison, Ray Kiernan and Simon Shaw were all involved in. I said I was, and he went on to say that all charges against the four of them were dropped and no further action was taken.'

'I'm sorry, you've lost me there. What charges?'

'Exactly. I didn't know what he was talking about, so I blagged it a bit and asked him to confirm the nature of the charges. He got a bit defensive, and sexist if I'm honest, and said, and I quote', Eleanor continued, referring to the notepad in her hand, '"Those birds had no proof that they had been sexually assaulted against their will. That's the problem when a high-profile English football team arrives in town, all the local girls want a bit of the action, if you get my drift".'

Rachel's heart was pounding. She could hardly believe what she was hearing. Simon Shaw, her friend Maddy's husband, had been accused of sexual assault. *How the hell am I going to break that to her?* she thought. 'Wow,' she said, trying to recover her composure, 'he sounds like a right charmer. I don't suppose you managed to get the names of the girls doing the accusing?'

'Unfortunately not. He wasn't forthcoming with that, assuming he actually knew their names in the first place. But I did get the name of the fourth person accused: Dave Cox,' she said, referring to her notebook. 'Kingsley even gave me his last known contact details, but it was what he said when he offered them that troubled me. He said, "Like I told that reporter lass, no one from the club has had any contact with any of these former players apart from Simon Shaw, because none of the rest of them are still in the game". It seems like someone else has recognised that there might be a link between the deaths of Edison and Kiernan, and Simon Shaw's crash.'

'Did Peter Kingsley say when the reporter had called?'

'No, Guv. I should have asked. Sorry, Guv.'

'Okay. Ring him back and ask him when he spoke to the reporter. I'll circulate an email reminding everyone to be very vigilant about who they talk to and what they say. The last thing we want is a smart-arse reporter making this a front-page story. If these events are connected, Dave Cox is potentially the next victim and a front-page story could force the killer to act quickly, putting him in even more danger.

'Hold on, Eleanor, on second thoughts, I want you working on the diary, so I'll get DI Wilson back here to follow up with the delightful Peter Kingsley. You'll just need to bring him up to speed on what you've uncovered so far.'

'Yes, Guv.'

'Like I said on the phone, if anything seems unusual in Mr Shaw's diary, I want to be the first to hear about it,' Rachel said, handing over the hessian bag.

'Am I looking for anything in particular?'

'Trust your instincts, Eleanor, they're usually pretty good.'

'Thank you, Guv,' PC Drake said, allowing herself a smile as she left the room and headed back to her desk.

Rachel typed a quick email to her team, reminding them not to divulge any information on cases they were working on, hit the send button and then called DI Wilson's number. He picked up on the second ring.

'How are the enquiries going, Graham?' she asked, before he had time to speak.

'Not great, if I'm honest. The church is at the end of a lane, so pretty isolated and no passing traffic. We do have one interesting lead, though. One of the parents, whose lad had been collecting up the cones and bibs at the end of last night's training session, said he noticed a motorbike pulling into the church car park as they were leaving.'

Rachel stiffened. 'Any description of the bike or the rider?'

'As luck would have it, Mr Connors is a motorbike enthusiast. He's pretty sure it was a Suzuki GSX600F Katana, circa 1999,' Graham said, clearly reading from his notebook.

'Well, that's pretty specific. Did we confirm the make of the bike involved in the M4 incident?'

'No. We were paying more attention to the passenger taking a potshot at Simon Shaw.'

'Right. I'll get on to Larry now and then we can cross-reference with Sergeant Turnbull's vehicle. I should have thought of that before sending DS Green off to Wales. Mind you, Turnbull could have borrowed or hired a bike if his is so distinctive. Did this witness say anything about the rider?'

'Not much, only that he seemed quite a slight build and was wearing leathers and a helmet, as you would expect.'

'Slight build? That doesn't sound like an army officer, does it? How sure do you think he was?'

'Honestly? I think he was paying much more attention to the bike than the rider.'

'Well, at least we got clear info on the bike. I want your team to carry on with the house-to-house enquiries, but I need you back here.'

'Guv?'

'PC Drake will fill you in when you get here, but there could be another potential victim if these incidents are all linked, and I need you to track him down before the killer does.'

'On my way.'

Rachel disconnected the call and was about to ring Larry for details of the motorbike from the M4 incident when Eleanor Drake appeared in her doorway again.

'Guv, you need to see this,' she said, walking across the room holding a piece of paper in a pair of tweezers and laying it down on Rachel's desk. On the sheet of white notepaper, written in capital letters in blood-red ink were the words:

IT'S TIME TO PAY FOR WHAT YOU DID

'Where did you get this?'

'It was tucked into the front cover of Simon Shaw's diary. Turn the paper over, Guv,' Eleanor said, handing Rachel the tweezers.

On the back of the sheet, scrawled in black pen, were four names: *Neil, Ray, Dave and Jimmy.* Rachel looked up. 'Who's Jimmy?'

'I don't know yet. I wanted you to see this straight away, but I'm going to check the rest of the Kings Park Rovers team who had their preseason in Porto, and hopefully that will give us the answer.'

'We also need the names of the two girls who reported the sexual assault. I don't know why they would have waited this long, but this is starting to look like one of them might be out to settle an old score. Bag this up and get it to forensics for examination while I get on to the Porto police department. It shouldn't be too difficult to check their records. And Eleanor.'

'Yes, Guv?'

'Before Graham gets back, can you check with Larry for the make and model of the motorbike on the M4 footage, and then pass the information on to DS Green? If it's the same as Turnbull's motorbike, I want him brought back here for questioning. There may not be any obvious connection between him and this historic accusation, but we can't afford to miss anything.'

CHAPTER TWENTY-THREE

12.10 p.m. – Wednesday

Maddy's mind was in a state of turmoil, and she had barely spoken to her daughter in the back of the police car on their journey to Charing Cross Hospital. As suggested, she had told Siena that the Yaris was playing up and that Rachel had kindly organised for them to be driven in to London in a police vehicle. Unbeknown to Maddy, Rachel had also asked the constable to stay with the two Shaw women throughout their visit and now, after parking his car, he was positioned outside Simon Shaw's private room.

'Do you think he knows we're here, Mum?' Siena asked, taking a seat in a chair on one side of her father's bed while her mother sat at the other.

'It's hard to say. His eyelids seemed to flicker slightly when you spoke just now, but maybe that's just wishful thinking,' Maddy replied, interlocking her fingers with her husband's and feeling a mix of emotions. She wanted to believe that Simon had been hiding things from her to protect her. She wanted to believe that he would never do anything to hurt her, but after what she had discovered she couldn't help wondering if she really knew him at all.

'I was looking up stuff about induced comas on my phone in the car on the way in,' Siena said. 'Apparently, it's not a bad thing if they don't bring them back to consciousness quickly. It gives the mind and the body time to heal. So long as Dad's vital signs stay constant, it's good. It's like he's having an extra-long, deep sleep.'

'It's funny how the medical team don't really explain all this. They must realise that most people these days are capable of looking at websites for information, and yet it would be so much better coming from them.'

'They're probably terrified of saying the wrong thing and then, if things don't work out as they expect, relatives could sue them. I guess they're just protecting their own backs.'

Maddy nodded distractedly. She couldn't help wondering if that's what Simon had been doing by not telling her stuff that she had a right to know. She shivered.

'Are you okay, Mum? You seem really quiet today.'

'I'm sorry, darling, I didn't get much sleep. I wasn't criticising the staff – far from it, I've got nothing but praise for the team here. Although the consultant hasn't said much, he has managed our expectations.'

'And the nurses have all been very caring and thorough. No wonder Rob was so critical of my job, and thought it was a waste of time. When you see the long hours and unpleasant things nurses have to deal with and realise how little they get paid to do it. Maybe that's why he finished with me and started dating that nurse. Maybe he was right about me, perhaps I am spoilt, and leading a charmed life—'

'Is that what he said?'

'On several occasions. If I ever complained about anything, he said I needed a reality check. He was always telling me that he thought you and Dad were paid far too much money for the jobs you do.'

Maddy couldn't help thinking that Rob had a point. She had often thought it was ludicrous to be paid more to read the news than the Prime Minister was paid to run the country, but it wasn't her decision. Television companies were prepared to pay top dollar to get the best, most professional people for the job, at least that's the way it always had been until recently, when it seemed any

Tom, Dick or Harry could set up online and call themselves a TV presenter.

'He's clearly under a false impression regarding how much, or should that be how little, lower-league football managers are paid.'

'I guess he based his assumption on the size of our house. He always hated going there, you know. He said it made him feel uncomfortable that three people shared such a huge amount of space when other people were sleeping four to a room.'

'You shouldn't have let him make you feel guilty just because your dad and I have talents that not everyone has, and are rewarded for making the most of them. Talent alone isn't enough. An awful lot of hard work and sacrificing the things that other people take for granted, like not going out drinking on a Friday night with your mates, and giving up Christmas morning to train for the Boxing Day fixture, make the difference between success and failure. Lots of people can kick a ball around, but only a few will ever become professional footballers because the others lack self-discipline,' Maddy said, trying not to sound too defensive.

The thought of Rob making Siena feel guilty about the careers she and Simon had worked so hard at made Maddy angry. There had been several times when Rob openly admitted that he hadn't gone into the army because of an overwhelming desire to serve and protect his country. He'd said that he wouldn't have wanted to follow in his father's and grandfather's footsteps down the coal mines, even if that option hadn't been removed by the massive pit closures of the 1980s and '90s. There was precious little opportunity in Redcar when he had left school, apart from the steelworks, so he had signed up to the army at the age of seventeen as a way out of a life he didn't want. *There was nothing wrong with that,* Maddy thought, *but he shouldn't make others feel bad about their life choices, especially as he was constantly claiming he wanted to get out of the army but didn't want to sacrifice his pension by leaving early.* Although the circumstances surrounding the way Rob had finished his relationship with Siena were not ideal, Maddy was relieved that he was no longer in their daughter's life. There was, however, still a question mark over whether or not he had some kind of involvement in Simon's accident. Maddy cleared her throat.

'Siena, I need to ask you something. Do you think Rob resented us enough to do either your dad or me harm?'

'Why do you ask?'

'Well, Rachel told me this morning that someone fired a shot at your dad while he was driving, and that it almost certainly caused the accident.'

Siena gasped. 'Are you serious?'

'Yes. The police forensics team found a bullet embedded in the driver's seat. It must have missed your dad by millimetres.'

'Oh my God,' Siena said, her face turning as white as the hospital bed linen. 'That's awful. But why would you assume Rob did it? He might not have related to you and Dad, but I can't imagine he disliked either of you enough to harm you. What makes you think it was him?'

'I don't necessarily, but the shot was fired by a passenger on the back of a motorbike.'

'Does Rachel think it was him? Is he a police suspect?'

'Let's just say they want to question him about his whereabouts on Monday morning. They're on their way to Wales now.'

'Is he in Brecon? I used to love going there to see him,' Siena said, a wistful expression on her face.

Maddy nodded. In some ways, her daughter was quite young for her age, the way she'd handled the break-up of her relationship with Rob being the perfect example, but in others she was incredibly independent. Maddy had hated Siena tackling the three-hour drive to the Brecon camp on her own in all types of weather, and had always insisted that she texted the moment she arrived. 'Apparently, he's been out on a training exercise since Sunday evening, but the police need to be sure he couldn't have slipped away without anyone noticing. What is it, Siena?' Maddy said, noticing her daughter's eyes widening.

'H-he couldn't have slipped away without the soldiers under his command noticing, but he might have unofficially swapped duties with another sergeant. He sometimes did that when I was visiting so that we could spend more time together. Oh God, Mum, I don't know what I'll do if it turns out Rob did this, and Dad doesn't pull through. What a mess,' she said, tears welling up in her eyes and trickling down her cheeks. 'I'm so sorry. I never meant for this to happen. If only I hadn't reacted to the break-up the way I did, Rob would never have rung the house on Sunday. I knew it was all my fault, I just knew it,' Siena said, sobbing.

Maddy moved to the other side of the bed to comfort her daughter, holding her head against her chest and resting her chin on the top of Siena's head. 'Shh, shh, it's not your fault. There's no point in jumping to conclusions. Rob is probably not involved at all, but the police wouldn't be doing their job properly if they didn't at least question him. He doesn't really have a strong motive. It seems a very extreme way of teaching your dad a lesson for threatening him on the phone, and anyway, Rachel isn't even sure whether or not the attack was targeted. She even suggested that your dad might not have been the intended victim.'

'What do you mean?' Siena asked, raising her chin to look into her mother's eyes.

'Dad was driving my car. Rachel asked me this morning if I had any enemies.'

'And do you?'

'I wouldn't say enemies, but there are a few people who wouldn't be upset if I retired early. I wouldn't jump, so maybe someone wanted to give me a little push.'

'You mean Byron Farley,' Siena said, brushing the tears away from her eyes. 'Do you really think he would go to those sort of lengths to get rid of you?'

'Honestly? I don't. If it had just been the motorbike driving erratically, I could have believed that he might have been trying to scare me, but I can't imagine him sanctioning me being shot at.'

There was a quiet tap on the door, and a nurse came in pushing a trolley.

'Bella?' Siena said, 'is that you? Mum, you remember Bella from Mountview, don't you? She was really kind to me.'

'She was really kind to me, too, on Monday while your dad was having his brain scan,' Maddy said, recognising the nurse who had brought her tea in the relatives' room while she was waiting for news.

'I'm so sorry that this has happened to your dad, Siena,' Bella said. 'How is he doing? I was off yesterday.'

'Pretty much the same,' Siena replied. The ventilator is still breathing for him, but one of the other nurses said the best thing for patients with this kind of trauma injury is rest. And she told us to talk to him, so I've brought a book to read to him by his favourite author.'

'I've also heard that's good,' Bella said, smiling. 'The consultant has started his rounds, so he should be here shortly, but there are a few checks I need to do.'

'Is it okay if we stay?' Maddy asked.

Bella hesitated.

'We don't have to. We could pop to the cafeteria for ten minutes, if you'd prefer us to be out of the way.'

'No, it's all right,' Bella said, placing the blood pressure cuff around Simon's arm and inflating it. She waited a few moments before saying, 'His blood pressure is fine.' The Velcro fastening strips made a rasping sound as she removed the cuff. 'I'm just going to check his eyes for his response to light,' she said, taking her torch out of the pocket of her tunic and easing Simon's right eye open while she shone the bright light into it. She did the same thing with his left eye before slipping the torch back in her pocket.

'Everything seems pretty stable,' she said, making a note on the chart before hanging it back on the rail at the foot of his bed. 'I'm so sorry you've got all this to deal with, on top of recent events.'

'Thank you, Bella. We'll get through this somehow,' Maddy said.

Bella smiled. 'You're so lucky you have each other for support.'

'I know,' Siena said, making eye contact with her mum.

'I noticed the policeman waiting outside. Simon's not in trouble for causing the accident, is he?' Bella asked.

'No, the police are certain the crash wasn't Simon's fault. The police officer is just waiting to drive us home later. My car wouldn't start this morning,' Maddy explained to Bella, careful to reiterate the story she'd told Siena. 'I'll suggest to him that he might be more comfortable in the cafe.'

'Good idea,' Bella said, heading towards the door. 'You wouldn't want other patients thinking your husband has done anything wrong.'

'She's so thoughtful,' Siena said once the door was closed. 'When I was in Mountview she was always saying how lucky I am to have people that care about me so much, even though I didn't show my appreciation at the time. What a coincidence that she should be here at Charing Cross Hospital, and even stranger that she should be on Dad's ward.'

'A happy coincidence,' Maddy said, smiling. 'At least we can be confident that he's getting the best care.'

CHAPTER TWENTY-FOUR

1.50 p.m. – Wednesday

DCI Rachel Hart tapped her pen impatiently on her notepad as she waited for the email from Captain Nunes to arrive following their brief telephone conversation. The switchboard had put her through to him after she explained the reason for her call, as he'd been a serving officer with the Porto police department since 1988. He'd said he remembered the case clearly because the accusations were made against players in a visiting English Premier League team and he was a keen football fan. He was adamant that there had been no case to answer against the footballers because the alleged rape hadn't been reported until five weeks after the team had returned to England, by which time any physical examination would have been pointless. 'Goodness knows how many other men these two young women would have had sex with in the interim period. That's the trouble with modern society – nobody has any moral standards any more.'

Rachel gritted her teeth as she swiped her computer screen to refresh the page. She had a problem with men who were totally dismissive of rape allegations. They seemed to have no understanding of the courage it took for women to admit that they had been violated, and the psychological damage it could cause them for the rest of their lives. She shuddered, recalling her attempts to try and comfort her six-year-old sister after she was returned to the cellar following each assault. Ruth would never again allow another man

to touch her in that way. The only time she had, she had been so
repulsed by what she had done that she had tried to take her own
life by slashing her wrists. That had been the start of the downward
spiral that had eventually led to her being a permanent resident
at Mountview. *No wonder I feel such guilt at the pleasure good sex
brings me*, Rachel thought.

There was always the possibility that the two Portuguese girls had
made false accusations. Rachel knew that it was sometimes a case of
a girl regretting that she had allowed things to go so far, but every
case deserved to be investigated and, from what Captain Nunes had
said on the phone, it appeared that this case had been dismissed from
the outset. She had wanted to challenge his attitude, but realised
that it would gain nothing and might even result in him refusing
to send her the information they held on file, which she needed if
she was to learn the names of the two accusers and eliminate them
from her enquiries. She had got off the phone with him as quickly
as possible once he had agreed to email her the case file.

Rachel refreshed her email for the tenth time in as many minutes
and was relieved to see a one-line email from the captain with the
all-important document attached. Rachel downloaded the file and
began to read the statement made on 13 August 1994 by Beatriz
Azevedo and Rosa Viegas, two eighteen-year-old girls who were
employed as waiting staff at the five-star Funchal Hotel in Porto.

The accusation was made against the occupants of two adjoining
rooms, 324 and 326, which hotel records at the time confirmed
were allocated to members of the Kings Park Rovers football
team. The alleged attack took place late at night after Beatriz had
entered room 324 to deliver two bottles of champagne following
their order of beers earlier in the evening. In her statement, Beatriz
said she was pushed onto the bed by a big man with dark hair
who placed one hand over her mouth to prevent her screaming,
while he lifted her skirt and pulled her underwear down with the
other. He had then thrust himself into her and she thought that

she must have fainted from the pain as she had never had sexual intercourse before.

Rachel could feel bile rising from the pit of her stomach and beads of perspiration forming on her forehead. The indignation she felt on Beatriz's behalf was tangible. *How dare this drunken brute force himself on someone who was simply doing her job?* She struggled to focus on the words on the screen as they started to swim before her eyes.

The statement went on to say that when Beatriz regained consciousness, a different man was on top of her and she managed to twist her head sufficiently to cry out. She said she couldn't remember exactly what had happened after she screamed, but she was aware that there were four men in the room and that one of them had ushered her towards the door saying, 'I think you should leave now'.

On the next page of the document, there was a list of questions with Beatriz's responses:

Q. Why did you wait so long to report the alleged assault?

A. I was afraid no one would believe me, and I didn't want to lose my job.

Q. Did you have a physical examination directly after the alleged assault?

A. No. I was in pain and bleeding. I told my friend, Rosa, my period had come early, and she got me some painkillers and made my excuses for not going to work for a few days.

Q. Why did you then come forward five weeks after the alleged assault?

A. I was terrified that I might be pregnant, so I bought a tester kit. When it was positive, I broke down and told my friend Rosa what had happened to me. She said we had to report it to the police. She said we couldn't allow them to get away with what they did, because they might do it to someone else.

Q. *Are you absolutely certain that you didn't go to that hotel
   room with the intention of willingly having sex with a famous
   footballer?*

A. *(no answer recorded – accuser began to cry).*

Rachel was struggling to comprehend the accusatory nature of
the questions. It was clear that whoever conducted the interview
hadn't believed Beatriz's story and had showed no compassion
or understanding of the trauma the eighteen-year-old must have
experienced.

Rosa Viegas was only asked one question:

Q. *Were you in room 324 or the adjoining room 326 of the
   Funchal Hotel when the alleged assault took place?*

A. *No.*

The statement sheet had been signed by both girls and the
interviewing officer.

Rachel scrolled down to the next page. It was a fax that had
been sent to Kings Park Rovers outlining the allegation and listing
the occupants of rooms 324 and 326 on the night in question. The
occupants of room 324 were listed as Dave Cox and Ray Kiernan,
while 326 was being shared by Neil Edison and Simon Shaw.
Rachel massaged her forehead with her fingers again wondering
how on earth she was going to tell Maddy that her critically ill
husband was potentially a rapist. Further down the page was a
short statement from the Kings Park Rovers Chairman:

*We treat allegations of this nature very seriously. The four accused
players have all been questioned and all strenuously deny having
any intimate contact with Beatriz Azevedo. They do admit to
ordering champagne on room service, but none has any recollection of the person who delivered it. Consuming large amounts of*

alcohol during a preseason training camp is not acceptable and could tarnish the reputation of our club, and as such the players in question will be punished with large fines.

Handwritten across the Chairman's statement were the words: 'Case dismissed due to insufficient evidence'.

Rachel sat staring at the screen for several moments. *That was it? No further investigation was carried out?* The football club had questioned the four players and the Portuguese police had accepted their response. The UK police were never informed. She could hardly believe it. She hit print and took a few deep breaths to calm herself before going out into the incident room.

'Can I have a bit of hush, please,' she said to the dozen or so officers who were either tapping away on computer keyboards or on the phone. Within a few seconds, there was silence and all eyes were on Rachel standing in front of a whiteboard. 'Thank you. I know you're all hard at work on what might seem like two unrelated incidents, but we now have reason to believe there could be a connection between the stabbing of Father Raymond Kiernan and the crash involving Simon Shaw,' she said, writing both their names on the board. 'They are both former professional footballers, as I'm sure some of you will be aware,' she added in response to a few mumbles of recognition, 'and both played at the same time for Kings Park Rovers. There is a third team member from the same period, Neil Edison, who died a few weeks ago in what was originally believed to be a suicide.' More mumbling. 'Because of information that has come to light, we now have reason to believe that there is at least one other member of the same squad who could potentially be in danger: Dave Cox,' she said, writing his name on the board with a question mark after it. 'These four players had sexual assault allegations made against them following a preseason training camp in Porto in July 1994.' Rachel surveyed the room, thinking that several of her officers wouldn't even have been born in

1994. 'The charges were dropped due to insufficient evidence, but it would seem there is a possibility that someone was not satisfied with that outcome and is now looking to exact revenge. How are we getting on locating the whereabouts of Mr Cox, DI Wilson?'

'No joy as yet, Guv. The landline the club gave us is no longer in use and the address in Ascot, which apparently used to be a Victorian house, was knocked down a few years back and is now a development of eight luxury apartments. I'm waiting for a call back from the utilities companies who may have had a forwarding address when he moved, and also from HMRC. They will have a record of his whereabouts, assuming he's working.'

'Okay, keep hassling. Time is of the essence for Mr Cox. If these attacks are all related to the historic sexual assault allegation, and we have a vigilante on the loose, he's potentially the next victim. There is another name that might also be relevant to the case. Did you find out who "Jimmy" is, PC Drake?'

'Yes, Guv. James Dawson was the club captain at Kings Park Rovers from 1989 to 1999. He retired after his testimonial year and now runs a gym in Bracknell called Muscles.'

'Would you like me to get down there and question him, Guv?' DI Wilson said. 'I can't do much more on Dave Cox until the utilities companies or HMRC get back to me, and I can stay on top of that on my mobile.'

'No worries, I'll do it. I'd rather not have another dead ex-footballer on our hands if at all possible, so you keep on trying to trace Dave Cox. Did you get the information from Larry re the M4 motorbike, PC Drake?'

'Yes, Guv. Larry confirmed it's the same make and model as the one reported by the eyewitness at the church in Little Waterton, and he's still working on trying to enhance the images of the number plate captured on the phone footage. I've emailed the DVLA for details on Sergeant Turnbull's motorbike, and I'm just waiting to hear back.'

'Good. Keep DS Green in the loop on any information you get re Turnbull.'

'Will do, Guv.'

'Does anyone here speak Portuguese?' A hand rose tentatively in the air. 'I'd like you to try and trace these two women,' Rachel said, walking across the room and placing the papers she had just printed out on PC Leverette's desk. 'They originated from Tavira on the eastern Algarve, and may well have returned there after the alleged sexual assault incident. I want to know if either of them is currently, or has recently been, in the UK.'

'Yes, Guv.'

'PC Harman, you're driving me to Bracknell. Get the car and I'll be down in two minutes. That's all for now. We'll have a debrief later this afternoon. Graham, a word, please.'

DI Wilson followed Rachel into her office and closed the door behind him. 'Is there a problem, Guv? I was only offering to go to Bracknell to interview James Dawson so that you could get on with other stuff. I wasn't trying to undermine you.'

'I know. Look, I didn't want to appear soft in front of the team, but I'm not heartless either. Wherever you are in tracking down Dave Cox at 4 p.m., you're to hand it over to another senior officer and go to meet your wife and family at Legoland. That is an order. Do I make myself clear?'

'Yes, Guv. Thanks, Guv.'

'It goes without saying that this is just between you and me.'

'Of course, Guv. You'll be back on my wife's Christmas card list.'

Rachel raised her eyebrows.

'Oh, and I forgot to mention in the meeting that I called Peter Kingsley at Kings Park Rovers,' Graham said. 'He says he received the call from the reporter at about quarter to eleven this morning, which is why he wasn't surprised when Eleanor Drake rang.'

'Did he get the name of the reporter or the publication or media company she works for?'

'He says not, and I believe him because he didn't ask for my name either.'

'It would seem to be a bit of a dead end, but I can't help wondering who would be making enquiries about this historic rape allegation and why.'

'Maybe it's to do with that rugby player who was convicted of rape a few years ago being released from prison yesterday. Perhaps she's putting together a story on rape allegations against professional sports people?'

'Possibly, or Maddy Shaw might not be the only one who has made a connection between these recent events.'

CHAPTER TWENTY-FIVE

2.15 p.m. – Wednesday

'Will you be okay if I pop outside for some fresh air for a few minutes?' Maddy asked. 'It's really stuffy in here, and I've got a bit of a headache starting.'

'You go, Mum. I'll make a start on reading this book to Dad.'

'What did you bring in the end?'

'*Playing for Pizza*,' Siena replied, flashing the cover in Maddy's direction. 'It's John Grisham. I know he's one of the only authors Dad reads.'

'And usually only on holiday. You'll have to fill me in on the story when I get back,' Maddy said, closing the door to the private room behind her. She was surprised to see that the constable who had driven them in to Charing Cross Hospital was back in the corridor outside Simon's room.

'Did you go to the cafe?'

'Yes, I got myself a sandwich and a bottle of water, but I didn't want to be away too long because my instructions were to wait outside the room and take you home when you're ready to leave.'

'Well, if they're your orders I guess you'll have to stick to them. I'm just going for a breath of fresh air, I won't be long.'

Maddy left the hospital via the main entrance and turned left down Fulham Palace Road, hoping that her memory served her correctly and there was a park a short distance away. She had known the area well when she was in her early twenties, as she used to live in a flat-share on Munster Road when she had come to live in London. In fact, that was where she'd been living when she'd first met Simon, and they had occasionally gone for a walk around the park if all her other housemates were at home and they had wanted some privacy. She was just starting to wonder if she had misremembered the park's location, or if it had been a casualty in the urgent need for new housing in London, when she spotted the familiar wrought iron gate. Although it was almost lunchtime and the early April sunshine was quite warm, the park was deserted apart from a weary-looking young woman pushing an infant on a swing and an older woman stooping to pick up the excrement her dog had just deposited on the path. Maddy made her way to a bench in the far corner, pulled out her phone and selected Cal's number. He answered on the second ring.

'Maddy. How are you? I tried to call you a few times yesterday, but it kept going to voicemail. I was worried sick about you. How's Simon? And Siena, how's she taking it?'

Maddy couldn't resist a smile. It was so like Cal to bombard her with questions and not give her a chance to answer, but that was what she loved about him. 'Slow down, Cal. You're making me breathless just listening to you.'

'Sorry, doll, it's just that no one at *News 24/7* seems to know what the hell is going on. I'll start again: how is Simon?'

'He's in an induced coma, but stable. I left Siena reading to him while I popped out to call you. The mobile signal in the hospital is a bit hit and miss.'

'Shall Josh and I come to the hospital? Simon's in Charing Cross, isn't he?'

'That's really thoughtful of you, Cal, but it's a bit pointless at the moment. Maybe when he regains consciousness, assuming he does,' Maddy said, her voice trembling.

'Hey! I don't want to hear any of that kind of talk,' Cal said. 'You have to think positive in these sorts of situations. Repeat after me, "Simon will be okay".'

'Do you really think so?'

'Yes, I do. He's a fighter, or he wouldn't have survived that smash. Come on, say it.'

'Simon will be okay,' she obliged, but her voice lacked conviction.

'That's more like it. So, how are you doing? And I mean truthfully. This is me you're talking to.'

'Okay, I think. None of this has properly sunk in yet. Have you heard that the police are saying it wasn't an accident?'

'Geez! Really? There have been a few rumours flying around the newsroom, but nothing concrete, and the police have been pretty tight-lipped if I'm honest. Byron's been pulling his hair out because he thinks we should get any information first as it involves the husband of his top newsreader.'

'Your words, not his, I'm sure,' Maddy said, raising her eyebrows.

'Actually, he's been saying some pretty nice things about you.'

'Well, that makes a change. I thought he was too besotted with Jordana to say anything nice about anyone else.'

'He's not too happy with her after last night.'

'What happened last night? Did she stand him up on a dinner date?'

'No. Kate Lander rang me an hour ago. She was fuming because Farley had moved her and Mike from prime time last night to the midnight slot in favour of Jordana and Blake, and then Jordana rang in sick at the last minute. Apparently, when Kate questioned his decision he said she knew what to do if she didn't like it. She rang because she knows we're good mates. She said for me to warn you that Farley is definitely trying to get rid of the old guard, so watch your back.'

'Poor Kate, but it makes me feel a bit better knowing that it's not only my shifts Byron is messing about with to give Jordana the best exposure. I thought it was a bit odd that Blake was on last night without her.'

'You were watching?'

'I just flicked on to see if you were working when you didn't pick up your phone.'

'You just missed me. I covered four till eight for them, so I must have been on my way home when you rang.'

'So what was wrong with Jordana, a broken fingernail? Or maybe a spot on her nose?'

'Nobody seems to know. Look, I hope you won't take this the wrong way, but this whole situation with Farley might not be Jordana's fault. I was chatting to Lizzy in make-up, after they got the call to say Jordana wouldn't be in, and apparently she's aware that she's putting other presenters' noses out of joint because of Farley pushing to get her to the top. Not only is she embarrassed by it, she's also worried by what's expected in return for her career progression. She's probably regretting turning up for the audition in January. I feel a bit sorry for her now that I know she didn't instigate the attention she's getting from Farley. When you're that young and drop-dead gorgeous, it must be tricky trying to balance your ambition and your moral standards.'

'I suppose I've never thought about it from her point of view,' Maddy said, feeling guilty about her sarcastic remark. 'Thankfully I'm too old now to have to deal with predatory males, but I had my fair share of unwanted attention when I was younger, and it's a horrible position to find yourself in. I hope she has someone she can turn to for advice. Her parents, maybe?'

'According to Lizzie, she doesn't speak to them. She was adopted as a baby, then brought to live in England when her parents split up, but she and her mum argued over something and don't speak now.'

'Is Jordana's father foreign, then?'

'Spanish, I think, or maybe Italian. He's from somewhere Mediterranean. To be honest, I tend to tune out when Lizzy's on a roll, but it's irrelevant because she's not in contact with him either.'

'It would explain her colouring, though,' Maddy said, thinking of Jordana's dark hair and eyes, and olive skin tone. She paused, wondering whether what she was about to suggest was too ludicrous to say out loud, even to her best friend. Taking a deep breath, she said, 'Cal, this might seem like a weird question, but you don't think Byron would do absolutely anything to further Jordana's career, do you?'

'Like what?'

'This has to stay between you and me.'

'Of course.'

'What if someone thought it was me driving the Jag on Monday morning? The police are pretty sure the accident was caused deliberately,' Maddy said, being careful not to give any detail. 'What if I was the intended victim, not Simon?'

She heard a sharp intake of breath.

'You can't be serious? Surely you don't think Farley's behind it? He's a coward of the first order, and besides, I don't think he's even got a driving licence, has he? He comes to work on a pushbike.'

'I don't mean that it was him riding the motorbike, but he could have paid someone to do his dirty work. He's been trying to get rid of me for a while and I've dug my heels in. What if he just reached the end of his tether and decided to apply a bit of brute force?'

'Honestly? I don't think even he would sink that low, but mostly because he would be shitting himself about getting caught. No, I think you're definitely barking up the wrong tree. That said, if I were you, and if you feel up to it, of course, I'd try and get your arse back behind the news desk as quickly as possible. It's a bloody cut-throat business we're in. Don't give Farley any opportunity to get rid of you.'

'Thanks, Cal. That's what I reckoned, but I just thought I'd run it by you. I'll email Farley about coming back for a couple of shifts at the weekend, so he won't have the satisfaction of firing me for being absent without leave.'

'Good girl. Let me know what shift they give you and I'll try and get scheduled for it too. And ring me if you need me.'

'Will do,' Maddy said, ending the call. She was relieved that Cal had dismissed the notion that Byron Farley would do anything to harm her, but it did resurrect all her concerns about who might have attacked Simon. After her conversation earlier, she felt certain she was right that the three former footballers had been targeted. The question was: by who?

Fifteen minutes later, as Maddy was approaching Simon's room, she heard Siena's voice. *Bless her, she's still reading to her dad. It's a good job Grisham's written a few books,* she thought, smiling, but a moment later she stopped dead in her tracks, the smile disappearing from her face. There was another voice, and she recognised it instantly. She flung the door open.

'What the hell do you think you're doing here?' Maddy demanded.

'Mum! That's a bit rude. Jordana just dropped by to deliver this fruit basket from *News 24/7* for Dad. Not that he's going to be eating it any time soon.'

'By *News 24/7*, I take it you mean Byron Farley,' Maddy said through gritted teeth. Despite what Cal had just told her about Jordana not encouraging Farley's attention, surely she must realise that turning up at the hospital was totally insensitive. *The woman is either thoughtless or heartless or both*, she thought.

'Actually, Gary suggested it. He feels really bad about shouting at you on Monday, under the circumstances. He asked if anyone lived near here, and I said I didn't mind doing a detour on my way in to work. I'm sorry if I've upset you, that wasn't my intention at all.'

Maddy could feel Siena's eyes on her. 'No, I'm sorry. I shouldn't have spoken to you like that. It's been a very stressful couple of days. Thank you for going out of your way to drop this off. Are you feeling better?'

'Better?'

'Yes. Cal said you called in sick yesterday.'

'Oh, that,' Jordana said, clearly surprised that Maddy knew she had been off. 'I had really bad period pains. I could barely stand up with the cramps in my stomach, but it's not the sort of thing that blokes like to hear, so I told them I had a migraine.'

Maddy wasn't sure why, but she had the distinct impression that Jordana was still not being truthful.

'I get those, too,' Siena said. 'I find anything with codeine in usually helps.'

'Thanks for the tip. Look, I should be going,' Jordana said, moving towards the door. 'I don't want to get in any more trouble with Byron by being late for my shift. I'm glad your husband's doing so well, Maddy, most people wouldn't have survived a crash like that. He was lucky.'

'Byron'. That was clearly for my benefit, Maddy thought, *just to underline that she has a special relationship with our boss*. Regardless of what Cal had said about Jordana being a victim of unwanted attention, Maddy got the impression that far from being innocent, she was manipulative and calculated.

'That was nice of her, Mum,' Siena said as the door closed behind Jordana. 'She didn't have to volunteer to come here.'

All Maddy could muster was a grunt. Clearly her daughter still had a lot to learn in terms of being a good judge of character.

CHAPTER TWENTY-SIX

3 p.m. – Wednesday

Rachel was about to drop her phone back into her handbag when it pinged, alerting her to yet another text message. She fully expected it to be Tim again, urging her to reconsider the decision she had reached late the previous night after she'd been dropped home by DI Graham Wilson following the stabbing of the priest.

Initially, Rachel had been furious that Tim felt he had the right to tell her what she should or shouldn't do in her professional life. *How dare he suggest that she was too intoxicated to make the best decisions.* She had fumed inwardly all the way to Little Waterton, but the moment she was at the crime scene all thoughts of Tim were forgotten as she and her DI had gone over the timeline of events with the distressed flower arranger who had found Father Raymond's lifeless body.

It was only later, after she had said good night to Graham and was dropping the teabag from the strong cuppa she had made herself into the bin on top of the freesias she had thrown away earlier in a fit of pique, that she allowed herself to consider why she was so angry with Tim. He was expressing his concern for her, showing that he cared about her on more than just a sexual level. He was getting too familiar, too close for comfort. She had been debating whether to sleep on her decision when she had received Tim's text message apologising for his behaviour, but saying that he only had her best interests at heart. It was a case of bad timing.

It underlined to Rachel that they were becoming too involved. She had texted him back immediately: *I'm sorry, Tim, but we're finished.*

Rachel had turned her phone off and gone to bed. When she had turned her phone back on in the morning, she had been disappointed that there was no communication from Tim. All that had changed an hour ago. She had now received four messages all saying the same thing: *Can't we at least talk about it?*

Rachel hadn't replied to any of the messages. She gave the screen a cursory glance and was surprised to see that the new message was from Maddy. If there was a problem with Simon, she was pretty sure Maddy would have rung, but she was still nervous opening the message up:

Thanks for the bodyguard, Rachel, but I honestly don't think we need him. I've just spoken to my closest friend at News 24/7 and he says Byron Farley is too much of a coward to put a hit out on me. I think he's right. Simon was the intended victim and I'm certain it has to do with his former teammates at Kings Park Rovers. I'm just going back to the hospital to sit with him. The signal in there is rubbish, but Siena and I should be home around 6.30 p.m. if you have any news. Did anything flag up in his diary? Maddy x

With the new developments over the past few hours, Rachel had almost forgotten that she'd suggested to Maddy that she may have been the intended target rather than her husband. That was before she discovered that sexual assault allegations had been made against Simon and his former teammates, giving a credible motive for the attacks. *I wonder if Maddy knows anything about it, particularly if it happened before the two of them met?* Rachel thought, pushing open the smoked-glass door leading into the reception area of Muscles gym. *It's going to be a difficult conversation if Simon never told her.*

The distinctive aroma of stale sweat that seemed to permeate the interiors of even the best-run gyms filled Rachel's nostrils as she approached a muscle-bound man standing behind a stainless-steel desk. He was wearing a vest so small that it was little more than a strip of orange fabric running down the centre of his torso. Rachel had always wondered what drove bodybuilders to distort their bodies to the point where they could no longer lower their arms to their sides, leaving them looking as though they were permanently halfway through a lateral raise. *Maybe they see something different when they look in the mirror?* she thought.

'Can I help you, love?'

Rachel cringed. She hated being referred to as 'love'. 'I'm looking for Jimmy Dawson. Is he here?' she replied, waiting for the inevitable question that she knew would follow.

'Who's asking?'

Her ID wallet was already in her hand before the man had finished speaking.

'Oh, right. I'll tell him there's someone here to see him,' he said, disappearing through a door.

James Dawson has clearly done all right for himself, Rachel thought, turning her back on the desk to watch at least thirty clients working out on treadmills, rowing machines and recumbent bikes in a huge open gym. Beyond that she could see a swimming pool, quite unusual in most independent gyms, in her experience, and various smaller studios, all with glass walls, where aerobics and spin classes were taking place.

'I take it you're not here to enquire about membership,' a voice behind her asked.

'It's a good job I'm not easily offended,' Rachel responded, turning round to face a tall, slim man in his early fifties who had either recently returned from holiday or made regular use of the gym's sunbeds. 'Do I look that unfit?'

'Not at all. Anyway, most people are not in great shape when they first join a gym, that's kind of the point of the membership. I don't suppose you would have felt it necessary to flash your ID unless you were here on some sort of official business.'

'Is there somewhere we can talk in private?' she asked.

'Sure. Follow me.'

Rachel did as asked, and found herself in a large, airy office with a bank of monitors on one wall. There were even more facilities than she had been able to see from the reception area. Jimmy sat down in a high-backed leather chair behind his desk and indicated for Rachel to take the chair opposite him.

'This is a pretty impressive set-up, Jimmy. You don't mind me calling you Jimmy, do you?'

'Everybody does, why would I make an exception for you?'

'Thanks. Did that start during your football career?' Rachel couldn't be certain, but she thought she noticed him tense slightly.

'Long before that. I think the only people who ever called me James were my mum, when she was mad at me, and my headmaster at Woodgate Secondary.'

'Well, I don't need to go that far back into your past, but I do want to ask you some questions about an incident that occurred almost twenty-four years ago. Are you okay with that?'

'Sure, fire away. I've got nothing to hide.'

Despite Jimmy's words, Rachel couldn't help thinking that he looked exactly like someone with something to hide. Beads of sweat had started to form on his shaved head, and he was tapping his fingers on the top of his desk.

'It's my understanding that you were the club captain of Kings Park Rovers in 1994.'

Jimmy nodded.

'Prior to the season starting, the team went to Portugal for a training camp in July during which an alleged incident concerning two young Portuguese waitresses occurred. Would you be able to tell me your recollection of what happened?'

'Nothing happened. As you said, some allegations were made against some of the lads, which were proved to be false. Unfortunately, it goes with the territory. As footballers' wages have risen, so have the number of allegations of improper behaviour.'

Nothing had been proven, Rachel thought, *because no proper investigation was ever undertaken*. She persevered. 'Do you remember the specifics of the case, in particular who the accusations were made against?'

Jimmy's brow furrowed, as though he was trying to remember. 'Let me see…' he said.

If he's pausing for effect, Rachel thought, *he's not impressing me*.

'Ray and our keeper, Dave, shared one room, and Simon and a young lad, Neil, shared the other. I think the complaint was made against all four of them, even though the girl said she had only been raped by two of them.'

Rachel's throat tightened. Clearly Jimmy was unaware of what he had just said: 'only been raped by two of them' were his actual words. *So, what? Didn't it count as proper rape unless it had been all four of them forcing themselves onto Beatriz?* She took a breath to calm her rising anger.

'Were you questioned at the time in connection with the allegations?'

'No. Why would I be? As far as I remember, there was absolutely no evidence of any wrongdoing, and the alleged incident didn't even warrant being reported to the British police.'

'You're absolutely right, it wasn't reported to us at the time or we might have had a closer look at things. It takes a great deal of courage for a woman to claim she has been sexually assaulted and, having read the case file this morning, it would appear that this case was dismissed without any kind of formal investigation.'

Rachel deliberately paused. Two could play at mind games, and she wanted him to think that potentially the case was being reopened. Although Jimmy's name had not appeared on the Portuguese police report, it was listed on the back of the anonymous letter found in Simon Shaw's diary. Rachel wanted to know why.

'Do you watch the news?'

'Not often. I'm pretty busy running this place, to be honest.'

'Are you aware that two of the people named in the historic rape allegation are now dead, and another one is in a coma after an attempt was made on his life?'

'I wasn't aware of that, no. Look, I'm sorry, but I don't see how this is relevant to me and I've got a client waiting for a personal training session,' Jimmy said, starting to get up from his chair.

'Just a couple more questions, Jimmy, if you wouldn't mind. Have you been in contact with any of these former teammates recently?'

'No, I haven't seen any of them for years, not since we all retired from the game.'

'I see,' Rachel said, also standing up so she could look him more closely in the eyes. 'Maybe I've got this wrong, and you're not the Jimmy listed alongside Ray, Neil and Dave on the back of a threatening letter that we found in Simon Shaw's possession.'

She noticed Jimmy's Adam's apple bob up and down as he swallowed several times before saying, 'I can't see why it would be me.'

'One final question. Would you happen to have any contact details for Dave Cox? We've been trying to trace him, but without much success at the moment. We believe his life could be in danger, if these incidents are all linked to the historic rape incident.'

'Like I said, I haven't seen any of them for years, so I'm afraid I can't help you.'

'Well, thanks for your time, Jimmy. If you do remember anything you think might be relevant, perhaps you could call me at the station or drop me an email,' Rachel said, handing over her card.

'Sure.'

Rachel was beginning to find his laconic use of the word 'sure' very irritating. 'I hope I didn't keep your client waiting too long.'

'No problem. I'm just sorry I couldn't be more helpful,' he said, holding the office door open for Rachel to pass.

'So am I, but you never know, something may happen to jog your memory,' she said, hoping that the something wouldn't be Dave Cox turning up dead.

CHAPTER TWENTY-SEVEN

3.30 p.m. – Wednesday

DS Errol Green checked his watch; it was half past three and he'd just finished a phone conversation with his wife who was about to leave for Legoland with their two young boys, Troy and Dean. He could hear their excited voices in the background and felt slightly aggrieved that they would be enjoying some family time while he was stuck in Wales, potentially for several hours, waiting for Sergeant Rob Turnbull to return from manoeuvres. Errol had an excellent working relationship with DCI Hart, but he sometimes thought she wasn't very understanding when it came to making allowances for her officers to be able to maintain some semblance of a home life. It didn't surprise him. She had no husband or children of her own, although, if rumour was to be believed, she did currently have a boyfriend. *Maybe that will soften her up a bit*, Errol thought, taking another sip of his lager shandy and grimacing at the insipid taste. It wouldn't do for him or his DC to be over the legal limit for driving, but they'd both needed something to take away the heat of the mutton curry they'd ordered for lunch.

When he and DC Broadbent had arrived in the small Welsh town of Brecon a couple of hours earlier, they had driven straight to the barracks. At the gatehouse they were told that the soldiers out on exercise weren't due back until later that evening, any time between 6 p.m. and 9 p.m. usually, depending on the weather conditions up on the Beacons, the hills that surrounded the town.

DS Green had asked if there was anywhere close by where they could get something to eat and that had rooms where they could possibly stay overnight, should the need arise. The gatehouse soldier had suggested The Bell, a pub in the centre of town, but he had warned them that the food wasn't up to much.

He wasn't joking, Errol thought, belching as he pushed his plate away. *I may have an iron constitution, but even I can't stomach that. How is it possible to make something so fiery-hot and yet, at the same time, flavourless?* he wondered, watching his colleague Phil Broadbent as he made his way back across the bar to their table by the window.

'Not the best, was it, Sarge?' he said, nodding his head in the direction of their half-eaten plates of food, as he slid back onto the high-backed wooden bench opposite his superior officer.

'Keep your voice down, Phil. I want to ask her if she knows Sergeant Turnbull,' he said, flashing his eyes in the direction of the approaching barmaid. 'She's not likely to be very forth-coming if she hears you slagging off the food. And don't call me Sarge in front of her. She doesn't need to know that we're police officers.'

'Right, Sarge, I mean... Errol,' he said, his voice barely above a whisper. 'Although it doesn't take a genius to work out that we weren't very impressed with the curry.'

'Let me deal with it.'

'Can I get you boys anything else?' the waitress asked, picking up their plates.

'No, thanks,' Errol replied. 'We shouldn't have stopped at the motorway services on the way down for coffee and a muffin, it's spoilt our lunch.'

'Eyes bigger than your belly, were they?' she joked. 'Are you down from London?' she asked, in her sing-song Welsh accent.

'Not quite that far. Reading.'

'What brings you here, then?'

Errol smiled at her directness, but he was ready with an answer. 'We've got a meeting at the barracks. Our company deals with electronic equipment used for tracking people.'

It wasn't a million miles from the truth.

'That's handy around here. People are always getting themselves lost when they're out hillwalking. Not so much the soldiers, mind, cos of their training. They're always out on manoeuvres.'

'It must be pretty good for business, having the army base here?'

'Yes. Quite a few of them come in here on their nights off. They're not very generous with their tips, though.'

'I suppose working behind the bar you're on first-name terms with some of them. We've an appointment with...' Errol looked at the screen of his phone, as though he were checking someone's name, 'Sergeant Turnbull.'

'You mean Rob,' the barmaid replied, keen to show that she was indeed on first-name terms with the soldier the 'salesmen' were there to see. 'He used to come in here a lot when he was stationed here, but I thought he'd been relocated?'

'I wouldn't know, I've never met him. You obviously know more about him than we do. What's he like? Are we likely to make a sale?' Errol asked, trying to keep the conversation light.

'Depends what kind of a mood he's in. He can be a bit grumpy. He's got a lovely girlfriend, though. You'd have made a sale to her, all right. Siena, she's called, and she's as pretty as her name. She always chats to us girls if he gets into a game of darts or pool. She worships the ground he walks on, she does. She's quite a bit younger than him – his mates used to tease him by asking where she'd left her white stick.'

Errol couldn't help thinking that the barmaid would never have got away with her un-PC comment if she worked in a trendy London bar.

'Well, let's hope he's in one of his better moods when he gets back from his training exercise.'

'I wouldn't bank on it. It's been raining and cold for the past few days, and it's always blowing a gale up on the hills. I hope I'm wrong, mind. Are you sure I can't get you anything else? Another shandy, perhaps?'

'No, you're all right, thanks. I wouldn't mind a coffee, though. Phil?'

DC Broadbent nodded agreement.

'Two coffees coming up,' she said, heading off towards the kitchen carrying the plates of half-eaten curry.

'I hope we don't have to stay here tonight, Sarge.'

'What did I say about not calling me Sarge?'

'Sorry. It doesn't feel right calling you Errol when we're on duty.'

'Well try. I think we'll make a decision on staying after we've tasted the coffee. I can't face the day without a decent fix of caffeine.'

'We won't have much choice if they're really late back. I can't imagine Sergeant Turnbull agreeing to an immediate police interview if he's tired, cold and hungry.'

'I was meaning about staying here at The Bell. There must be more welcoming establishments, even if they're further away from the barracks. I'm just nipping outside to try PC Drake again. I don't want to be overheard after we've just told the barmaid we're salesmen. Stick the saucer over my cup if the coffee arrives before I'm back. Weak coffee is one thing, but cold, weak coffee would just about finish me off.'

Less than ten minutes later, DS Green slid back onto the bench on his side of the table.

'The good news is that the coffee is pretty good, S... I mean Errol,' Phil Broadbent said, removing the saucer from the top of his DS's cup. 'Any updates from Eleanor?' he added, emphasising the PC's first name.

Errol took a sip of his coffee and nodded his approval. 'Just as well it's half decent as we might be drinking a lot of the stuff over the next few hours. Drake was about to call us. The motorbike in the M4 incident is definitely the same make and model as Turnbull's, but she's waiting to see if Larry can clean up the images of the number plate on the phone footage. Drake transferred my call to DCI Hart. She thinks there's enough evidence for us to take Sergeant Turnbull back to the station for questioning rather than interviewing him here. We're to drive him back to Reading tonight, regardless of the time.'

'I guess that's a case of be careful what you wish for. It looks like it's going to be a late one,' DC Broadbent said.

'Look on the bright side – at least you'll be sleeping in your own bed tonight.'

CHAPTER TWENTY-EIGHT

After her meeting with Jimmy Dawson, Rachel got back to the police station at around 4.15 p.m. From his body language, she was pretty sure Dawson had been hiding something in relation to the rape allegations, and she was confident that he was the Jimmy on Simon Shaw's list. Rachel also believed he had been lying when he had said that the former teammates had not been in touch with each other recently. There was no date on the threatening letter, and no envelope with a postmark on it to ascertain when it had been sent, but Simon Shaw's diary entry had been in late January, a few weeks before Neil Edison had taken his own life, if indeed he had. On the way back to the office she had called the team in Richmond who had investigated Edison's death, asking if they would share their case file and allow her officers to examine his personal effects, which had been bagged up and stored. She hadn't been asked what her interest in the case was. As far as they were concerned, Neil's death was a suicide and the case had been closed. They were happy to oblige.

Her team in Little Waterton who were going through Father Ray's effects had, so far, not found a similar letter to the one Simon had received. *It doesn't mean he didn't receive one*, Rachel thought, dropping her bag onto the chair in her office and sitting down at her desk to check if Edison's case file had been sent through. *Maybe we haven't found it yet. Or he could have disposed of it?* It was still early days; the priest had only been dead for a few hours and, according to DI Graham Wilson when he had returned from Little Waterton at lunchtime, Father Ray's office was awash with paperwork that was going to take some time to sift through.

As instructed, Graham had already left for the day when Rachel got back, telling his colleagues he had to rush to a forgotten dental appointment. She had rung him to let him know she was on her way back to the office and asked him to leave anything pertaining to Dave Cox on her desk rather than getting anyone else involved. *That's how things get missed*, Rachel thought, scanning the hand-written notes Graham had left for her. *Handing over information to another officer who hasn't been in the loop from the start is where mistakes can creep in.* Not all of her officers were as thorough as they might be when it came to paperwork. She cast an eye over the files she had been going through and signing off on Monday morning because there had been a lull in active investigations. *Was it really only two days ago that I was moaning to Tim about being stuck at my desk underneath a mountain of paperwork? So much has changed since then, not least my relationship with him*, Rachel reflected. She had deliberately left her phone on silent and in her handbag. *What was the point of knowing whether or not he had texted again?* She had made her decision to finish things with him, and nothing he could say or do would change that.

Her DI hadn't come up with much on Dave Cox, although he had established that Cox and his wife were going through divorce proceedings around the time that he seemed to have disappeared off the face of the earth. Graham had been in contact with the DVLA, but they held no current vehicle details linked to him on their system. As yet, the utilities companies hadn't responded with any current account information, and HMRC weren't as useful as he had hoped, as it appeared that Dave Cox had not been paying UK tax for over six years. Everything seemed to coincide with him selling his house in Ascot. *You don't just disappear without trace,*

Rachel thought, *unless, of course, you want to.* It was possible that he had taken the money from the house sale and gone to live abroad, which would account for why they were having such difficulty tracing him. She was just writing a note asking Graham to contact the UK Passport Office when he was back at work the following morning, when there was a tap on her door.

'Come in.'

'Guv, have you got a minute?'

It was PC Drake. 'Yes, Eleanor, what have you got for me?'

'We've already had confirmation that Turnbull's motorbike is the same make and model as the bike at the scene of our two incidents, and now Larry has been able to make out a partial on the number plate. The first and last two letters match, Guv.'

'I think we can safely say that it was Turnbull's bike. Our next job is to prove that it was him riding it. Have you passed this information on to DS Green?'

'Just about to, Guv. I wanted to let you know first.'

'Good work, Eleanor. Can you get me the details for the senior commanding officer at the Brecon camp, and I'll contact him to arrange for DS Green and DC Broadbent to have access to look around for the motorbike and impound it if they find it.'

'What about Turnbull, Guv? Do we have enough to bring him in for questioning?'

'Absolutely. Until we have proof to the contrary, we have to assume that Turnbull was riding his own motorbike. We won't arrest him, unless he proves difficult – we'll just question him under caution. Please relay that to DS Green.'

'On it, Guv.'

Rachel opened the email from the Richmond team and clicked on the icon to open the attached PDF of the Neil Edison case file. She selected print and the machine in the corner of her office spluttered into life. *We're definitely getting somewhere*, she thought, as the printer spat out sheets of paper, *but I still can't see how Turnbull is involved in all this, unless… someone has employed him as a hitman.*

Maddy had said that Turnbull took a mechanic's course because he couldn't afford the repairs on his motorbike. His motive could be money, pure and simple. He was army trained and had access to weapons, so he had the means to kill in a variety of different ways, particularly with his background in Afghanistan. Opportunity was the only stumbling block. Two of the attacks were committed while he was on a training exercise in Wales, giving him the perfect alibi. *I'm looking forward to questioning you, Sergeant Turnbull,* she thought, crossing her office to collect the sheaf of papers. If he was responsible for the attacks, Rachel knew they were only one step away from finding out who ordered them and why.

Rachel had gone through the Neil Edison file with a fine-tooth comb and could find nothing in it to suggest that his death was anything but suicide. None of his colleagues had a bad word to say about him, other than that he was a bit of a loner. He was very good at his job and very knowledgeable about the plants in his care. He was always extremely careful around dangerous plants, and none of his co-workers believed that he had accidentally poisoned himself by handling a toxic plant without proper protection. To a man, and woman, they were all saddened by his death but not particularly surprised, as he had experienced episodes of severe depression previously. The only thing that was bugging Rachel was that none of his colleagues had said that he seemed depressed on the morning when they had last seen him at work. In fact, several had commented on what a good mood he had been in because he loved the planting part of his job and that was what he had been doing that morning. One female colleague, Lydia Cantor, had made particular reference to his good humour, noting that he had had a bout of depression about six weeks before, but added that he seemed to be back to his usual self. Rachel made a note of Lydia's contact details after checking the time. It was almost 6 p.m. and she had arranged a debrief with the teams working on the different elements of what now appeared to be the same case. Contacting Lydia would be on her list of things to do the following morning, along with interviewing Sergeant Turnbull. She closed the lid on her computer and walked into the buzzing incident room.

'Let's try and keep this fairly brief if we can, people. DS Parker, have you uncovered anything of significance which may suggest a motive for stabbing Father Raymond Kiernan?'

'No, Guv. We've been going through his personal effects, and also the paperwork in his office. Father Ray was a bit old-school, so there's a fair amount of it, but it's mostly notes for sermons as far as we can tell at this point. The church is fairly remote, at the end of a lane on the outskirts of the village, so our line of questioning with the villagers has predominantly been focusing on whether anyone has noticed any unfamiliar faces in the village recently.'

'And?'

'Nothing really, apart from a woman sketching in the graveyard, but apparently that's not so unusual.'

'Was there any description of the woman?'

'Slim with long dark hair was the best we could get,' she said, consulting her notebook.

'Okay. Maybe see if there are any CCTV cameras on the roads in and out of the village that might have footage of a woman matching this description arriving or leaving.'

'Yes, Guv. The murder weapon is with the forensics team, but they've said there are no fingerprints, so either the assailant was wearing gloves or it's been wiped clean.'

'Only to be expected, I guess,' Rachel replied. 'There's nothing further to report on Simon Shaw. He's still in an induced coma, but stable. Earlier this afternoon I interviewed James Dawson, the owner of Muscles gym in Bracknell, who we believe might have been the Jimmy named in the list on the back of the threatening letter found in Simon Shaw's diary,' she continued, adding his name to the whiteboard with a question mark at the side of it. 'He couldn't or wouldn't help with any of my enquiries, and it did seem as though he wasn't being entirely truthful. We'll leave it a couple of days, and then maybe pay him another visit at the gym. Neither DI Wilson nor myself have had any luck in tracing Dave Cox. He appears to have done a vanishing act in 2013 shortly after selling his home. I suspect he might have gone abroad. DI Wilson will pick up on that in the morning. Talking of going abroad, have you been able to establish if our Portuguese waitresses returned to their home town following the alleged assault, PC Leverette?'

'Yes, Guv. Both Rosa Viegas and Beatriz Azevedo returned to Tavira in early January 1995. We already know that Beatriz was pregnant following the alleged rape, but it transpires that Rosa was, too.' There was a muttering around the room. 'I'm waiting to hear back from the hospital with any information they may have surrounding the births, but I have to say they're not very forth-coming in divulging personal information to the British police.'

'If they continue to be obstructive, we'll have to approach them through the local police in Tavira. Did you establish whether either Rosa or Beatriz has visited the UK recently, or is potentially still here?'

'I've been in touch with the UK Border Force and neither name has flagged up as entering the country in the past six months. I've also put in a call to the Portuguese passport authority, but I haven't heard back from them yet.'

'Keep plugging away at it. So, I've just been going through the case file of our other footballer accused of rape: Neil Edison. To be honest, it does seem like a pretty open-and-shut case of suicide, but the timing suggests that it may still be linked to our investigations even if the gardener did take his own life. I'm going to have another look at that in the morning, when we're also expecting to be able to interview Sergeant Turnbull. Following confirmation that the motorbike used in the M4 attack and seen in Little Waterton around the time of the stabbing was the same make and model as Turnbull's, we now have a partial number plate match. Any further news from Brecon, PC Drake?'

'Yes, Guv. DS Green has reported back to say they've not been able to locate Turnbull's motorbike at the Brecon barracks. I've been in touch with the traffic division for any sightings of it travelling west on the M4 since it was seen in Little Waterton last night at around 7 p.m. They haven't come back to me as yet, but will continue to check footage. I've stressed the urgency, Guv.'

'Good. Has DS Green confirmed whether Turnbull and his soldiers are back from their training exercise?'

'They weren't when I last spoke to him. They're due back between now and 9 p.m. and I've asked him to call me as soon as they've made contact with Turnbull and are on their way back to Reading with him.'

'Please let me know as soon as you hear from him.'

'Yes, Guv.'

'So, to summarise: up to this point, it's probably seemed like we had a number of individual cases, but I'm fairly confident that we will be able to start linking the various lines of enquiry together once we've interviewed Sergeant Turnbull. He seems to figure prominently in at least two of these incidents, now all we have to ascertain is why. That's it for tonight. Please make sure you hand over all relevant information to the late-team members. I'll see you all bright and early in the morning,' Rachel said, heading back into her office.

Eleanor Drake followed her. 'Guv, some of us are going to the pizza place round the corner for a bite to eat. Would you care to join us?'

'Thank you, but no, Eleanor,' Rachel replied, then added as an afterthought, 'I already have a prior engagement.'

'Another time, maybe. Night, Guv.'

Rachel had no idea why she had found it necessary to lie to Eleanor Drake; usually she simply declined such invitations without feeling the need to explain herself. *I could drop in on Maddy on my way home and then I wouldn't be lying,* she thought, slipping into her jacket and throwing her bag over her shoulder. *It would be preferable for her to hear about the historical rape allegation from me, and I'd rather have that conversation with her face to face.* But Rachel knew Maddy would be bound to ask questions about the case, in particular any developments regarding Rob Turnbull, and she wasn't at liberty to share that information, even with her friend. Instead, she sent Maddy a quick text, but not before she noticed that there had been no further communication from Tim after his earlier flurry of messages. *Well, he seems to have taken the hint,* she thought, trying to ignore the disappointment welling up inside her, while tapping the words out on her phone screen and pressing send: *Hi Maddy, nothing much to report I'm afraid. I'll catch up with you tomorrow x*

Rachel stopped off at the Little Waitrose service station on her way home to fill up with petrol. She treated herself to *penne arrabbiata* for one, a bottle of red wine and a bar of Lindt dark chocolate with sea salt. Not usually in the habit of drinking alone, it was a familiar pattern when she had dumped a boyfriend. She parked opposite her house and was just turning the key in her front door when she became aware of the pungent aroma of freesias.

'I really am very sorry.'

Rachel turned around to be confronted with the biggest bunch of freesias she had ever seen, totally obscuring the person holding them. She stood rooted to the spot, not knowing what to say.

'Can we at least talk?' Tim said, lowering the huge bunch of flowers to waist level, pleading with his eyes.

'I'm not sure there's much to say,' Rachel replied, recovering her composure. 'I've been on my own too long to allow someone else to come into my life and start telling me how to live it. Honestly, it's better that you find out now how stubborn and selfish I am. You shouldn't have wasted your money on more flowers – I threw the others in the bin.'

'I won't give up. I'm just as stubborn as you say you are. We're both Capricorns, remember?'

Rachel thought about the contents of the flimsy plastic bag she was holding. *Do I really want to spend the rest of my life dining on meals for one in front of the television? Haven't I punished myself enough? I like Tim and he obviously likes me, or he wouldn't be here.* She could feel herself wavering.

'You'd better come in.'

CHAPTER TWENTY-NINE

7.30 p.m. – Wednesday

'It makes you wonder why they do it, doesn't it, Sarge,' DC Broadbent said, as he and DS Green watched the steady stream of soldiers returning to their base after three days and nights exposed to the elements in the Welsh mountains. They were unshaven, soaked through and bent forward against the wind as they carried their equipment in huge rucksacks that were incredibly heavy, according to one of the soldiers they had been conversing with while they were waiting.

'People probably ask the same question about why we join the police force. There's never just one reason. For some it's a career that runs in the family, for others it's because they want to serve their community or in a soldier's case their country, and for others it's the only job going: a guaranteed pay cheque at the end of the month.'

'That looks pretty brutal, though, Sarge, and that's just the training – without an enemy trying to kill you. I'll bet they're glad to be back.'

'Most of them, although I'm not so sure Sergeant Turnbull will be glad to be back when he finds out he has a welcoming committee. He'll probably wish he'd stayed out on the mountains. Come on, let's get ourselves out there and make ourselves known to him.'

The soldiers were forming orderly lines as though they were on the parade ground rather than just back from a gruelling training exercise, as DS Green approached the figure at the front who was barking out orders, most of which were being carried away on the buffeting wind.

'Sergeant?'

'Who are you?' The man's tone was brusque but wary.

'I'm DS Green and this is DC Broadbent. We're from the Reading police division, and we need to ask you to accompany us there for questioning with regard to an incident which took place early on Monday morning.'

'You've got the wrong man. I've been out on a training exercise with this lot since Sunday night, so whatever the incident is, I had nothing to do with it.'

'I'm sorry sir, but we have clearance from your commanding officer to take you back to Reading with us.'

'I've got thirty witnesses who will all testify that I've been with them for every minute of the past seventy-two hours, isn't that right, lads?'

'Yes, sir,' was the communal response.

'I'm sorry, Sergeant Turnbull, but we are just obeying orders, and our orders are to escort you to Reading for questioning in connection with two very serious incidents.'

'You've got the wrong man, I'm afraid. I'm guessing you're looking for Rob Turnbull?'

DS Green and DC Broadbent exchanged a look.

'That's right. We were told he was the sergeant in charge of this training exercise.'

'He was supposed to be. Bully and me have been mates for years. We were out in Afghanistan together, and I always knew he had my back. Just after he arrived here on Sunday afternoon, he had a call from his girlfriend to say that his mum was ill. He told me he'd used up all his leave so he couldn't go and see her. I could see he was worried sick, and a soldier in that frame of mind can be a danger out on a training exercise when you need everyone to be on their toes. I offered to swap with him, but it was pretty last-minute, so I haven't had time to fill in the paperwork.'

'So, you are?'

'Sergeant Will Edridge. Whatever you think Bully's done, he didn't do it. I'd stake my life on it.'

'We're going to need you to come with us to confirm your identity with a senior officer. We're investigating a very serious matter and, like you, we have orders to carry out.'

'Fine. I'll probably get a rollicking for changing places without it being approved in advance, but that's not your problem. Bully would do the same for me. Let me just dismiss this lot first.' He turned to face the bedraggled soldiers in front of him. 'Company, stand at ease,' he bellowed. 'Company, dismissed.'

Half an hour later, after receiving confirmation that the sergeant who had been out on field exercise for the past three days and nights with D Company was indeed Will Edridge, DS Green rang PC Eleanor Drake to tell her the news.

'Well, that was a bit of a wild goose chase,' he said.

'Sorry, Sarge, I didn't catch that. It's a bit noisy in here, let me just pop outside.'

'Where are you, Drake?'

'In Pizza Pronto. A group of us stopped off in here when we got off shift.'

'It's all right for some. DC Broadbent and I have had the day from hell and you lot are gallivanting around.'

'Sorry, Sarge. It's been a bit full on, so we just wanted to let off a bit of steam.'

'Is the Guv with you?'

'No. We invited her, but she said she had a prior arrangement.'

'Did she indeed. It's a shame she cancelled my prior arrangement for today. It wouldn't be so bad if Turnbull had been here, but he's not, which would explain why his motorbike isn't here either. He was supposed to take D Company out for the training exercise, but apparently got a call on Sunday to say his mother was ill. He left Brecon at about 3 p.m. on Sunday afternoon. It's not clear if he went straight up to Redcar, where his mother lives, or whether he stopped off at the barracks in Windsor first.'

'Do you think the story about his mother being ill is true?'

'It's hard to say. The sergeant he swapped his duties with was certainly taken in by it and they're best friends. I got the feeling that if we hadn't been there to meet Turnbull, the swap in duty would never have come to light and made it into official army paperwork. I think it was just a mate covering for a mate, and now we've landed him in a spot of bother. It would have been the perfect alibi for Turnbull if we hadn't discovered the switch.'

'I'd better let the DCI know.'

'Yes. I think her instinct about Turnbull has been right all along.'

'Night, Sarge, drive safe.'

Errol disconnected the call, smiling at his handset.

'What's so funny, Sarge?' DC Broadbent asked, not taking his eyes off the treacherous winding road for a second.

'PC Drake. She's so by the book on everything, and then she comes out with "drive safe". I think we've just discovered that she is a human being after all, and not the perfectly programmed police robot she comes across as being at work.'

'That's a bit harsh, Sarge, she's just very thorough.'

'You mark my words, she's a PC on a mission. She wants to be the next DCI Hart, and I'll bet money that she'll make it ahead of you and me. What does the satnav give as our ETA?'

'9.45 p.m.'

'Oh well, at least we'll get a bit of overtime out of this pointless jaunt. Shout if you need me, I'm going to try and grab forty winks.'

CHAPTER THIRTY

7.35 p.m. – Wednesday

Rachel quickly changed out of her work clothes into a pair of leggings and an oversized lightweight sweater and made her way downstairs. It felt strange knowing that someone was sitting on her sofa, sipping wine and watching television, when she normally had the house to herself. For some unfathomable reason she felt nervous as she rounded the turn at the bottom of her staircase.

'I hope it's okay,' she said, indicating Tim's glass of wine, 'it's just a cheapie I grabbed at the petrol station.'

'Do you want me to lie, or shall I be honest?' he replied, pressing the button on the remote control to turn the television off.

'I think honesty is always the best policy, don't you?' she said, heading behind the kitchen counter and pouring herself a glass of the wine in question.

'In that case,' he said, 'I've tasted better.'

Rachel took a sip. It was sharp and on the vinegary side. 'Me too,' she said, walking into the lounge carrying the bottle and purposely sitting in the armchair rather than next to Tim on the sofa. 'So, what did you want to talk about?'

'Us.'

'There is no "us", Tim. I've really enjoyed going out on dates with you, and the physical side of things has been great,' she said, feeling the warm glow of a blush, 'but I never promised you anything more, and I'm sorry if you think I misled you.'

'I'm the one that should be apologising, and I am. I – I guess I got ahead of myself and thought you wanted the same thing as me: a relationship where we spend more time together and get to know one another. But if that's not what you want, I'll take what I can get. I just don't want you not to be a part of my life. I like you being in it.'

'You're making this difficult for me.'

'I don't mean to. I know I overstepped the mark the other night, and I'm truly sorry. Work is work, and it's none of my business what decisions you make. I would be pretty cross with you if you tried to tell me what the best line of defence was for a client. I just didn't want the evening to end when it was going so well… at least, I thought it was going well.'

Rachel could feel Tim's eyes on her, seeking affirmation, but she didn't speak, taking another big gulp of the unpalatable wine instead.

'You're the best thing that's happened to me in a long time, Rachel,' Tim continued. 'The minute I walked into that interview room last November, I felt a connection. It was so difficult to concentrate on what you were saying when all I wanted to do was bury my face in your hair. I couldn't believe my luck when you agreed to go out for dinner with me. Honestly, I had a spring in my step for days, and then I nearly blew it by being late. You gave me a second chance then, when I really didn't deserve it, and now I'm asking you for another one. Please, Rachel, please say you will.'

It wasn't the first time Rachel had heard this type of plea after she had dumped a boyfriend, but the difference was that she actually really liked Tim. *What's not to like?* she thought, lifting her eyes to connect with his and feeling a shudder of desire running through her body. *He's handsome, thoughtful, clever, funny and he likes me. But that's the problem. He doesn't really know who I am and what he would be taking on. What if he stops liking me after I've allowed him to get close? I can't cope with that. I can't deal with being rejected.*

'I'm sorry, Tim, I just can't. I'd been thinking about finishing things with you anyway, and your actions the other night just brought it about sooner.'

'But why? Why would you finish things when we get along so well? I don't understand. Are you saying you don't have feelings for me?'

'Exactly. That's exactly what I'm saying. We had some fun together, but it's run its course.'

'I've changed my mind about this wine. It's delicious. The best wine I've ever tasted.'

'What are you talking about? It's cheap plonk.'

'You asked me to be honest about the wine, and I was. I thought you liked honesty. I just want you to be truthful about your reasons for not wanting to see me any more.'

Tim had backed her into a corner and Rachel knew it.

'All right. You win. I do have feelings for you, quite strong feelings, actually, but I can't let you get any closer because I don't want to be hurt if you have a change of heart. It's simple, really. It's self-preservation.'

'But I won't have a change of heart, Rachel,' he said tenderly, placing his wine glass on the coffee table and reaching for her hand. 'I've been looking for you all my life, and now that I've found you, I never want to lose you.'

His words sounded so sincere. Rachel looked into his eyes and the sincerity was matched there. She could feel herself wavering. She wanted to believe him, but it was such a risk. *What are you so afraid of?* a voice whispered in her head. *Why can't you accept that someone loves you and wants you? Take a chance, Rachel*, the voice in her head persisted, *don't let him slip through your fingers*. She reached out to place her wine glass next to his and allowed him to take her hand.

'If we're going to do this, there are some things you need to know about me.'

'We all have things in our past that we're not proud of, but I don't care. That was before I met you.'

'It's not what you think. You need to know these things because sometimes they overwhelm me, and I need to know you would be able to handle it.'

'Love conquers everything, Rachel. I'm a good listener if you want to talk?'

'God, I wish I had a decent bottle of wine in. I could do with some Dutch courage.'

'I've got some in my car. I didn't want to seem too presumptuous, so I thought I'd start with the flowers as a peace offering. Do you want me to fetch it?'

Rachel nodded. 'Are you hungry?'

'A bit.'

'I can offer half a pasta *penne arrabbiata* microwave dinner, and chocolate for dessert.'

'Sounds perfect,' Tim said, scrambling to his feet. 'Shall I take your key to let myself back in while you're preparing our banquet?'

'Good idea. You've got about four and a half minutes. I hope you're not parked too far away.'

'I'll be back before you know it,' he said, pulling her front door closed behind him.

I hope I'm doing the right thing, Rachel thought as she pierced the film lid and placed the tray on the microwave turntable before setting the timer. It was a huge leap of faith, one she had never taken before, but maybe she had finally found the person she could share her life with.

Rachel watched the gentle rise and fall of her white cotton duvet, beneath which Tim lay sleeping. It was 6 a.m. and she knew her alarm would be going off soon, marking the start of another busy day. Despite having had very little sleep, she wasn't feeling at all tired. She felt as though a massive weight had been lifted off her shoulders.

*

The bottle of wine Tim had brought in from his car was infinitely superior to the service station plonk. After they'd shared Rachel's microwave dinner for one, she had settled back into the armchair while Tim sat on the sofa.

'Would it help if I start?' Tim had asked.

'Start?'

'Is it easier for you if I tell you a bit about me first?'

Rachel had nodded. Even after polishing off the good wine and refilling their glasses with the lesser-quality stuff, she had been wondering how she was going to start the conversation about what had happened to her and Ruth.

'I know I told you that I grew up in a series of foster homes, but I didn't tell you why. I never really knew my mum. She ran off with a bloke who worked in the bank when I was two and a half. Apparently, I had a really bad case of the "terrible twos". She told my dad she couldn't cope with me any more, and that she wished I'd been a girl because they were easier to deal with. I don't think my dad ever forgave me. Although I tried my hardest to please him, nothing I did was ever good enough. Eventually, he couldn't stand the sight of me, so he sent me away.'

'Oh, Tim, that's awful,' Rachel had said. 'It wasn't your fault your mum couldn't cope with a boisterous boy. Were you an only child?'

'Yes, and it's probably just as well or we would most likely all have ended up in care. I just think maybe my mum wasn't the maternal type, if there is such a thing. How about you? Have you got any brothers or sisters?'

Inadvertently, Tim had opened up the conversation for Rachel.

'I have a twin sister.'

'Really? An identical twin?'

'Yes.'

'I'm surprised you haven't mentioned her before. I thought twins were virtually inseparable.'

'We are very close,' Rachel had said, 'but my sister isn't well. She lives in the residential wing of a hospital.'

'I'm so sorry to hear that. Is she terminally ill?'

'She – she doesn't have a physical illness. Something happened to us when we were young, and it's affected her psychologically.'

'Do you want to talk about it?' Tim had asked gently.

'Not really, but I think it's only fair that you should know what you're getting into.'

Tim had patted the sofa and Rachel had gone to sit next to him, leaning her head into his chest so that she didn't have to look in his eyes.

'Take your time,' he had said, 'we've got as long as it takes.'

Rachel had struggled at first to find the words. Most of the people she worked with knew about it because they knew of the case, but she had never spoken about it to any of them. She didn't want to appear emotionally weak, and she couldn't guarantee she wouldn't cry.

'My sister and I have always been very close. We did everything together, the good things and the naughty things. If I took a biscuit from the tin without asking, she would take one too, so that if we were found out we would both be in an equal amount of trouble. Don't get the wrong idea, most of the time we were pretty well behaved, but, like all kids, there were occasions when we could be mischievous. One afternoon, we were helping our mum to bake a cake when I accidentally dropped one of the eggs on the floor. Mum was really cross because then we didn't have enough for the cake mixture. We were covered in flour, so instead of getting us washed and changed, she told us to play out in the back garden while she went to the supermarket for a box of eggs. We were only six. She shouldn't really have left us on our own. Not long after she went, our next-door neighbour stuck his head over the fence and asked us if we would like to pick some apples from his tree. He put a ladder over the fence, and we climbed up our side and he lifted us down the other.'

Rachel had paused as she felt Tim's body tense up. 'It was a really warm day, and we got hot and thirsty very quickly, so he invited us inside his house for a drink of orange squash. I – I don't know what happened after that. The next thing I remember was waking up in a very dark room that had a horrible smell. I was lying on a mattress on the floor. There was something in my mouth to stop me crying out, and my hands were tied behind my back. My sister wasn't there.'

As though she was reliving the moment of terror, Rachel had started to cry, tears seeping from the corners of her eyes.

'Hey,' Tim had said. 'You don't have to go on with this if it's too upsetting for you.'

'I think maybe I need to. I was alone for what seemed like a very long time before I heard a door open and a shaft of light illuminated a steep stone staircase. That's when I knew I was in the cellar. We had one the same in our house, but Mum and Dad used ours to store things, so we never went down there. He was carrying my sister. I thought she was dead at first because she was all floppy like a rag doll. He put her down gently at the side of me on the mattress and then turned around without saying a word, went back up the stairs and shut the door. I wriggled my body closer to my sister so she would know I was there. When she stirred, she started kicking out, but then I think she must have realised it was me. The next time the door opened, I was terrified. I thought he was going to take me, but he didn't. He took my sister again. He always took my sister. It was like he didn't want me. It was like I wasn't good enough.'

'Hey, come on, that's nonsense,' Tim had said, trying to comfort her. 'You were just lucky.'

'My sister always said that, all through our childhood – in fact, she still does. But I don't think so. It tortures me to think of the physical abuse she suffered at the hands of that monster.'

Rachel had noticed that Tim's hands had formed into fists and his knuckles had turned white.

'I couldn't share her pain and I couldn't ever truly know how she had suffered. I've been weighed down with the guilt of it my whole life. I don't know why he chose her and not me, but it must be my fault, right?'

'Wrong. You've got to stop blaming yourself. Neither of you did anything to deserve what happened to you.'

'It's you who's wrong,' Rachel had said, lifting her head away from his chest and searching his face for reassurance that what she was about to confess was the right thing to do. 'Ruth didn't want to climb over the fence to pick the apples. It was me who said yes.'

Rachel had started to sob uncontrollably, and Tim had rocked her like a baby. She had never felt able to trust anyone sufficiently to tell them her guilty secret: not her mum and dad, nor the medical professionals who she and Ruth had seen for years after the trauma of the abduction. Until that moment, the only people who knew what had happened that sunny afternoon were Ruth and their next-door neighbour. Ruth had never betrayed her sister, but deep in her heart Rachel knew she blamed her and it had changed their relationship. As Tim had held her close, saying over and over, 'It's not your fault, she could have said no,' Rachel realised why she had never previously allowed a man to get too close. She was terrified that Ruth would deliberately ruin things by telling them what a wicked person she was, because she didn't want to share her sister's love. Now someone else knew and didn't blame her, Rachel had felt an enormous sense of relief.

*

A shrill piercing sound cut through the air, startling Rachel. She reached across Tim to turn off the alarm.

'I have mine set to Smooth Radio,' Tim said, sleepily. 'That certainly is a wake-up call.'

'I was already awake. I was watching you.'

'That doesn't sound in the least bit creepy,' he said, reaching for her under the covers. 'How are you doing this morning?' he added, gently planting a kiss on her lips.

'Better.'

He looked at her quizzically.

'I mean, better for sharing,' she explained. 'Thank you.'

'Thank you, for giving me another chance and for telling me about your sister. I'd like to meet her one day.'

'Would you really?'

'Yes, I wouldn't say it if I didn't mean it. I thought we agreed last night that honesty is the best policy.'

'I visit her on Sundays. You can come with me this weekend, if you'd like.'

'I would like that.'

'Well, that's a date then.'

'It's going straight in my diary.'

'Do you still keep a diary?'

'Does anyone these days? It was just a turn of phrase.'

Rachel thought of Simon Shaw's oversized desk diary that had provided them with such useful clues in her current case. Without it she might not have made the connection between the former footballers.

'Some people do,' she said. 'Look, I'm sorry to be a party pooper but I'm going to have to throw you out so I can get in to work. I've got a pretty big day ahead. Do you want coffee and toast before you go?'

'I'll do it while you have a shower.'

'I could get used to this,' Rachel said, heading off towards the bathroom.

'That's what I'm hoping,' Tim said, under his breath.

CHAPTER THIRTY-ONE

7.55 a.m. – Thursday

'Morning, Guv,' DI Graham Wilson said as Rachel stopped by the kitchen to get herself a coffee en route to her office.

'Morning, Graham. How was Legoland?'

'The kids really enjoyed it, and to be honest the adults were pretty impressed, too. I think Errol's a bit pissed off that he missed out, particularly as it was a wasted journey down to Wales.'

'What are you talking about?'

'Didn't you see PC Drake's message? She copied it to me to keep me in the loop. Our Sergeant Turnbull wasn't on a training exercise after all. He left Brecon in the middle of the afternoon on Sunday.'

While Graham had been talking, Rachel had reached into her bag for her phone. Sure enough, there were two messages from PC Drake, the second one checking to see whether she had received the first. *Shit*, Rachel thought, *I turned the bloody sound off when Tim kept texting yesterday.* She scanned the content of the first message.

'Are we really expected to believe that his mother is sick?' she said. 'That's an alibi if ever I heard one. I think we need to issue a warrant for his arrest. There are far too many coincidences surrounding his recent actions.'

'On it, Guv.'

'Is Errol in?'

'He's on his way.'

'Right. I want to see him in my office before the morning meeting. I don't suppose I need to ask if Eleanor Drake is in?'

'At her desk since 7.30 a.m.'

'Tell her to wait for me in my office while I get myself a strong coffee, would you?'

'Late night was it, Guv?'

'You know I'm not a fan of gossip, Graham.'

'My lips are sealed, but you are entitled to a private life, you know.'

'Thank you so much for your approval. Maybe tell that to PC Drake, because she doesn't appear to have one.'

'Guv.'

Rachel poured the boiling water onto the coffee granules, gave her drink a quick stir and headed towards her office, where she could already see Eleanor Drake standing across the desk from her seat.

'Sit down, Eleanor,' she said, closing the door behind her. 'Firstly, I'm sorry I didn't get back to you after your first message last night. You were right to follow up with a second.' *Is it my imagination*, Rachel thought, *or did she just breathe a sigh of relief? Am I really that scary?* 'As we now know, Sergeant Turnbull hasn't been in Wales for the past four days, which means I'm even more anxious to trace the whereabouts of Dave Cox, as his life is potentially in danger. I want you to work with DI Wilson on this.'

'Yes, Guv.'

'As I said in the meeting yesterday, the lack of UK tax information on Cox would suggest that he's probably been abroad. You could start by checking with the UK border authorities to see if he has re-entered the country in the past few months. I'll let DI Wilson know that you're picking up this part of the investigation. Have you already applied to become a detective, Eleanor?'

'Not yet, Guv.'

'But you'd like to?'

'Yes, Guv.'

'Well, if this case goes well, you'll have my recommendation after your input. That's all for now.'

'Thanks, Guv.'

As Eleanor Drake left Rachel's office to return to her desk, Errol Green knocked at Rachel's door.

'Come in, Errol, and sit down,' Rachel said. 'Look, I know you're not best pleased with me for sending you off to Wales yesterday, but if Sergeant Turnbull had been there, as expected, you were the best man for the job because of your physical presence. I have to call things as I see them, and I'm sorry it interfered with a social arrangement. I hope you don't see it as a wasted journey because if you hadn't been there to confront the other sergeant, Turnbull would have had an ironclad alibi. One of the possibilities I have been considering is that he's some kind of hired killer, and if that does turn out to be the case, you will have been instrumental in helping us bring him to justice.'

'Yes, Guv.'

'Are we all good?' Rachel asked, surprising herself that she had bothered to ask when her DS had merely been doing his job. *Maybe Tim is bringing out a caring side in me*, she thought.

'Of course, Guv.'

'We're issuing a warrant for Turnbull's arrest. After our morning meeting, I want you to go to the Windsor barracks and ask around a bit. We need to know more about his private life.'

'I put out a few feelers at the pub in Brecon where Broadbent and I had lunch. Not an establishment I would recommend, by the way. It seems that while he can be a bit moody, he has a really friendly girlfriend, a few years younger than him by the sound of things.'

Rachel immediately realised that DS Green was referring to Siena Shaw. 'I think that may be his ex-girlfriend,' she said.

Errol Green raised his eyebrows.

'I'll clarify in the meeting, but we want to know more about a recent girlfriend. One he's only been seeing for a few weeks.' She checked her watch. 'Right, let's not keep everybody waiting.'

CHAPTER THIRTY-TWO

10.25 a.m. – Thursday

Bella's hand was shaking as she handed over her boarding pass to be checked by the ground staff at the departure gate. She had run through the terminal building with the final call for passengers for her flight spurring her on. She was hot, sweaty and still breathing heavily when she took her place on the waiting aircraft. Moments later, the cabin crew were closing and cross-checking the cabin doors and within ten minutes of her taking her seat, the plane was pushing back from the stand.

'Are you all right?'

Bella turned to look at the anxious face of the woman sat next to her who had asked the question, not realising until that moment that she had tears streaming down her face along with trickles of perspiration. The woman was offering her a tissue.

'Thank you,' she said, taking the tissue and mopping the tears from her cheeks before wiping her eyes. 'I just had some bad news about my grandmother. She's dying, and I don't know if I'm going to make it home in time.'

The woman placed her hand gently on Bella's forearm. 'Try not to worry,' she said, 'it won't make the plane go any faster. I'm sure she knows you love her whether or not you make it in time to say your final goodbyes.'

Bella's eyes filled with tears again. The doctors had warned her that her grandmother was very frail and might only have days to live. *I should have changed my flight and stayed with Vovo last Saturday*, she thought. *There was no real urgency to come back to London, nothing that couldn't wait and certainly nothing as important as being at Vovo's side in her final hours on earth.* She was aware the woman was still looking at her.

'You're right,' Bella said, 'my grandmother raised me, so she knows she's the most important person in the world to me.'

'Would you like to change places with me and sit by the window? I sometimes find it calms me to simply stare out at the bright blue sky when I'm feeling upset.'

'That's really kind of you. Are you sure you don't mind?'

'Not at all. I lost my dad a few months ago, so I know how you're feeling. Once we're in the air and the seatbelt signs are off, we can swap places. Have you got far to go the other end?'

'No. Tavira is only about twenty-five minutes from the airport, thankfully.'

'Ah, that's where I'm going, too. It's a lovely little town, so much nicer than the tourist resorts when you head west along the Algarve. I'm Debbie, by the way.'

'Bella. I was born in a little village near Tavira, so it's home for me.'

'It's a home from home for me. I bought a derelict farmhouse up in the hills a few years ago, so I come back regularly to check on how the building work to restore it is going. It's a beautiful part of the world, I'm surprised you moved away.'

'It wasn't really by choice, but I'll soon be going home for good.'

Ten minutes into the flight, Bella and her kind-hearted fellow passenger swapped seats.

'Let me know if you need anything else, I've got plenty more tissues. And try to think positive thoughts,' Debbie said.

'Thank you,' Bella replied, turning her head to look out of the window and effectively ending their conversation. She was a pleasant enough person, but Bella didn't really feel much like

talking. She closed her eyes, thinking back to the email she had
received from Beca earlier that morning:

Bella,

   *I don't want to worry you, but I think you should come home. I
called in to see Vovo this morning and she has taken a turn for the
worse. The doctor has recommended calling the priest. I think you
need to get a flight home today if you can.*

Beca xx

The email had been sent a little after 7.15 a.m., which would
have been an hour later in Portugal, and Bella was thankful she
had checked her emails while she was eating her breakfast, or she
would have been at work the whole day knowing nothing about
the drama unfolding in Tavira. She had immediately gone online
to book a seat on the 10.45 a.m. flight to Faro, and once it had
been confirmed, and she had checked in, she had emailed her
three-word response:

On my way. Bella xx

It had been a mad rush to grab a few clothes and toiletries and
throw them into her hand luggage, before rushing to the station
to catch the next train, already packed with commuters on their
daily trek into London. Bella had stayed near the train doors as
she would only be on for two stops, despite the train driver urging
people to move along the carriages and her fellow passengers glaring
at her for taking luggage on an early-morning commuter train.
She had straddled her small case and hung onto the overhead rail
with one hand while she had called the Melrose Nursing Agency
from her mobile in the other. Unsurprisingly, no one had been
in the office to take her call, as it was still before 9 a.m. Unlike

the medical workers they organised shifts for, the agency office staff adhered to strict nine-to-five working hours, although the answering machine was checked remotely to deal with emergencies. She had left a voicemail apologising that she wouldn't be able to make her shift that day at Charing Cross Hospital, explaining that there was an emergency back home and she didn't know when she would be back.

Bella opened her eyes and looked out of the plane's oval window at the blue sky, which seemed to stretch to eternity. *Is this what heaven is like?* she wondered. *Please, please, universe, let me make it to Vovo's bedside in time.*

CHAPTER THIRTY-THREE

10.45 a.m. – Thursday

Now that Rachel's morning was free, as there was no Sergeant Turnbull to interview, she decided that rather than talking to Lydia Cantor on the phone, she would drive to west London and speak to her face to face at the botanical gardens, but not before she had rung to make sure Lydia was at work. She had also asked if there was any CCTV footage from the Palm House where Neil Edison had been working on the day he had gone home sick from work. Once she had finished her business at the botanical gardens, Rachel was planning on dropping in to Charing Cross Hospital to check on Simon Shaw and have a quick catch-up with Maddy and Siena.

She parked her car in the staff car park at the botanical gardens and went to the Arboretum Restaurant where she had arranged to meet Lydia Cantor. Moments after sitting down with a cappuccino and a chocolate-chip cookie, a tall, slim woman in her late thirties approached her table.

'DCI Hart?' she asked.

'You must be Lydia,' Rachel said, getting up to shake her hand. 'Thanks for agreeing to meet with me this morning. I just have a few questions to ask you surrounding the death of your colleague, Neil Edison.' Rachel noticed that the woman's eyes started to water. *Could they have been more than work colleagues?* Rachel wondered. 'Would you like to sit in here, or shall we go outside as it's such a lovely morning?'

'Outside might be better. It gets busy in here around morning coffee time, and it's very noisy because of the echoey high ceilings. It's not really the sort of thing we want to be shouting about.'

Holding her plate and cup and saucer, Rachel followed Lydia out onto the terrace and they sat down in the furthest corner to minimise the chances of being overheard.

'I thought the police had concluded that Neil took his own life?'

'All the evidence points to that, but something in your statement is bothering me,' Rachel said, taking a sip of coffee. 'You said he seemed to be in good spirits on the last day he was at work? In fact, you said that following a bout of depression six weeks previously, his mood had been very upbeat. Do you know why?'

'No, not really.'

'But you have your suspicions?'

'I – I think it may have been something to do with someone he was chatting to on an online dating app.'

Rachel was watching Lydia closely. There was a small twitch in the corner of her mouth as she spoke.

'From all the statements taken from his colleagues, I understood that Mr Edison was a loner. I wouldn't have thought he was the type for online dating.'

'He's exactly the type. He was very shy around women. It took him a couple of years before he could look at me eye to eye when we were having a conversation. I – I think it may have been something I said that made him join the dating site.'

'Really?'

'I'm not going to lie,' Lydia said, swallowing hard, 'I really liked Neil. He was different from most men. I know how difficult it is to meet people because I'm quite shy, too. About a year ago, I told him I was going to sign up to an online dating website, Nice to Meet You, and I joked that he should do the same. I said, "Maybe we'll come up as a perfect match". He didn't seem to get the hint that I'd like to start seeing him out of work, but a couple of days later he asked me to help him with his profile.'

'And it was after that that you noticed an improvement in his mood?'

'Not straight away. His behaviour was pretty much the same as usual until about a month before he died. It was after a particularly low episode, where I was fearful he might do himself some harm.' Lydia stopped speaking and swallowed hard. It looked as though she was battling to hold back tears.

'So, Neil had actually attempted suicide previously?'

Lydia nodded. 'But he'd been seeing a therapist, and it seemed as though he had got past all that.'

Rachel was only too aware that mental health issues were not that easily dealt with. There were times when Ruth appeared as normal and well-adjusted as the next person, but a tiny trigger could send her spiralling back down into the depths of depression. 'Things are not usually that straightforward with mental health issues,' she said. 'What do you think may have happened to lift his mood?'

'Well, he didn't actually say that he'd met someone, but maybe just being online and having people like the look and sound of him gave him a bit more hope for a less lonely future,' Lydia said, the sadness in her voice echoing in her eyes.

'I'm sorry it didn't work out quite as you'd hoped,' Rachel said, trying not to feel guilty about her own recent breakthrough with Tim.

'It doesn't matter. He obviously didn't have the same feelings for me that I had for him. You can't make someone like you. I just keep wondering if maybe I'm in some way responsible for him killing himself.'

'How do you mean?'

'What if he'd met someone online and then, when he met them in real life, they were a disappointment to him? Maybe that's why he killed himself. Maybe it is my fault,' Lydia said, brushing a tear away with the back of her hand.

'Don't blame yourself. Whatever happened, you only had his best interests at heart,' Rachel said, resisting the urge to put her arm around Lydia, who was clearly struggling. 'Did you manage to locate the CCTV footage I asked for?' she said, before Lydia became too emotional.

'Yes. We can view it in the security office. Do you want to go there now, or would you like to see where Neil was working that morning?'

'Perhaps we can go to the Palm House first, if it's close by,' Rachel said, finishing her coffee and standing up, having not touched her biscuit.

'It's on the way.'

Rachel was relieved to enter the air-conditioned security office following the oppressive heat and humidity of the huge glasshouse. It would make a fascinating day out, but she was there on business, and there was very little to see apart from the area where Neil had been working. Lydia had already communicated to the security guard the location they specifically wanted to look at, so he had the correct camera footage ready to view.

'As a matter of interest,' Rachel said, 'why do you have security cameras in the glasshouses? There's nothing of any value to steal, is there?'

Lydia looked at her in disbelief. 'You must be joking! Some of those plants are incredibly rare.'

'I get that, but I was meaning of monetary value.'

'Precisely. Imagine the worth of something that doesn't exist anywhere else on the planet.'

'But you could never admit to having it because people in the know would be aware that it was stolen.'

'That doesn't put collectors off. The rarer something is, the better. Think of missing pieces of artwork, or even vintage wine. You wouldn't drink the stuff, it would be completely unpalatable, but it's merely the knowledge that you have the last bottle of a particular year from a vineyard of repute.'

'Point taken,' Rachel said, while watching Neil on the slightly fuzzy footage systematically digging a hole, dropping a plant into it and then moving along to the next planting position. It was slow and repetitive, and she was about to ask the security guard to fast-forward when a woman entered the picture and appeared to be talking to Neil, although it was impossible to tell because she had her head lowered. A few minutes later, she seemed to be showing him something on a sketch pad.

'Wait a minute, stop,' Rachel said suddenly. 'Can you play that bit again?'

The security guard obliged.

'What is it?' Lydia asked.

'Did you notice Neil jerk his arm in towards his body? Stop – there. What do you think happened?'

'Perhaps she caught him with her fingernail while she was turning the pages of her sketch pad. Or maybe with the nib of her pen,' Lydia said, squinting at the frozen picture on the screen.

'That's what I thought.' *Could the woman have deliberately caught Neil's hand with her pen to administer some kind of poison?* Rachel wondered. *It was a bit far-fetched, but it was certainly a possibility if she had deliberately targeted him.* 'Do you have a camera pointing down the walkway towards the direction she came from?'

'Give me a minute,' the guard said.

Rachel wanted a closer look at the artist. All they could see at the angle they had been looking from was the top of her head.

'Here we go,' the guard said. 'I've taken the time code back by a minute.'

Rachel watched for a few seconds as the woman, her head down, clearly concentrating on her artwork, made small drawing movements with her pen.

'There,' she said. 'Can we go back a couple of frames? Stop.'

There was a tiny upward tilt of the head, as though the girl had noticed Neil, but she hadn't raised her head sufficiently for them to see her face.

'Would it be possible for you to send across all your CCTV footage from first thing that morning for my team to have a look at, please?'

'No problem,' the guard said.

'Do you think she had something to do with Neil's death?' Lydia asked.

'Probably not, but I'd like to eliminate her from our enquiries.'

What Rachel didn't reveal to Lydia was that a woman with long dark hair had been seen sketching the gravestones at the church in Little Waterton in the days prior to the stabbing of Father Raymond Kiernan. It could be a coincidence, but somehow Rachel doubted it. If they could get a clear CCTV image of the woman seen drawing at the botanical gardens and show it around to the residents of Little Waterton, maybe they would get clarification that they were the same person.

Rachel had just driven over Kew Bridge, on her way to Charing Cross Hospital to visit Simon Shaw, when her phone rang. It was DI Wilson.

'Guv, you need to head back here.'

'Have you found Dave Cox?'

'Not yet, but you'll never guess who just walked into the station, asking for you?'

'Not Rob Turnbull?'

'No, still no news on him. It's Jimmy Dawson.'

'Did he say what he wants?'

'No, just that he wanted to speak to you.'

'I'm on my way,' Rachel said, indicating to pull into the left-hand lane at the Chiswick roundabout to go west on the M4 rather than heading east towards Hammersmith and the hospital. 'Whatever you do, don't let him leave.'

CHAPTER THIRTY-FOUR

2.20 p.m. – Thursday

'Can I get you a cup of coffee, Mr Dawson?' Rachel asked, indicating for him to take the seat opposite her at her desk.

'Not for me, thanks, your DI has already offered several times. I don't drink the stuff – it's poison. Well, not exactly poison, you understand. It's not going to kill you instantly, or anything, like a poison dart. It's just not very good for you. I'll stick with water, thanks.'

Rachel raised her eyebrows. She had just come from viewing footage of Neil Edison's encounter with the mystery artist that suggested he might have been killed by poison administered via a pen nib. *Surely Jimmy Dawson wouldn't have said something like that, risking arousing my suspicions unless, of course, he's being disingenuous because he thinks he's got away with it.* She gave him a long hard look before deciding to let the comment pass. His body language, head lowered and fiddling with his fingers, was completely different from his demeanour at the gym, where he had been cocky and arrogant, and he sounded nervous.

'So, what brings you here?' she asked pleasantly.

'I wasn't exactly truthful when you came to see me at Muscles.'

'Oh?' Rachel said, feigning surprise.

'You caught me off guard a little, and I didn't want to say anything that might incriminate me before I'd had time to think things through.'

'I see. So now you've had time to get your story straight… in your head, that is.'

He looked up sharply. 'I didn't have to come here, you know.'

'Yes, I realise that, but you obviously wanted to, or you wouldn't be here. Would you be more comfortable if we went along to an interview room and recorded our conversation?'

'I think that's probably a good idea.'

'Follow me,' Rachel said, getting up from behind her desk. 'PC Drake, can you join us in interview room one, please,' she said, crossing the office with Dawson in tow.

As he took his place on a plastic chair in the interview room, Jimmy asked, 'Do I need a lawyer?'

'It's your choice. I don't know what information you are about to divulge. You're not under arrest, and we haven't called you in for questioning. I offered to record our conversation so that we get all the information accurately logged. Would you like a lawyer present?'

'I don't think so, but can I request one at any time?'

'Absolutely. Right, let's get started. What is it you wanted to talk to us about?' Rachel said as Eleanor Drake pressed the record button on the machine.

'First of all, I need to set the record straight regarding the night of the rape allegations. Although the four players accused were the ones registered to the two adjoining hotel rooms in question, Simon Shaw wasn't actually in his room that night.'

Jimmy had immediately grabbed Rachel's attention.

'May I ask how you know that, Mr Dawson?'

'I know because I'd let him have my room that evening. Simon was my best friend in the Kings Park Rovers squad, and he'd fallen hook, line and sinker for a waitress who worked behind the bar. I mean, *really* fallen for her. All he could talk about was bringing Rosa back to England and marrying her.'

He must be talking about Rosa Viegas, Rachel thought.

'They'd had a bit of a kiss and cuddle and a fumble around, but he was sharing a room with Neil Edison and he didn't want to embarrass the boy by bringing a girl back to their room. Trust me, Simon was a decent guy. Not all players would have been that considerate.'

Rachel was working hard to disguise her feelings of disgust. *How could anyone entertain the thought of having sex while someone else was present in the room?*

'I was the team captain, so I had my own room. It's strictly against the rules to change accommodation without permission, but Simon was my mate, so the five of us agreed to keep it quiet and I went in with Neil for the night.'

'So, let me get this straight. You were the fourth man in this rape allegation, not Simon Shaw,' Rachel said, relief flooding through her that now she wouldn't have to find a way to tell Maddy that her husband was a suspected rapist. *What a good job I didn't go round there last night piling unnecessary worry on her*, she thought. 'He wasn't involved in this at all?'

'That's right, but when the four of them were hauled in for questioning by the club, we all agreed to stick to our story that Simon was in his room with Neil. We figured that if the club thought we'd kept that quiet, they might think we were being less than honest about the sexual assault allegations.'

'And were you?'

'Can I come back to that later?'

'If that's what you want, but I do want answers. It appears, from what you've just told me, that you were at the very least a witness to what went on.'

'I was a witness, nothing more, I swear.'

Rachel had little choice but to allow him to continue telling his story the way he wanted to. 'All right. But I will want to question you in depth about that night.'

'I realise that, which is part of the reason I wanted to gather my thoughts about recent events before I came to the police station.'

'Go on.'

'It's all such a long time ago, and I genuinely hadn't been in touch with any of my former teammates for years prior to January of this year.'

'Even your best mate, Simon Shaw?'

'Yes, even Shawsy. Our friendship was never quite the same after what happened in Portugal. It was a night we all wanted to forget, and not seeing each other made that easier. Then in early January, completely out of the blue, Dave Cox turned up at Muscles. He said he'd seen an article in the paper about my success story with the gym and thought he'd look me up for old times' sake. You can imagine my surprise. The last I'd heard of him was that he'd done a runner after selling his house in Ascot because he didn't want to give his wife half of the money in a divorce settlement.'

It's nice to be right, Rachel thought, allowing herself a half-smile.

'We went for a drink and he was all friendly, but the drunker he got, he started getting a bit loose-lipped. He asked how much his silence was worth.'

'His silence?'

'Yes. It turns out that he'd been abroad for over five years and the money from the house sale was long gone – most probably he'd drunk his way through it. He'd come back to England homeless and penniless and the idiot had borrowed money off a loan shark to try and get himself back on his feet. Not only that, he'd always been a bit of a gambler, and he'd gambled some of the money he borrowed hoping for a big win. By the time he came to see me, he was in debt to the tune of a hundred grand.'

'That's a huge amount of money, which presumably he didn't have the means to repay. So, I'm assuming his reason for getting in touch with you was blackmail?'

'Exactly. He said he wanted fifty grand from each of us to keep quiet about what had gone on in Portugal or he was going to the police. He knew Simon was managing Beechwood Town, but he needed my help to find the other two. I'd heard Ray had gone into the priesthood, and I was able to track him down quite easily, and Ray knew that Neil was working as a gardener because Neil had turned to him for help with his mental health issues. Dave Cox arranged for us all to meet at a grotty maisonette he was renting in Windsor. Basically, he gave us an ultimatum. He said if he didn't get the money from us he'd be a dead man anyway, so he might as well turn himself in and take the rest of us down with him. What a bastard. We'd all worked hard to put together a decent life after our playing days were over, and he was about to ruin it all. Against my better judgement, I said I'd give him the money, but none of the other three had that sort of money lying around. He said he had to have at least a hundred grand, and pretty sharpish, to clear his gambling debt. I volunteered to pay Neil's share as the lad was completely innocent in the whole business, and Simon said he could raise the other hundred grand to pay his and Ray's share by remortgaging his house.'

So, that's why Simon remortgaged the house without telling Maddy, Rachel thought.

'And once he'd got his money, he left you alone?'

'Far from it. About a month after Simon and I had given him the money, I received a threatening letter like the one you found at Simon's. We all had them. The four of us agreed to meet at Muscles to discuss what to do next, but Neil never showed up. When I heard on the news that he'd killed himself, I couldn't believe it. I'd spoken to him on the phone a couple of days previously to arrange the meeting, and although he was upset about receiving the note and having the whole rape accusation surface again, he certainly didn't sound suicidal. In fact, he told me he was more hopeful about his life than he'd been in a long time because he'd met somebody online, and he was looking forward to meeting up with her in real life.'

Which is what Lydia said. Did the idea of his new girlfriend finding out about his past push him over the edge and make him take his own life, or was he poisoned by the nib of a drawing pen? Rachel wondered. Neither possibility could be ruled out. 'What did the three of you decide to do at the meeting?'

'We couldn't agree. Shawsy was all for the truth coming out and, to be honest, I could see his point. He wasn't even in the room, and yet he'd had to bear the weight of suspicion from the hierarchy at Kings Park Rovers, who were probably never entirely convinced that nothing went on. You have no idea how many times I wish we'd just been honest from the start, instead of trying to protect two of our teammates who were as guilty as hell.'

'Do you want to tell me what happened?'

'That's why I'm here. When I heard about Shawsy's accident, I hoped it was just a terrible coincidence, but when Ray got murdered, the penny dropped and I realised Dave would be coming after me next.'

'You think Dave Cox is responsible for killing Raymond Kiernan?'

'What other explanation could there be? When you came to the gym and said you were looking for Dave because you thought his life was in danger, I nearly laughed out loud. He's not a nice person, and he should have been made to answer for what he did to that poor girl.'

Rachel could feel her heart thudding in her chest.

'Like I said, I agreed to let Shawsy have my room for the night while I went in with Neil. Our room had an interconnecting door with Dave and Ray's room, which was open because we'd been having a few beers in there and playing poker. Neil was only seventeen, just a kid really, and he asked if we could go back to our room for a game of FIFA, which we did. The other two carried on drinking and when they'd finished all the beers, they called through and said they'd ordered champagne from room service. We'd finished playing all the preseason games and were due to fly home the next day, so I didn't think it would hurt. It would be them who had to deal with raging hangovers on the plane. I didn't even hear the room service arrive because Neil and I were so engrossed in our game. The first we knew that there was anything wrong was when the girl cried out. I rushed into the next room with Neil behind me, and the sight that met my eyes made me want to throw up. Dave was stood at the end of the bed with his pants and trousers around his ankles and his tackle hanging out. He was swigging from a bottle of champagne while Ray was ramming into the waitress with his hand over her mouth. It was disgusting. They were like a pair of depraved animals. I yelled at Ray to get off her, but he ignored me until he'd climaxed. Then he climbed off the girl and said, "Don't be so bloody impatient, mate. Now it's your turn". He still had his hand over her mouth to stop her crying out again, but I'll never forget the look of terror in her eyes.'

Rachel could feel her skin turning cold and clammy. Without drawing the attention of Eleanor Drake, she needed to breathe deeply or she would faint. She could only imagine what it must be like to be pinned down, having someone thrusting into you against your will, but, just like Beatriz, her sister Ruth knew.

'I don't remember my exact words,' Jimmy continued, 'but I pulled the girl up off the bed and asked her if I could do anything to help. She just stood there for a few moments in a state of shock with blood running down her legs. I turned on Dave and said something along the lines of, "What do you think you were doing?" and he said, and I'll never forget these words, "She was gagging for it, wasn't she, Ray?" To his credit, at least Ray had some decency. Seeing her standing there crying and bleeding seemed to sober him up, and he started to cry too. I think that was what stopped

me reporting it. I couldn't point the finger at Dave without getting
Ray in trouble, too.'

'But they raped her, and you were a witness to it. How could you
live with yourself?' Rachel blurted out, unable to control her revulsion.

'Guv,' Eleanor said, 'do you want me to carry on in here while
you take a moment?'

Rachel took another deep breath, struggling to control her
pounding heart. 'No, I'll be fine, thank you, PC Drake,' Rachel
said, her eyes fixed on Jimmy, who had his elbows on the table
with his head resting in his hands. 'What happened to the girl,
whose name was Beatriz, by the way?'

'I got her a towel from the bathroom and she wiped her legs,
pulled her skirt down and backed towards the door. She didn't
say a word. To be honest, I don't even know if she spoke English.
She never turned her back on us as she reached behind her for
the door handle. It was as though she was frightened she might
be pounced on again. She slipped out of the room leaving the
four of us staring at the bloodstained towel and bed sheets. I was
pretty sure she would report it to the hotel management, but Dave
said it would be her word against ours. Provided we all stuck to
the story that she had willingly engaged in sex with them, she
wouldn't have a leg to stand on. It was a horrible night, waiting
for the knock on the door, but it never came. Even the next day
while we were at the airport waiting for our flight home, I was fully
expecting the police to come and arrest us. But they didn't. When
the club finally called us in for questioning, Dave told us to deny
that the girl had had sexual intercourse with any of us. He said
that because the report was so long after the event, there would
be no evidence. Neil nearly bottled it, but I managed to persuade
him not to say anything because what had been done couldn't be
undone, and although he had nothing to do with the assault, his
career in football would be over. The sad irony is that two months
later, his leg was broken in three places in a horrendous tackle,

so his career was over anyway. I'll always remember going to visit him in the hospital after the doctors had told him he would never play again. He said, "I deserve this. This is my punishment for what happened to that girl". It really messed with his head, and no wonder. We're all responsible for his death, not only Dave Cox.'

Rachel couldn't disagree. The mental health issues Neil Edison had suffered, that most people probably assumed were caused by his career-ending injury, were more likely to do with the guilt he felt for not reporting his colleagues. *If only he'd been brave enough to tell the truth*, she thought, *he might still be alive today*. 'Has Dave Cox been in touch with you since Father Raymond Kiernan's murder?'

'No.'

'Have you got the address of the property in Windsor where you all met up in January?'

'Yes, 23 Runnymede Court. What happens now?'

'I'll send some officers down there to bring him in for questioning, but as I'm sure you probably realise, it will be your word against his.'

'That's why I was nervous about coming in, but to be honest, if he's capable of stabbing a man of the cloth, he's capable of anything, so I'm prepared to take my chance.'

'With regard to the historic rape case, I'm not sure how we will proceed with that. There might be a case of perverting the course of justice for you to answer, so I would ask that you don't attempt to leave the country, as we may well want to bring you in for questioning.'

'Does my wife have to know about any of this?'

'That's entirely up to you, Jimmy, but in my experience, honesty is always the best policy in the end. Thank you for coming in to the station with this information, which, for the record, was completely voluntarily. Interview terminated,' she said, indicating that PC Drake should turn off the machine.

'Do you think I'm safe?' Jimmy asked as he got to his feet.

'Well, we'll go and pick up Dave Cox now. Has he ever given any indication that he knows where you live?'

'No. He's only ever contacted me at Muscles.'

'Then my suggestion is just to be extra vigilant and maybe give work a wide berth until we notify you that he's in custody.'

'Sure, I'll do that.'

'Can you show Mr Dawson out, please, PC Drake, and then I want to see you in my office.'

'Yes, Guv.'

Rachel walked back along the corridor and stopped off at DI Wilson's desk on the way to her office.

'This is Dave Cox's last known address, Graham. Errol is already in Windsor, asking around the barracks for any information on Sergeant Turnbull. I suggest you call him and get him to meet you there to bring Cox in for questioning.'

'Questioning? I thought Cox was a potential victim?'

'Apparently not. Jimmy Dawson has just put him very firmly in the frame as our prime suspect. Maybe I was wrong about Turnbull, and his mother is sick after all.'

She continued through to her office and sat at her desk. Moments later, Eleanor Drake appeared in the doorway. 'Come in, PC Drake, and shut the door behind you.' Rachel could see that the young police officer was nervous. She didn't ask her to sit down. 'I like you, Eleanor. You have a tremendous work ethic and you're very thorough and intuitive. But don't ever undermine my authority in front of a member of the public in that way again. Do I make myself clear?'

'Yes, Guv. Sorry, Guv. It's just I thought—'

Rachel raised her hand to stop Eleanor from speaking. 'That's all, PC Drake.'

She watched the young officer leave the room, as angry with herself and her inability to control her emotions as she was with Eleanor Drake for drawing attention to it.

CHAPTER THIRTY-FIVE

4.05 p.m. – Thursday

'What do you reckon?' DI Graham Wilson said.

'It doesn't look like there's anyone here,' DS Green replied.

The two police officers had arrived at 23 Runnymede Court a little after 4 p.m. First they had rung the bell and then tried hammering on the door, but there was no reply.

'Do you reckon there's a back entrance?'

'I wouldn't have thought so. I grew up on an estate like this and usually the front door on these maisonettes leads straight on to a flight of stairs with all the accommodation on the first and second floors,' Errol replied.

'So, no outdoor space?'

'No. We had to go down to the park if we wanted to play outside.'

'Not really ideal for families, is it? Obviously the architect who designed estates like this didn't have kids.'

'Or couldn't have cared less about poorer families, because he was probably swanning around in a big house with a garden the size of a field for his own kids to play in. What do we do now, Guv?'

'Rather than heading straight back to the station, I think we should knock on a few doors and find out if the neighbours have seen Dave Cox lately.'

'Good idea. I'll take the other side of the road.'

Graham watched his burly colleague cross the street. He was a bit rough around the edges, but he had a heart of gold, and the two of them had become good friends since Graham had transferred to the unit three years earlier. He walked up the short path to the next-door neighbour's property and knocked on the door. Moments later, the door opened a crack and Graham could see the safety chain was on, which he had to concede was probably a good idea in the area they were in.

'I don't buy anything from door-to-door salesmen,' an elderly woman said.

'That's good to hear,' Graham said, 'you never know if it might have dropped off the back of a lorry, and then you'd be breaking the law. I'm with the police,' he said, flashing his warrant card. 'I'm just wondering if you've seen your neighbour today?'

'If you're with the police, why aren't you wearing a uniform? You conmen think you're so clever, but you can't fool me,' she said, starting to close the door in his face.

'I'm a plain-clothes detective, but it's good to see you're cautious about strangers at your door.'

The old lady pulled the door back open to the extent of the safety chain. 'What is it you say you want? Has someone else been mugged? It's not safe to go out round here.'

'Your neighbour; have you seen him today?'

'Which one?'

'Number 23.'

'That's not what I meant. I mean which man, the older one or the younger one?'

'Dave Cox?'

'I don't know any names, just what they look like.'

'Would it be possible to step inside for a few minutes, please?' Graham asked.

The woman looked him up and down. 'I suppose. But I'm keeping the front door open and I've got my panic button in my hand,' she said, unlooping the chain and opening the door to let him in.

The stench of cat urine and rotting food was almost overpowering as Graham followed her into her living room, which looked out to the road at the front of the property.

'Get down off there,' she said, wafting her arms at two overweight cats who were sleeping on the threadbare sofa. They obediently followed her instruction. 'There you go,' she said, indicating for him to sit down. 'I'm Edith, by the way.'

He perched right on the edge of the seat. 'Thank you, Edith.'

'I'd make you a cup of tea, but I haven't any fresh milk.'

'No worries, I won't keep you long anyway.'

'So, what have they done wrong?' she asked.

'Nothing. Well, as far as we know. We're just trying to locate Mr Cox to help us with some enquiries.'

'So, is he the younger one or the older one?'

'He's in his late forties.'

'The older one, then. I haven't seen him in a couple of months.'

'Has he moved out?'

'I wouldn't know for sure, but I don't think so. When he came to live here just before Christmas, he didn't have a lot of stuff, but I think I would have noticed him taking it out again. He kept to himself and lived on his own until about a month after he moved in, when the woman appeared on the scene. She wasn't here all the time, though, just for a few days at a time, usually. I can see the comings and goings to their front door cos it's right by my window, you see,' she said, indicating her perfect view of next door's path.

'Can you describe the woman?'

'I couldn't really see much of her because she was always wrapped up in her winter coat and hat, but she was slim and appeared to be quite young. Mind you, everyone's young compared to me. I'll be eighty on my next birthday.'

Although she looked every day of her seventy-nine-plus years, Graham offered the obligatory compliment, 'Well, you don't look it, Edith,' while noting down the vague description of the woman. 'And you say you haven't seen Mr Cox for a couple of months?'

'No. About a month ago the woman seemed to be around a bit more, but with the younger man. She always seemed a bit young for the older one, so maybe they were just friends and he was letting her live there, and then she got herself a boyfriend. Perhaps that was what the argument was about.'

'Argument?'

'Yes. I think it might have been Monday, or maybe Tuesday, I lose track a bit these days. Anyway, there were raised voices, but I haven't heard anything since, so they must have sorted it out.'

'Can you remember when you last saw either the woman or the younger man?'

'The day after the argument, I think. He went out around teatime on that damn noisy motorbike, but I didn't see her leave.'

'Well, you've been most helpful, Edith,' Graham said, getting to his feet and reaching into his pocket for his card. 'If either of them turns up, or you see Mr Cox, would you be kind enough to call me on this number at the police station?' he said, heading for the front door and the opportunity to breathe some less fetid air. As he walked out of the door, Errol crossed the road in his direction.

'Any luck, Errol?'

'I think the Guv will want to hear about this. The neighbour over the road says she doesn't think Cox lives there any more. She reckons she hasn't seen him in a couple of months, but she has seen a slim woman go in and out from time to time with a younger man who she assumed was her boyfriend.'

'That's exactly what the next-door neighbour said, but I don't see why this would be of so much interest to the Guvnor.'

'I'm getting to it. Mrs Lynch says she had to have words with the woman's boyfriend because his motorbike is noisy and wakes her baby up when he goes tearing off on it. I must have motorbikes on the brain, because I spent all yesterday afternoon looking for Turnbull's bike down in Wales while you were enjoying Legoland.'

'Don't be bitter, Errol, it doesn't suit you.'

'That was my pathetic attempt at humour, which obviously fell flat. Anyway, I asked her if she could describe either of them and he sounded exactly like our missing soldier, so I showed her his photo and it was a positive ID. How random is that?'

Graham could feel the hairs on the back of his neck stand up. Surely Rob Turnbull dating a woman who was living in the same house as Dave Cox couldn't be a coincidence. DCI Hart had suggested that maybe Turnbull had been paid to be a hitman. *Was it possible that Dave Cox had engaged him?* It was more than possible; it was highly likely.

'We need to call this in to the Guvnor right now, and she needs to get a search warrant, pronto. I think we may accidentally have just solved this case. All we need now is to find and arrest Turnbull and Cox.'

CHAPTER THIRTY-SIX

4.30 p.m. – Thursday

Bella paid the taxi driver and stepped out into the bright late-afternoon sunshine, cursing herself for forgetting to pack her sunglasses, such had been her rush earlier that morning. She carried her overnight bag rather than wheeling it over the bumpy cobblestones of the alleyway that led to her grandmother's cramped town house behind the square in the centre of Tavira.

Pushing aside the colourful strands of the beaded curtain that helped keep flying insects out of the house, she stepped into the cool, dark interior of her childhood home and gave her eyes a moment to adjust. Very little had changed in over twenty years, despite her grandmother's modest win on the lottery when she was eleven years old. There were two armchairs with sagging seats and a small sofa in front of the open fireplace, which was the only source of heat in the house. Bella shivered, remembering herself and her best friend, Beca, huddling together on that sofa under crocheted blankets to keep warm during long winter evenings.

Leaving her case at the side of the dining table, which was covered in a white cloth with flowers lovingly hand-embroidered by her grandmother before she had become so ill, Bella climbed the narrow staircase up to the bedrooms, her shoes making an echoing sound on the wooden surface. At the top of the stairs she turned to her right and tapped lightly on her grandmother's bedroom door before pushing it open and going inside. She had texted Beca on her way from the airport to say she had arrived safely, and Beca had responded saying that Vovo was sleeping, so she was going to go and get herself a late lunch in one of the cafes in the square, giving Bella some precious time alone with her grandmother.

Bella moved across the room and sat on the rickety wooden chair at the side of her grandmother's bed, reaching for her hand as she did so. Her skin felt dry and papery and very cold, but beneath her fingertips Bella could feel the slow, faint beat of her pulse. 'Vovo,' she whispered, 'I'm here.'

The old woman's eyelids flickered at the sound of the familiar voice, but she didn't open them. It was almost as though the effort was too great. Finally, she said in a voice barely more than a whisper, 'Rosa?'

Bella's heart contracted. It saddened her that her precious grandmother would assume it was her absentee daughter, rather than the granddaughter who had been a constant in her life until a few months ago. 'No, Vovo,' she said gently, 'it's Bella.'

The muscles in the old woman's cheeks twitched and the lines deepened as her thin, pale lips formed a half-smile. 'You came.'

'Of course. Beca was worried about you, so I got on the first plane home. How are you feeling?'

'Not good. My time is nearly done,' she croaked, opening her pale blue eyes with an enormous effort, 'but it will be a relief to go to my Maker.'

'Don't say that, Vovo,' Bella said, unable to prevent the tears rolling down her cheeks.

'Don't cry, Bella. I've had a good life, but I'm tired and often in pain,' the old lady said. 'I'm ready to go, but I wanted to see you one last time. I need you to promise me something.'

'Anything.'

'Forgive your mother.'

Looking down at her frail grandmother, the woman who had given up the peace and tranquillity of her senior years to raise her granddaughter, Bella knew she couldn't refuse, but she couldn't bring herself to speak.

'She made a mistake, Bella. Her life was ruined by what happened in Porto, but that was her own doing and she shouldn't have blamed you. She knows that now. She is so sorry for the things she said to you, but it was the drink talking.'

Bella still could not speak. It wasn't only the words her mother had used on her eighteenth birthday; it was the pure hatred in her eyes when she had spoken them. That look was imprinted in Bella's mind. In an effort to erase it, she focused her gaze on the painting of the belladonna plant that hung above her grandmother's bed. She wanted this beautiful woman to rest easy in her grave in the knowledge that her daughter and granddaughter had been reconciled, but it wasn't that simple to undo twenty-three years of hurt.

'When your father went home to England and she never heard from him again, her heart was broken.'

Bella could feel the quickening of her pulse. *Why would Rosa be heartbroken that she'd never heard from the man who had raped her?* Her grandmother must be confused with all the pain relief she was taking. 'Did he know about me?'

'No. Rosa didn't tell anyone about the baby until she and Beatriz came home. She was already suffering, and then Beatriz died. It's little wonder that she turned to drink to dull her pain and guilt. It was a terrible time, but it's all so long ago. I know she hasn't been a good mother to you, but she is still your mother, and with me gone, the time is right for you two to try to get to know one another.'

'You're the only mother I've ever known, Vovo,' Bella said, struggling to stay calm. 'You have been my mother, my father, my grandmother, my everything. I don't know what I'll do without you. I'm so angry that she forced me out of my home when all I wanted to do was stay here and look after you. I know I promised you anything, but I don't know if you realise just what you are asking from me.'

The old lady seemed exhausted after all the talking. Her eyes closed again, and her voice faded to a whisper as she said, 'At least promise me you will try. To forgive is so much harder than to punish, but in the end, you're the one who will benefit the most.'

'I promise I will try. That's the best I can do.'

'Good girl. You have always been such a good girl. I need to sleep now,' she said, her voice trailing off.

Not always, Bella thought, watching her beloved vovo drift back to sleep.

CHAPTER THIRTY-SEVEN

6 p.m. – Thursday

The information from DI Graham Wilson and DS Errol Green had come through too late to organise a search warrant that night, but one had been promised for the next day. Until Rachel could get another member of the team down there to take over, she had asked Errol Green to watch 23 Runnymede Court in case Turnbull, Cox or the woman returned. None of the neighbours questioned had been able to provide a fuller description of the woman, but the neighbour with the baby did mention she had seen her wearing leathers when she went out on the bike with Turnbull. That had set Rachel thinking: *Could she have been driving the bike when Turnbull took his potshot at Simon Shaw? Is she also the artist from the graveyard in Little Waterton and the Palm House? Maybe Turnbull used his girlfriend to recce his targets…*

Rachel was about to leave for the day when her phone rang. It was Maddy.

'Hi, Maddy,' she said, answering the call, 'I was going to pop in and see you and Siena earlier. I was over at the botanical gardens, so in the neighbourhood, really. But, as usual in my line of work, I had to change my plans and hotfoot it back to the station. Any news on Simon?'

'That's one of the reasons I'm ringing.'

'What is it, Maddy? Is everything okay?'

'Some good news at last. The consultant says Simon's vital signs are so positive they're going to attempt to bring him out of his coma on Saturday.'

'That's fantastic,' Rachel said, wondering why Maddy didn't sound more excited by the prospect.

'I know. Apparently, there's a small risk attached, but they feel pretty positive that he's going to respond. He looks so much better than he did when we first saw him on Monday. Not so grey. Siena's been reading to him constantly, and the nursing staff think that has contributed.'

'Try not to worry,' Rachel said, thinking that must be why Maddy sounded a little tense. 'I'm sure the consultant wouldn't try it if he didn't think it was for the best.'

'No, I know that. The other thing I was ringing for was to see if you fancied coming to supper with us tonight. There's something I want to talk to you about.'

Rachel had half hoped that Tim would text to suggest dinner after their breakthrough the previous evening, but he hadn't. *He's probably as busy as me*, she thought, deciding to accept Maddy's invitation.

'I'd love to,' she paused, hoping Maddy would understand, 'but you do understand that I won't be able to discuss the case with you now that it's a major investigation.'

'That's not what I want to talk about. But could you just answer me one question? Are you any closer to finding out who did this to Simon and why?'

Being as ambiguous as she could, Rachel said, 'We've had a couple of breakthroughs today. I'm hopeful that we should have some news I can share in the next couple of days.'

'I hope it doesn't break while I'm on air,' Maddy said. 'I don't think Byron Farley will tolerate another mute episode from me.'

'You're going back to work so soon? Are you sure, Maddy? Yours is a bit different from most people's jobs. It's not just a case of turning up and going through the motions. You're in the spotlight.'

'To be honest, I don't really have much choice if I want to keep my job.'

'Aren't you on compassionate leave, or something?'

'I think you're only entitled to that when someone has died. Farley hasn't actually said anything, but he's trying to fill my shoes with his latest girlfriend's stilettos and I'm damned if I'm going to let that happen. I'd already offered to do Saturday and Sunday mid-shifts before the hospital told me they were going to try and bring Simon round from his coma. I'll try and get out of Saturday, but if I can't, I should be able to get to the hospital by half past four.'

'And I thought police work was tough.'

'It's a different kind of tough, Rachel. There's no way I could do what you do and see what you see. I'd never be able to sleep again.'

'You become immune to most things after a while.' *But not all*, Rachel thought, *not when they're close to home*. Her sister's six-year-old face swam before her, her eyes filled with shock, horror and pain. *I'll never know what she had to endure*, Rachel reflected, shaking her head to try and free herself of the image. 'So, what time shall I come over to yours?'

'Is seven thirty all right for you?'

'Perfect. I'll see you then.'

Less than five minutes later, Rachel received a two-word text from Tim:

Tonight, gorgeous? X

Brilliant timing, she thought, a wry smile on her face. *But maybe it wouldn't do to appear too keen…* She replied:

Sorry Tim, I already have plans for dinner with Maddy and Siena. Tomorrow maybe? Or Saturday if you're busy, then we can go to the hospital straight from mine on Sunday morning X

Rachel's phone immediately pinged with Tim's reply:

No problem, I'll text you tomorrow and see how you're fixed. Pencil me in though X

Will do X

Rachel dropped her phone into her bag, grabbed her jacket from the hanger on the back of her office door and was walking through the main office when PC Leverette called out to her.

'Guv, I've finally been able to get some information from the hospital in Tavira. They should be able to send confirmation in writing tomorrow, but I've just got off the phone with a woman who was a ward sister back in 1995. She seems to remember Beatriz Azevedo and Rosa Viegas. Apparently it was a bit of a scandal at the time that two local girls had got themselves pregnant.'

'They hardly "got themselves pregnant",' Rachel said, irritation creeping into her voice. 'I wonder if all the people who were so judgemental about it had lived a completely mistake-free life. Somehow I doubt it.'

'That's what I thought, Guv. Learning from our mistakes is all part of the journey.'

'Very philosophical. Sorry, I interrupted you. Did the ward sister remember anything about the babies? Boys, girls, one of each?'

'She's going to check the hospital records for me, but what she did remember is that one of the young women died during childbirth, along with her baby. She haemorrhaged, and despite their best efforts, they couldn't stop the bleeding.'

'Does she remember which girl?'

'Beatriz Azevedo. She's going to confirm everything in an email tomorrow once she's checked on the sex of the other baby.'

'Good work, PC Leverette. You may as well head home now, there's not much more you can do tonight.'

'Yes, Guv. Night, Guv.'

Rachel headed down the stairs and out into the fading light, the first signs of a glorious sunset adding tinges of pink to the deepening blue sky. *Poor Beatriz*, she thought. Not only had she not been believed when she had reported the sexual assault that had led to her pregnancy, but she had paid the ultimate price for the actions of others. *When we do find Dave Cox, I'll do everything I can to get justice for her.*

CHAPTER THIRTY-EIGHT

'I think I'm going to head up to bed if it's okay with you guys,' Siena said, stretching her arms above her head and suppressing a yawn.

'It's only 9.15 p.m. Anyone would think you were eighty-two rather than twenty-two,' Maddy said, smiling indulgently at her daughter.

'It's all that sitting around in a building that doesn't have windows that open. Not to mention reading for hours on end. Not that I'm complaining. I've really got into *Playing for Pizza*, and I want to know what happens next. I don't suppose it will matter much to Dad if I've moved on by a few chapters when we go in tomorrow.'

'It would shock you if he opened his eyes and said, "Hey, you've missed a bit", wouldn't it?' Rachel said.

'I wish he would. I hate seeing him just lying there with that horrible machine sucking and blowing.'

'Well, it might not be for much longer,' Maddy said. 'If everything goes to plan on Saturday we could have him home sooner than we thought.'

'Saturday can't come quickly enough. Shall I help with the dishwasher first?'

'No, it's fine, I can manage,' Maddy said, giving her daughter a kiss on the cheek.

'Night, Siena,' Rachel said.

'Night, thanks for coming round to keep our spirits up. I hope we didn't quiz you too much about lover boy,' Siena said, winking.

'Close the door on your way out,' Rachel responded.

'You didn't mind us asking you about Tim, did you?' Maddy said as she cleared the plates off the table and stacked them in the dishwasher.

'No, of course not, although it feels a bit weird talking about him as a boyfriend because I don't usually let things get that far.'

'Why not, if you don't mind me asking?'

'I think I've always been worried about Ruth's reaction to sharing me with someone,' Rachel said. 'But I have a feeling she'll like Tim. I've never taken anyone to the hospital with me before, but he's coming with me this Sunday.'

'How did she react when you told her?'

'I haven't yet,' Rachel said, a note of doubt creeping into her voice. 'Anyway, let's move the spotlight off me and my love life. You said you had something you wanted to talk to me about.'

'It's a bit of a confession, really.'

'Don't tell me you've got illegally tinted windows on the Yaris as well…'

'Hardly. Nobody bothers peering in to see who's driving that. No, it's something I did after you left with Simon's diary yesterday morning,' Maddy said, part of her fervently wishing she hadn't. 'I got the feeling you didn't really believe me when I suggested there was a connection between what's happened recently to Neil, Ray and Simon.' She hesitated, hoping Rachel wouldn't be too annoyed with her for meddling in police business. 'So I took matters into my own hands and rang the Kings Park Rovers press office to speak to Peter Kingsley, because I know him from when Simon was a player there. It's quite easy to get information out of him if you know which buttons to press – he loves to feel important.'

'I wish you hadn't done that, Maddy. I had everything under control, and that could have compromised our investigation.'

'I wasn't trying to undermine you, Rachel, I just wasn't sure that you were taking my suggestions seriously, so I was looking for some proof.' Maddy paused, waiting for a reaction, but Rachel's expression gave nothing away, so she pressed on. 'All I had to go on was that the three of them only played in the team together for a couple of months before Neil's injury. I told Peter Kingsley that I was writing a piece about Neil's suicide and asked him his opinion on why Neil had formed such a close bond with players who were a good deal older than him rather than his contemporaries, and he came right out with it.'

'Right out with what, Maddy?'

'There was a sexual assault allegation made against four Kings Park Rovers players while they were on a preseason tour in Portugal in 1994,' Maddy said, 'but I don't suppose I'm telling you anything you don't already know.'

Rachel shrugged her shoulders.

'When I rang Kings Park Rovers, it was to try and establish why anyone would want to attack three former teammates, my husband among them. I was completely on their side – outraged on their behalf because I couldn't imagine what they could possibly have done that would warrant such a reaction all these years later. Imagine my horror when I found out that my husband of twenty-three years is potentially a rapist. I felt sick to my stomach with the language Peter Kingsley was using about the accusers. He called them lying little tarts, out to make a fast buck by falsely accusing wealthy footballers of sexual assault. But all I keep asking myself is why Simon wouldn't have told me about something so momentous in his life, even though it happened before he met me, if he was innocent. We made a pact, Rachel, to tell each other all our secrets before we got married, so there would be no surprises, and now I find out he's been keeping this from me. I don't know what to think,' Maddy said, her voice faltering.

'I don't know what you want me to say, Maddy. You know I can't talk about the case, I told you that on the phone.'

'But it's not really the case, Rachel, this is my life we're talking about,' Maddy replied. 'The thought that Simon, my Simon, could have been party to something like this has completely devastated me. If you know anything, anything at all that would reassure me that this was a false allegation by those girls, please tell me, I'm begging you, because I'm not sure I can spend another moment with a man who could do something like that,' she said, a note of hysteria creeping into her voice.

Rachel was torn. She could set Maddy's mind at rest to a degree after Jimmy Dawson's admission earlier that afternoon that Simon had been nowhere near the hotel room when the assault had taken place. But an assault had taken place, and he could have spoken up for Beatriz and yet he chose not to. There was also the reason he wasn't in his own room; he was in a different room making love to a girl who he had intended to bring back to England and marry. A girl who, nine months later, gave birth to a baby which was most likely his, while he had moved on and proposed to somebody else. There was desperation in her friend's eyes, but although she recognised that Maddy needed to know the truth, Rachel believed it needed to come from Simon.

'I'm sorry, Maddy, but I can't discuss it with you.'

'Please, Rachel. It's torturing me. I keep looking at Simon lying in that hospital bed and wondering if I ever knew him at all. I'm begging you.'

Rachel got up from the dining table and went to stand behind Maddy's chair, resting her hands on her shoulders. 'The only thing I can tell you is that Simon's name should not have been included in the rape allegation. I'm going now, but here's my advice, for what it's worth. When he does come out of his coma, you two need to have a long conversation about what happened in Porto. Goodnight, Maddy.'

CHAPTER THIRTY-NINE

DS Errol Green drained the last of his takeaway coffee, crushed the cardboard cup and added it to the small bag of litter in the footwell of his car by DC Broadbent's feet. The two officers had arrived at Runnymede Court at 7 a.m. to relieve the overnight surveillance team, who had nothing to report. No one had entered or left number 23 and no lights had been switched on at dusk, suggesting that nobody was home. *The sooner we have the search warrant the better*, he thought. *If neither Turnbull or Cox are there, we're just wasting time hanging around, giving them a chance to get away.*

Since DCI Hart had issued a warrant for Rob Turnbull's arrest on Wednesday evening, the border forces had been on the lookout for him but, as a soldier, he was trained in the art of surviving in the wild and he would be expert in keeping a low profile. It was also possible that he and Cox had slipped out of the country and fled to the continent before they became persons of interest.

'Looks like we're on,' DC Broadbent said, indicating the arrival of DCI Hart in an unmarked car, and two further police vehicles, one of which was a van, parked across the entrance to the cul-de-sac to prevent any cars entering during the operation. They got out of the car to meet her.

'I take it you haven't seen anyone entering or leaving number 23?' she said.

'No, Guv.'

'Are you two wearing your stab vests?'

'Yes, Guv.'

'Right then, let's do this. DI Wilson said there's no rear entrance, but they could potentially jump from a first-floor window, so DC Broadbent, you take one of the uniformed officers around the back. Errol, you're with me.'

They approached the front door of number 23 and rang the bell, followed by rapping on the door and announcing their presence.

'This is the police. Open up. We have a warrant to search the premises.'

There was no response, apart from the twitching of curtains as people around Runnymede Court watched the events unfolding from the safety of their own homes. Rachel nodded towards the officer holding the cylindrical metal battering ram. He swung it in the direction of the lock and the door burst open, allowing DS Green to rush forward and up the stairs with two further officers close behind, repeating his announcement as he went, 'This is the police, we have a warrant to search the premises.'

Rachel followed them up the stairs and as she arrived on the landing, the stench hit her. She had been a police officer long enough to recognise the smell of death, but at that point she had no idea what she would be confronted with. Putting her hand across her mouth and squeezing her nostrils slightly between her thumb and forefinger to restrict the flow of foul air which she could already feel activating her gag reflex, she stepped into the living room. Errol was alone, standing next to the body of a man who was lying face down in a pool of dried blood. He appeared to have been shot through the back of the head.

'Dead?' Rachel asked by way of confirmation, even though it was obvious.

'For at least a couple of days I'd say, Guv, but we won't know for sure until the forensics team gets here.'

'Is it our missing ex-footballer?'

'Again, we'll have to wait for their confirmation, but it seems likely.'

'Stay here with the body while they finish searching upstairs,' she said, acknowledging the banging around on the upper floor. 'I'll ring this in and get the area cordoned off.'

As Rachel made her way down the stairs, she wondered if she had been played by James Dawson. He'd come to her office and told her not only the facts in the historic sexual assault case, but also that Dave Cox had been blackmailing them. He turned Cox from potentially the next victim to the perpetrator. *But what if all that had been a lie? With no one left to confirm or deny what had happened in Porto, maybe Jimmy was himself the rapist and he was the one doing the blackmailing? Perhaps Muscles wasn't doing so well after all and needed an injection of cash*, she thought, tapping Graham's number on her phone.

'Have you got him, Guv?'

'We've got a dead body, but no ID as yet. I need you to get the forensics team here ASAP.'

'We were too late, then.'

'It looks that way. From what we can see it was a single gunshot to the back of the head, execution-style.'

'Something a soldier who'd been in Afghanistan would be familiar with.'

'Precisely,' Rachel replied. 'With three of these ex-footballers dead, I think we need to put an armed guard on Simon Shaw's hospital room. There's no saying that Turnbull won't try to finish the job he started. The only thing I'm concerned about now is whether it was actually James Dawson who employed Turnbull as a hired killer, rather than Cox. Why would Turnbull turn on the person who hired him?'

'Maybe he didn't pay him? Or maybe he did pay him, then Turnbull shot him so there would be no witnesses to the whole scheme?'

'That's one too many maybes for me. It seems a bit convenient that Dawson suddenly developed enough of a conscience about the historic rape to come forward and point the finger at Dave Cox when it would have been his word against Cox's. Why would he risk that?'

'Unless he knew that Cox was already dead.'

'Exactly what I was thinking. Can you go to Muscles and ask Mr Dawson to accompany you back to the station for questioning? I'll meet you back there when we've cordoned off the area. The last thing we want is the press getting hold of any of this until we've got a few more answers,' she said, terminating the call.

'Guv!' DS Green shouted from the top of the staircase. 'You need to see this.'

Rachel quickly gave instructions for a cordon to be put in place, then hurried back up the stairs. 'Have you found some ID, Errol? Is it definitely Cox?'

'No ID, Guv, but it looks as though we've got another body, wrapped up in plastic sheeting in a chest freezer in one of the upstairs bedrooms. I've told the guys not to touch anything. Are forensics on the way?'

'Yes,' Rachel said, skirting past the first body on her way to the stairs leading to the upper floor.

'In here, Guv.'

Rachel turned left at the top of the stairs and entered what had clearly previously been a little girl's bedroom, although it was now empty of furniture apart from a large chest freezer against the wall opposite the door. The walls were painted pink and someone had stencilled fairies and stars on the ceiling, making the contents of the freezer seem even more gruesome. The two officers were standing either side of the freezer holding the top open, both looking shocked by their discovery.

'You haven't touched anything?' Rachel asked, peering down.

'No, Guv.'

'Okay, you can leave this with me. Tell DS Green on your way out that I want him at the front door, and no one is to enter until forensics get here.'

'Yes, Guv.'

Rachel turned her attention back to the contents of the freezer. The second body was face down and folded almost double, reminiscent of the position you would adopt if you were scared or hiding. It was impossible to be certain, but judging by the clothing she could make out through the thick plastic sheeting, Rachel believed the victim was another male. It wasn't what she had expected to find when she had knocked on the door ten minutes earlier armed with a search warrant. *We need to know the identities of these two*, she thought. *It's likely that one of them is Dave Cox, but who's the other one and where does he fit into the case? One thing is for sure – we clearly have a very dangerous killer on the loose, but is his job finished now, I wonder? If not, we need to try and work out who his next victim is before he gets to them.*

CHAPTER FORTY

1.40 p.m. – Friday

Bella had sat at her grandmother's bedside for most of the night, leaving her only when she needed the toilet and to have a bowl of soup and some bread that her friend Beca had prepared for her. Occasionally, she had dozed off, her head dropping forward onto her chest, only to wake herself up with a start. The doctor had called in at half past eight, but Vovo had barely opened her eyes, refusing even the sips of water to take her medication. He had given her an injection, but as he packed his things back into his bag he had made eye contact with Bella and shaken his head.

The sound of cars honking their horns and loud conversation as people went about their daily business in the town square was in stark contrast to the stillness of Vovo's bedroom. Bella sat watching the almost imperceptible rise and fall of the frail old lady's chest, illuminated only by shards of sunlight forcing their way into the dim room through closed shutters. Every now and then she would take the cotton cloth from the bowl of water on Vovo's bedside table and gently stroke the old lady's forehead to keep her cool. As the life ebbed away from the only person who had ever shown her true love, Bella's thoughts kept returning to the promise she had made. Reconciling with her mother wasn't going to be easy, but she had promised she would try.

When Bella heard a noise behind her she knew that her mother was at the entrance to the bedroom. Slowly she turned. The figure in the doorway was even more shrunken and aged than when she had last seen her. There was a gasp, and she realised with shock that it had come from her.

The two of them warily maintained eye contact for a few moments before Rosa asked, 'How is she?'

'Dying,' was all Bella could say in reply.

'It's sad to see her like this. She was always the strong one, the person everyone turned to for help, before the cancer got her. Has she been awake at all?' Rosa asked, taking a few steps into the room and standing at the end of her mother's bed.

'Yes, on and off, but just for a few minutes each time. She says she's had enough of the struggle, that she's ready to leave.'

'I know how she feels.'

Bella felt a ball of anger in the pit of her stomach. 'No. No, you don't,' she said, glaring up at Rosa. 'Vovo didn't cause her cancer, she was just unlucky. She didn't deserve to live the final days of her life like this.'

'But I deserve everything I get? Is that what you're saying?'

Bella shrugged.

'Maybe you're right. Maybe it would be for the best all round if I died, too. That would give you a clean start without the handicap of having me as your mother.'

'I don't think of you as my mother. Yes, you gave me life, but nothing else. A mother is someone who teaches you and comforts you, and is there when you need her. You were none of those things. You're a stranger to me because that's how you wanted it. I'm only talking to you now because I promised Vovo I would,' Bella said, looking back to her grandmother lying on the bed, seemingly wasting away before her eyes.

'She made me promise, too. Of all the people in the world, she wanted you to be here with her these past few months, but that wasn't an option when I showed up to try and make my peace with her. Because of me and the way I have always behaved around you, you couldn't be here when she needed you most. I'm so sorry, Bella. When I'm drinking, I don't realise how selfish I'm being,' Rosa said, moving to the opposite side of the bed from Bella and perching on a chair.

Bella looked up sharply. *Had she heard Rosa correctly? Did she just say, 'When I'm drinking'? Does that mean she is trying to stop?* she wondered.

'Over the past few days, your vovo's drifted in and out of sleep, but every time she was awake, she told me that I needed to forgive myself before I could forgive you. It's hard, though. I didn't only ruin my life and yours, I ruined Beatriz's, too. If it wasn't for me she would never have got pregnant in the first place, and she would still be alive now. But you have to understand, I didn't do it on purpose. I thought I was helping my best friend by getting her a job when there was nothing for her here in Tavira. How could I know what those animals would do?' Rosa said, shuddering. 'But the worst thing was that nobody believed our story, apart from Vovo. It was so hard for us both returning here, unmarried and pregnant, but I was lucky in that I had Vovo's support, whereas Beatriz's parents disowned her. She had no one else to turn to, so she lived with us and she would cry for days at a time. At least you were born out of love, but all Beatriz could remember of the conception of her baby was the pain and the stench of alcohol as they took turns to force themselves on her.'

'What do you mean, I was born out of love? You told me both you and Beatriz had been raped.'

'Did I?' Rosa asked, confusion clouding her eyes. 'Why would I tell you that when it's not true? You must be mistaken.'

'No, no mistake,' Bella said, her voice becoming high-pitched. 'It was on my eighteenth birthday, when you also said you wished I'd never been born and you wouldn't care if you never laid eyes on me again.'

'I would never have said that to you. I know I haven't been a good mother, but you're my own flesh and blood.'

'But you did say those things,' Bella insisted. 'I can still visualise the look of hatred in your eyes when you did.'

'I don't hate you, Bella. I wanted to love you, but I couldn't allow myself to after what happened to Beatriz. She was the one who was raped, and then she died giving life to Beca. If she had never been born I would still have my best friend,' Rosa said, rocking herself backward and forward in a trance-like state as though the memory was too painful to relate while she was fully conscious.

As though a fog was lifting, everything started to make sense to Bella. 'Are you saying that Beca is Beatriz's daughter?'

'I thought you knew. I felt sure Vovo would have told you.'

'No, she told me that Beatriz's baby was stillborn. She always said that it was a blessing in disguise because she would never have been given a proper chance in life.'

'That's what Vovo wanted everyone to think. She wanted Beca to have a fresh start, unencumbered by her past. Even the hospital records say that Beatriz's baby died in childbirth because Vovo paid someone to falsify them. The baby was supposed to be sent to Lisbon for adoption, but when Luisa Cadiz adopted a two-month-old baby girl two months after Beatriz gave birth, Vovo realised that something must have gone wrong with her plan. She went out of her way to form a friendship with Luisa, so that you two girls would grow up as best friends just like me and Beatriz, but I could never stand the sight of Beca, even as a baby.'

'Oh my God,' Bella said, 'you thought you were talking to Beca that night. You were so drunk you couldn't even recognise your own daughter. You have no idea of the damage you've done, Rosa.'

'I'm so sorry, Bella.'

'Does Beca know any of this?'

'No, and please don't tell her. What would she gain by knowing that she was the product of her mother being brutally raped?'

Rosa said, raising her gaze to look at her daughter, her eyes filled with pain and guilt.

Bella had only ever thought of her mother as a selfish drunk, giving no thought to the catastrophe in her life that had started her drinking habit. For the first time she could begin to understand the reasons behind it. The guilt Rosa must have felt, knowing that she was responsible for her best friend's death, must have been an unbearable burden.

'The drinking doesn't help, you know. It just dulls the pain. Eventually it will kill you before your time, and those animals who raped Beatriz will have claimed another victim.'

'I know. I'm trying to stop, really I am, but I don't know if I can do it on my own. I'm not strong like you and your grandmother. I need help.'

'Are you asking me for help?'

Rosa looked down at her hands. 'I want to stop, and you are a nurse. Can you find it in your heart to forgive what has happened in the past and help me?'

Bella looked from the emaciated woman who had given birth to her to the frail figure lying on the bed who had shaped her life. *Vovo brought me up to be a kind and caring human being, and yet forgiveness is something I struggle with. Maybe it really is time to forget the past and get on with the rest of our lives.* She lifted her gaze back to Rosa, whose face was full of hope. 'I'll try, but it will only work if you truly want it to.'

There was a faint rasping sound from the bed and Bella knew immediately that her beloved vovo had taken her last breath.

After the doctor confirmed Vovo's death, Bella tried to comfort Rosa, but she felt awkward and she was struggling with her own grief. When the two of them eventually went downstairs, Bella purposely made her mother a cup of coffee rather than allowing her alcohol. Not feeling able to talk about Vovo without crying, she changed the subject to her father.

'Why didn't you contact the English man and tell him about me, if you were so in love with him?' she asked.

Rosa took a sip of the bitter black liquid. 'Because I didn't think he'd believe me that the baby was his. Maybe I was just a stupid girl who believed him when he told me he loved me and wanted to spend the rest of his life with me. I wanted to remember what we had, even if it was only for a few days – I didn't want to tarnish the memory.'

'But what about after I was born, when everyone was being so awful to you? Couldn't you have reached out to him then to take you away from the hatefulness?'

'I didn't deserve to be happy. I was responsible for what had happened to Beatriz. If it wasn't for me, she wouldn't have died giving birth to a child that she must have hated from the moment of conception. I wanted to die as well – I wanted to kill myself, but I wasn't even brave enough to do that. I despised myself. I went away to give you the chance of a better life. I'm so sorry, Bella – so sorry it has taken my mother's death and the terrible grief I feel after everything I put her through, for me to realise how much I love you. I would do anything to undo the hurt I've caused – anything.'

Bella looked at the shrunken figure across the table from her, hunched forward with her hands clasped around the coffee mug. *It's not her fault*, she thought, *none of this is her fault.*

'I have to go back to London to tie up a few loose ends, but when I get home we'll start by trying to get you sober, Mum,' she said, using the word for the first time in her life.

CHAPTER FORTY-ONE

9 a.m. – Saturday

Despite being in the middle of a triple, possibly quadruple, murder investigation, Rachel had already decided that she wasn't prepared to miss her regular visit to her sister at Mountview Hospital. She remembered only too clearly the terrible state Ruth had got herself into the last time she had missed a Sunday visit, when she had been desperately searching for a missing child. *There's no such urgency with the current case*, she thought, heading into the incident room. *The only person missing is James Dawson, and Graham is perfectly capable of coordinating the search for him.*

Dawson hadn't been at Muscles gym when her DI had arrived there to take him back for questioning on Friday afternoon, but, in fairness, Rachel herself had suggested that he should stay away from his gym when she had believed Dave Cox was behind the killings. The staff had told Graham that it wasn't unusual for him to go away to the continent for the weekend if he didn't have any personal training clients booked in, the thought of which had irritated her. He had potentially ignored her request not to leave the country. But then he had a few irritating habits, not least the excessive use of the word 'sure'. After checking that he wasn't at his home address either, DI Wilson had immediately contacted the border authorities to check whether or not he had left the UK from any of the airports or ferry ports, but it appeared not, unless he was travelling under false papers. They had, however, been contacted by Heathrow Airport late on Friday afternoon, but that was nothing to do with James Dawson.

PC Drake had previously circulated details of Rob Turnbull's Suzuki Katana motorbike and had received a call to say that it was parked in one of Heathrow's long-stay car parks, where it had been since 9.30 p.m. on Tuesday. Rachel had been working on the assumption that Turnbull had managed to flee after killing Father Raymond Kiernan, although he must have been travelling under a false passport as there was no record of him leaving the country, but that all changed five minutes into the morning meeting. She was just thanking the gathered officers for giving up their weekend to work on the case when she received a call from the forensic pathologist, Rajesh Malik. She put her phone on speaker so that she wouldn't have to repeat the information to her team.

'What have you got for me, Rajesh?'

'We already had a blood match for the body found shot dead in the living room of 23 Runnymede Court, but we were waiting for confirmation from DNA samples and dental records. I can now confirm that the deceased is Sergeant Rob Turnbull.'

There was an audible gasp from the assembled police officers, and Rachel could feel her own pulse quickening. 'Well, I wasn't expecting that,' Rachel admitted. 'There goes my prime suspect. Any idea on the time of death?'

'We're still running tests to be able to narrow it down further, but we can safely say it was at some point on Monday and probably between 10 a.m. and 4 p.m.'

DS Green's hand shot up.

'Yes, Errol.'

'When we were questioning neighbours on Thursday, the woman across the road said she had seen Turnbull leaving on his motorbike in the late afternoon on Tuesday.'

'How sure was she?'

'Very. The noise of it wakes her baby.'

'In that case,' Rachel said, 'we have to assume it was not Turnbull riding the bike, because he was already dead, which is perfectly possible as the rider would have been kitted out in leather and wearing a helmet, as described by the witness at Little Waterton. It also means that he wasn't responsible for stabbing the priest.'

There was more muttering around the room.

'Although we don't have the gun,' Rajesh continued, 'we have found the bullet embedded in the wall. It passed straight through Turnbull's head from beneath the skull at the back in an upward trajectory, suggesting that the killer was shorter than the victim, and it left the body via his right eye socket.'

Rachel was fairly sure she heard someone murmur 'Gross'. 'Can we all just stay focused please?' she said. 'Is it a match for the bullet fired at Simon Shaw?'

'It's too early to confirm whether they were both fired by the same weapon, but it is the same type of bullet.'

'What about the body found in the chest freezer?'

'Also male. At the moment we can only roughly estimate how long he's been dead, because the body hasn't thawed sufficiently to perform an autopsy, but my best guess would be between six and eight weeks.'

'Which would tie in with what the next-door neighbour said about not seeing Dave Cox,' Graham said. 'Do you think it might be him, Guv?'

'I think it's highly likely. Any idea how he died, Rajesh?'

'That's a bit trickier. The body was frozen in the foetal position, so his hands are currently obscuring his face, preventing a visual ID. From what I can see, there are no outward signs of trauma and no wounds. It could actually have been something like a heart attack, and for some reason someone wanted to cover up the fact that he'd died.'

'Or?' Rachel asked, thinking that Rajesh sounded less than convinced with his own theory.

'Or, he could have been poisoned. We'll check for a needle wound in the post-mortem examination and also for signs of ingesting poison, although we would expect to see some residue of frothing around the mouth if that was the case. Some poisons are almost undetectable, and some can cause symptoms very similar to those of a natural death, so it could take a while to determine whether or not this man was killed deliberately.'

Although there was no hard evidence to support it, Rachel's gut feeling was that this was Dave Cox's body and he had been poisoned. And she couldn't help thinking that maybe the autopsy report on Neil Edison hadn't been thorough enough, because it had been assumed that they were dealing with a suicide rather than a cleverly disguised murder.

'Thanks for all that, Rajesh. Let me know when you have a confirmed ID on the second victim. Obviously, it goes without saying that the identity of both is to be withheld from the public and particularly the press until we issue a statement.'

'Of course,' Rajesh replied, sounding slightly offended. 'I'll get back to you as soon as I have anything more concrete.'

'Well, that throws a different light on things,' Rachel said. 'If the other body is confirmed as Dave Cox, it would seem that he was the first to die out of the four accused of rape, and if Rajesh's estimate of six to eight weeks is accurate, it's unlikely that Rob Turnbull committed that murder.'

'What makes you say that, Guv?' Errol Green asked.

'Seven weeks ago, Rob Turnbull flew out to the Dominican Republic for a holiday with Simon Shaw's daughter.'

'So he probably wasn't responsible for Dave Cox's death, and he couldn't have killed Father Ray because he was already dead himself,' Graham said. 'Is it possible, Guv, that he's just another victim in all this? Somebody used him to plant an evidence trail to throw us off the scent, and when he was no longer useful, or when he twigged what was going on, that same somebody shot him to tie up loose ends?'

'Very possible, and at the moment we have two main suspects,' she said, turning back to the whiteboard. 'We need to identify and track down Turnbull's new girlfriend. We have video evidence of a slim, dark-haired woman talking to Neil Edison hours before his death, and an eyewitness placing a similar female in Little Waterton. I believe that woman is Turnbull's girlfriend. Can we be absolutely certain that this woman is not Rosa Viegas seeking revenge for the death of her friend, Beatriz Azevedo? We know she hasn't left Portugal under her own identity as she doesn't have a passport, but it's possible she's travelling with forged documents. PC Leverette, I need you to liaise with the Tavira police and have them send officers to her last known address to confirm her whereabouts.'

'Yes, Guv.'

'The other suspect is James Dawson,' Rachel said, tapping her marker pen against his name on the whiteboard. 'He had a lot of front coming in here yesterday with his perfectly rehearsed version of events, but the question remains, why would he kill his former teammates now? What has happened to make him feel like he has to destroy everything linking him to the historic rape case? Yes, PC Drake.'

'Dawson said in his interview that Simon Shaw wasn't pre-pared to pay Cox again after they all received the letters and was threatening to blow the whistle on the whole affair, which would presumably be very damaging for Dawson's business. When Shaw didn't die in the crash, Dawson may have decided that the best way to remove the threat of Shaw revealing the truth was to offer his version of it to us. What if it *was* him involved in the actual rape, instead of either Cox or Kiernan? By volunteering his "true version of events", saying he was a witness and nothing more, nobody would ever be able to prove otherwise.'

'Apart from the woman who was raped and, as we know, Beatriz is dead. You may have something there, PC Drake. As a precaution, I've got an armed guard on Simon Shaw's hospital room in case the killer decides to try again. They're going to try and bring him out of his coma this afternoon and, provided he hasn't lost his memory, we may have some answers sooner than we think. Our priorities now are to identify and find the dark-haired woman and to track down Dawson. I want a private word with DI Wilson in my office, and then you're all to liaise with him for your specific roles.'

Graham followed Rachel into her office and closed the door.

'Are you okay to take the lead on this for the rest of the weekend?'

'Of course, Guv.'

'Thanks. Maddy Shaw had made herself available for a shift at *News 24/7* today, before she knew the hospital were going to attempt to bring her husband out of his induced coma.'

'Surely if she explained the circumstances she'd be able to get out of it?'

'Apparently not. I've offered to take her daughter to the hospital so that she won't be on her own if they try to bring her dad out of his coma before Maddy can get there after work. If Simon does come round successfully, it won't hurt to be there to ask him a few questions.'

'Good thinking. What are his chances of a complete recovery?'

'Pretty good, according to Maddy, but you never know with this sort of thing.'

'Do you want the whole team in on overtime tomorrow?'

'Ask for volunteers, but I would try and have PC Drake in if she's willing. She's come up with a compelling theory there.'

'I don't think we need to worry about Drake being willing. I think she'd sleep here if you let her.'

'She's a good police officer, Graham.'

'I can't argue with that. Do you want to be kept up to speed, or shall we just have a meeting early on Monday?'

'Call me after the morning meeting tomorrow to keep me in the loop, and obviously if there are any major developments, but apart from that, Monday will suffice. Sunday is my day for visiting Ruth, and any change in routine really upsets her. I'm quite happy that I'm leaving things in safe hands.'

'Thanks, Guv.'

CHAPTER FORTY-TWO

12.07 p.m. – Saturday

Rachel had picked Siena up at her house at 11 a.m. and they'd arrived at the hospital around midday. All any of them knew was that the plan was to bring Simon out of his induced coma at some point in the afternoon, so they were prepared for a lengthy wait if necessary. When Siena started talking about the bodies the police had discovered in the maisonette in Windsor the previous day, Rachel felt very guilty about withholding the fact that Siena's ex-boyfriend was one of them.

'You expect stuff like that to happen in some of the inner-city parts of London,' Siena said, 'but not in Windsor. Do you think it's drug-related?'

'We don't really know at the moment, and even if we did, I wouldn't be allowed to discuss it with you,' Rachel said.

Siena pulled a face. 'I thought we were friends?'

'We are, and as my friend, I'm sure you wouldn't want me to get fired for leaking classified information.'

'Point taken, although it must be difficult not being able to talk about your day at work with your other half when you get home.'

'It's never been a problem for me, but that's mostly because I've never really had an "other half", as you put it.'

'But you have now,' Siena said, smiling.

'I wouldn't exactly call him that yet, but yes, I do like him a lot.'

The talk over dinner at the Shaws' house on Thursday evening had revolved around Tim. Both Maddy and Siena had asked probing questions, which surprisingly Rachel hadn't minded. When did they meet? Where did they meet? Was she instantly attracted to him? Where did they go on their first date? Did she love him? She'd stumbled on that final answer, because the truth of the matter was she didn't really know what love felt like, having never previously allowed herself to get so deeply involved with anyone.

'It feels good being in a relationship, doesn't it? That's one of the things I really miss about being with Rob. I know we had our problems, and it wasn't nice the way he dumped me, but weird as it may seem, I still love him, and I've got a tiny glimmer of hope that he'll tire of his new girlfriend one day and come back to me.'

Rachel couldn't look Siena in the eye. She was tempted to break the rules and tell Siena that it was never going to happen because her former boyfriend was currently lying dead on a mortuary slab. She stopped herself because nothing would be gained by telling her; it wasn't going to bring Rob back to life. Instead of giving her false hope, Rachel changed the subject.

'I take it you finished reading *Playing for Pizza*? What John Grisham are you on now? I used to be a big fan, but I haven't had much time for reading lately.'

It seemed to do the trick.

A little before 2 p.m., there was a knock at the door and the nurse entered the room to check Simon's vital signs, which were holding up well.

'Is there any word from the consultant?' Rachel asked while the nurse went about her business.

'Not yet, I'm afraid. Mr Carraway is still in theatre, but Simon is first on his list once he gets out. My shift is finishing now, but one of the other nurses will be along in a while.'

'Is Bella back?' Siena asked.

'She's not in today, but I think I saw her name on the roster for tomorrow. It's my day off, so she'll probably be on this ward, as the hospital try to keep a degree of continuity with the critical patients. I hope you don't have to wait too much longer for Mr Carraway,' she said, pulling the door closed behind her.

The consultant still had not appeared when Maddy arrived at the hospital at quarter to five, after her shift at *News 24/7*, and peered anxiously around the door.

'He hasn't been yet, Mum.'

The look on Maddy's face was a mix of disappointment and relief. Clearly, she hadn't known what to expect.

Mr Carraway finally arrived just before 6 p.m., apologising profusely for keeping them waiting.

'I'm afraid I've only just got out of the operating theatre. It was a more complicated procedure than I thought. I'm so sorry, but it's too late to try and bring Simon round from his coma today because we don't have the same level of staff on overnight, and he needs to be monitored closely for the first few hours. I'm not in tomorrow, but we can pencil it in for Monday.'

'Will it be all right to leave him in the coma until then?' Maddy asked anxiously.

'Absolutely, just think of it as an extra few hours' sleep, which I'm sure we could all use.'

'I know you told us on Thursday, but what are his chances of a full recovery?'

'Very good. If we're talking in percentages, I would say around eighty-five per cent.'

After the consultant left the room, Maddy said, 'I'm sorry you've had a wasted afternoon, Rachel.'

'I haven't. It's been good to spend some time with Siena, but I'll have to make a move now.'

'The lawyer?' Maddy asked with a twinkle in her eye.

'Yes, the lawyer,' Rachel replied, 'but don't go getting any ideas, it's early days yet.'

'It doesn't matter how long you've known someone. When you find the right person you never want to lose them, even if they don't always do what you expect them to.'

Rachel guessed that Maddy was referring to herself and her intention to give Simon a chance to explain why he had kept secrets from her, but she couldn't help noticing Siena flinch behind her mother's back. *Poor Siena*, she thought, heading down the stairs to the exit, *she believed she'd found her 'one', but not only had he not felt the same way, the hope that he might change his mind was now extinguished forever.*

CHAPTER FORTY-THREE

11.03 p.m. – Saturday

'Are you sure you'll be okay on the sofa bed? You can sleep in with me if you prefer,' Bella said, fluffing up one of the pillows from her bed and placing it at the top of the multicoloured sleeping bag.

'I'll be fine. I think we could both do with a good night's sleep, and if I come in with you, we'll be talking all night, which is not good when you've got work in the morning,' Beca said, climbing inside the sleeping bag and wriggling her way down. 'It's actually quite comfy.'

'Good. You're probably right. These past couple of days have been shattering both physically and emotionally, and it wouldn't do for me to go into work tomorrow and not be fully alert. Mistakes cost lives in hospitals.'

'Which hospital are you working at tomorrow?'

'I'm back at Charing Cross,' Bella said, perching on the edge of the metal frame of the sofa bed and eyeing the thin foam mattress, doubtful that it was as comfortable as her friend was making it out to be.

'Oh yes, I remember you saying you'd been looking after a road accident victim who was in a coma.'

'That's right. He was in a pretty bad way when they admitted him on Monday. Goodness knows how he survived. I guess I'll find out if he made it when I go in tomorrow.'

'Will you be on the same ward then?'

'Probably, they like to keep continuity of care where possible. When I rang the agency to say I was going home to live in Portugal, they virtually begged me to stay and do another week, but I told them I could only work until Wednesday, as the funeral's on Thursday. Thanks for offering to come over here with me to help pack everything up. I haven't really got that much stuff, but I'm not going to have much time now that I've agreed to work.'

'That's what friends are for, and anyway, I've always wanted to come to England.'

'Well, hopefully you'll still have time to do some sightseeing even with my packing to do. I'm sorry I won't be able to show you around much.'

'I'll be fine. I'm used to finding my way about places. I'll buy myself a tourist map and get on a bus or the underground train.'

'I hope I've done the right thing leaving Rosa on her own until the funeral. I don't think it's really sunk in yet that Vovo has gone, but when it does, I don't want her reaching for the bottle to drown her sorrows.'

'You'll have to get her on the hot milk instead. Don't let yours go cold,' Beca said, indicating Bella's mug. 'I'm glad you two are talking again.'

'It was Vovo's dying wish. As hard as it is for me, I made Vovo a promise and I won't let her down,' Bella said, blowing on her hot drink before taking a sip.

'Do you think you'll ever be able to call Rosa "Mum"?' Beca asked.

Bella thought back to the previous afternoon when she'd uttered the word for the first time in her life. 'She's never really acted like a mother to me.'

'But at least you have a real mother.'

'True, although I don't know if it's better to have a real mother who has always hated the sight of you, or an adoptive one who loves you like her own.'

'If you're talking about Luisa, she didn't really,' Beca replied. 'It was fine to begin with, but after Cristiano was born, she lost interest in me. That's why I always spent so much time at your house. I think Vovo loved me more than Luisa did.'

'She had her reasons,' Bella said, almost under her breath, but Beca heard her.

'Beatriz and the rape, you mean?'

'You know about it?' Bella said, surprised.

Beca nodded.

'Who told you?'

'Your mum.'

'I don't understand. Rosa told me you didn't know.'

'Don't look so hurt, she wasn't lying to you. She believes that's true. When she turned up out of the blue last year to try and make her peace with your grandmother, Rosa got really upset when you told her she wasn't to be in the house at the same time as you. She drank herself into a stupor and I had to help her upstairs to the bedroom. As I was tucking her into bed she clung onto me and started to sob hysterically, thinking I was you. She begged forgiveness for the awful way she had treated you. The whole story came pouring out about getting Beatriz the job in Porto and how guilty she felt when she had only been trying to help her best friend.'

'I can't believe you've known all this time that Beatriz was your mum and you didn't tell me,' Bella said.

'She wasn't.'

'What do you mean?'

'Beatriz wasn't my mum. After Rosa inadvertently told me what happened, I assumed I must have been Beatriz's baby put up for adoption after she died because of the way Vovo had always looked out for me, but when I checked with the hospital I discovered that both Beatriz and her baby had died in childbirth.'

'That wasn't true,' Bella said, reaching for her friend's hand. 'Vovo had a friend who worked at the hospital. She gave them money to falsify the records and say that the baby had died too. You were supposed to be sent away from Tavira for adoption. Vovo thought it would give you the best chance of a happy life.'

'But I didn't know that. As far as I knew, I couldn't be Beatriz's baby because it had died, but the story encouraged me to find out who my birth mother was. The short trips away I've been taking over the past few months were to search for the woman who gave me life and then gave me away. I wanted to find her to ask her why she didn't want me. I wasn't having much luck, so I hired a private detective and he found her and my father living in Albufeira with their five children.'

'Oh my God, Beca, that's incredible! I'm so glad Vovo was wrong. I can't believe you have a proper family. I'm so happy for you,' Bella said, putting her half-empty mug down and throwing her arms around her friend.

Beca pulled away from the embrace. 'I haven't introduced myself to them yet, and I'm not sure I'm going to.'

'Why not?'

'They seem so happy, so settled. I don't want to spoil things for them. The investigator told me that they were both little more than kids when she fell pregnant with me. She was forced to give me up for adoption by her parents. I don't want to open up old wounds.'

'I can understand why you might think like that, but if it was me, I would want to meet the daughter I was made to give away. When we get home, I'll come with you to meet them if you like. I'm sure their other children would love to have a big sister like you.'

'I'll think about it. There's no real rush, now I know who my parents are.'

'I suppose you're right. I'm just so happy for you that you're not Beatriz's daughter. Wherever she is, she's blissfully unaware of where she came from. It would be terrible knowing that you're the product of a sexual assault,' Bella said, remembering how she had felt when she had mistakenly believed she was. The initial horror had quickly been replaced by self-loathing and a desire for revenge. 'It would be worse still if you were aware that the parent who could have loved you lost their life while giving you yours. Imagine the psychological damage that would cause.'

'Yes, just imagine.'

Bella yawned. 'I'm sorry, Beca, I'm going to have to call it a day, I can hardly keep my eyes open. Thanks for making hot milk for me,' she said, picking up her mug. 'See you in the morning.'

'Night, Bella, sleep tight.'

CHAPTER FORTY-FOUR

Rachel cast a sideways glance at Tim as they waited for the receptionist at Mountview Hospital to print their visitor passes. She was aware of the admiring looks he was attracting, and felt a little surge of pride that she was the one by his side. The previous night over dinner, a takeaway from India Dining on Tim's recommendation, they had discussed how they were going to approach today. Rachel had been starting to get cold feet about taking him with her to visit Ruth, but he was having none of it. 'It won't get any easier,' he had said. 'The first time is always going to be the most difficult for all of us.' In the end, he had agreed to go to the cafeteria and wait until Rachel came to fetch him after she had told Ruth that she had an extra visitor.

Once they had their visitor passes, Rachel walked Tim through to the cafe and bought him a latte, before heading off to Ruth's room. She knocked gently and opened the door. The room was empty, but she could hear the shower running. Rather than going back to the cafe to sit with Tim where she knew she would get increasingly nervous about the situation, she decided to sit and wait for Ruth.

'What are you smiling about?' Ruth asked, emerging from the bathroom a few minutes later, her freshly washed hair dripping onto the shoulders of her fluffy towelling dressing gown.

'Nothing.'

'You're lying. You know I can always tell when you're lying.'

'Can't a girl have any secrets?'

'Not from her twin sister. Have you just solved a big case?'

'No. I'm in the middle of one, actually, but I asked my DI to deal with it today because I didn't want to disappoint you by not visiting. In fact,' Rachel said, deciding to take the bull by the horns, 'I've brought you an extra visitor today.'

Ruth was immediately wary. 'Who? You know I only like seeing you.'

'It's someone I like… a lot.'

'A man. I thought we agreed you wouldn't ever bring any of your boyfriends here.'

'That was because they weren't really boyfriends, they were just people I went on a few dates with. But Tim's different. I think you'll like him.'

'I won't. And I don't want him contaminating my room.'

'Please, Ruthie. Can't you just give him a chance?'

'Why? I don't have to like him, and you don't have to bring him here. If you'd rather spend time with your boyfriend than me, that's fine. You can bugger off.'

'Don't be like that. You know you've always been the most important person in my life, and you always will be. Look, if you don't want him in your room, why don't you come to the cafe? He's probably on his third latte by now.'

Ruth hesitated. 'I'll have to dry my hair and get dressed and put some make-up on. He'll be tired of waiting by then.'

'No, he won't. He's really looking forward to meeting you. He's never met any twins before, and he wants to see if we really look alike.'

A sly smile crossed Ruth's face. 'All right, he can come to my room. But I want you to do something for me in return.'

'Of course,' Rachel said, relieved that her sister had changed her mind, but wary of what she was about to demand.

'I want you to dry my hair like yours and maybe show me how you do your make-up and then we really will look alike.'

Rachel relaxed. It seemed a small price to pay for Ruth to allow a stranger into her sanctuary. 'No problem, we'll be like two peas in a pod, just like we were when we were little.'

Twenty minutes later, Rachel went to fetch Tim from the cafe. On the way back to Ruth's room she briefly explained about drying her sister's hair in a similar style to her own so that the two of them looked more alike.

'No one could blame her for wanting to look more like you.'

Rachel felt her heart flutter. 'You will be gentle with her, won't you? She can be a little bit—'

'Stop worrying,' Tim said, interrupting her. 'We talked about this last night. She might not like me, she could be rude to me or she may be completely the opposite and be over-the-top friendly. Just relax. It'll be fine.'

Rachel took a deep breath and opened the door to Ruth's room. She was standing looking out of the window.

'Ruth, this is Tim.'

Ruth turned slowly and, as she did, Rachel heard Tim catch his breath.

'You're the image of your sister,' he said, 'it's almost impossible to tell you apart.'

A smile spread across Ruth's face. 'Be careful, Rachel, or he might take me home with him and leave you locked up here.'

Rachel watched as her sister walked across the room and peered into Tim's face while he was shaking her hand. 'Don't I know you? Are you a doctor here?'

'No. I'm a lawyer, and I'm pretty sure I'd remember meeting someone who is the double of my girlfriend. I hope you don't mind my asking, but may I use your bathroom? Those coffees while I was waiting have gone straight through me.'

'Help yourself,' Ruth said.

The moment the door was closed, Rachel said, 'Well, what do you think, Ruthie? He's nice, isn't he?'

'Do patients in hospital have lawyers?' Ruth said, ignoring the question.

'Sometimes, I suppose. Why?'

'He looks familiar, particularly his eyes. I recognise him from somewhere, I'm sure I do.'

'Perhaps you've seen his picture in a magazine or a newspaper when he's been photographed after winning a court case? Or maybe he just has a really familiar face? Do you think you might grow to like him?'

'The most important thing is that you obviously do, so I'll try.'

'Thank you,' Rachel said, hugging her sister as the door to the en suite bathroom door opened; she broke the embrace when her phone started to ring.

'Sorry, Ruthie,' she said after glancing at the screen, 'but I need to take this call. Hi Maddy, is everything okay?'

'Thank God you answered,' Maddy said, her voice agitated. 'I'm at the studios about to go on air and we've just received some inside information about the bodies in the Windsor flat. Is it true? Is one of them Rob?'

Shit! Rachel thought. *How the hell has that leaked to the press?*

'It's classified information. I can't tell you. Who was your source?'

'I have no idea. They're typing it into the autocue now. Did you know yesterday? Why the hell didn't you tell us? We're supposed to be friends.'

'You can't run the story, Maddy. We haven't issued a statement to the press yet,' Rachel said, ignoring her questions.

'Tell that to Byron Farley, he's virtually wetting himself because he's got this scoop. Not that I care about him, it's Siena I'm thinking of. I know Rob dumped her, but they were together for two years. She still loves him, for God's sake. She was getting a cab to

Charing Cross Hospital at eleven. She should be arriving around now. She shouldn't be alone when she hears this, and I can't leave with Farley breathing down my neck.'

'Okay Maddy, stay calm. If I leave now, I reckon I can be there in under thirty minutes.'

'Thank you, Rachel. Please break it to her gently and I'll be there as soon as I can.'

Ruth was glaring at her sister as she disconnected the call. 'Be where in thirty minutes? This is my day to see you.'

'I know, Ruthie, but something's happened and we've got to go. I'm sorry, but I'll make it up to you another time, I promise.'

'You don't have to go. You could get someone else to do whatever it is.'

'No, I can't. You remember meeting Siena when she was in here after hurting herself? Well, her dad is in hospital in a coma and now I need to break some more awful news to her before she finds out some other way.'

'So Siena is more important to you than me?'

'Of course not. If I didn't have to go I wouldn't, and I think you know that. I've already said I'm sorry. Come on, Tim, I can drop you at the train station.'

'He's not going to the hospital with you?' Ruth asked.

'No. It's police business.'

'Then he can stay here with me. I can get to know him better.'

'Stop playing games, Ruthie. I haven't got time for this.'

'It's all right, Rachel,' Tim said in an attempt to defuse the situation. 'I'll stay for a while and take Ruth for some lunch, as she's ready.'

Rachel hesitated for a moment before saying, 'If you're both okay with that, then it's fine with me. I'll be back as soon as I can,' she added, rushing from the room.

CHAPTER FORTY-FIVE

Rachel was out of breath when she arrived outside Simon Shaw's hospital room door, having run from the car park in her attempt to get to Siena as quickly as possible. She took a moment to catch her breath, exchanging a few words with the armed guard before fixing a smile on her face and going into the room. Siena was at her dad's bedside, reading to him.

'Rachel. What are you doing here?' Siena asked, surprise evident in her voice. 'I thought you were at Mountview today, introducing Tim to your sister?'

'I have been. In fact, they were getting on so well I decided to leave them to it for a couple of hours and pop over to see how your dad is doing.'

'He's pretty much the same, to be honest. I've made a start on the *Runaway Jury*,' she said, indicating the John Grisham book she was holding. 'I don't know about Dad, but I'm finding this one a bit complex.'

'Do you want to take a break from it? We could grab an early lunch, if you fancy it?'

'That sounds good. We normally have a cooked breakfast on a Sunday, but Mum's working so I just had a bowl of cereal after she left. We won't be long, Dad,' Siena said, leaning forward to kiss her father on the forehead.

*

Walking along the corridors towards the cafeteria, Rachel was hoping that the television in there wouldn't be tuned to the news channel. She was in luck. The few patients and visitors who were actually watching the TV had selected a cookery chat show called *Brunchtime* for their entertainment. After paying for Siena's chicken salad and her own tuna melt sandwich, she guided them over to a corner where they wouldn't be able to see the television if someone decided to change the channel. She allowed Siena to get stuck into her salad, mindful that Maddy had said she wasn't eating much, before she steered the conversation around to her real reason for being there.

'Siena, I'm going to come clean. I've actually got another reason for being here other than just checking on you and your dad.'

'You're sounding very serious and "policey". Have I done something wrong?'

'No, of course not.' Rachel took a deep breath. 'You know we were talking about the Windsor killings yesterday?'

'Yes, and you said you weren't allowed to discuss the case, even with friends,' Siena replied, putting another forkful of salad into her mouth.

'Well, we've got a positive ID on the bodies, and I'm afraid one of them is someone you know.'

Siena had been about to continue eating, but she stopped, her fork clattering onto her plate. 'Who?' she whispered.

'I'm so sorry, Siena, but one of the bodies is Rob.' Rachel watched the shock build in Siena's eyes as the impact of her words registered.

'N-not my Rob?' she stammered, as though hoping for confirmation that she had either misheard or misunderstood.

'Yes, your Rob,' Rachel said, reaching across the table to take hold of Siena's hand.

Siena shook Rachel's hand off impatiently. 'No, that can't be right. He can't be dead,' she said, a note of hysteria creeping into her voice. 'You must have made a mistake.'

'I know it must be a terrible shock for you, but I'm afraid it's true.'

Tears were streaming down Siena's face and dropping onto her half-eaten salad. Rachel got up and moved around to the other side of the table to put a comforting arm around her shoulders, not knowing what to say. Gradually, the flow of tears subsided.

'I can't believe I'm never going to see him again. I wrote him a letter to tell him how much I still love him, and now he's never going to see it. He'll never know that I hadn't stopped loving him even after what he did. Mum and I have had time to talk about things since Dad's accident, and I can see now that he wasn't the best boyfriend in the world, but I never gave up hope that he would realise he'd made a mistake and come back to me.'

'I think he knew how much you loved him,' Rachel said, pulling her chair into a position where she could sit next to Siena while keeping her arm around her shoulders.

'Do you mean that? Or are you just saying that to make me feel better?'

'I think you know I don't do that.'

'Yes. Yes, I do. Can you tell me what happened?'

Rachel was fully aware that she shouldn't divulge the specifics of the case to Siena, but whoever had leaked the story to *News 24/7* had probably also tipped them off that Rob Turnbull had been murdered. 'I shouldn't really be telling you this, but I don't want you to hear it from anyone else. He was shot, Siena, and possibly with his own weapon.'

'Shot? By who?'

'I wouldn't be able to tell you that if I knew, which I don't.' What Rachel didn't mention was that in the brief conversation she'd had with her DI that morning to update her on progress, it had been confirmed that the bullet found was fired from the same gun as the one that had narrowly missed her father.

'I don't understand. Why would anyone kill him?'

'I was hoping that maybe you would be able to help me with that.'

'You don't think I did it?'

'No, of course not. What I mean is, you've seen more of him over the past two years than anyone else, with the possible exception of the soldiers under his command. I want you to try and remember if he mentioned someone to you that he didn't get on with or felt threatened by.'

'He got on okay with most people, with the possible exception of my dad.' Siena looked panicked for a moment. 'It couldn't have been my dad, could it?'

'No. The time of death has been confirmed as late morning on Monday, so after your dad had his accident.'

'Then I can't think of anyone. He could be quite harsh at times with some of his subordinates, but they respected him for that. They knew that he was only preparing them for the conditions on the battlefield to give them the best chance of survival.'

'What about away from the army? Was there anyone you met when you were out socially with him?'

'I can't think of anyone,' Siena said, furrowing her brow in concentration.

Rachel took a deep breath. 'I hate to have to ask this, but how much do you know about his new girlfriend?'

Siena flinched.

'Siena?' Rachel urged.

'Her name is Izzy. He accepted her as a friend on Facebook at the beginning of February.'

'Can you show me a picture of her?'

'No. He unfriended me and blocked me when he finished things between us,' Siena explained. 'He said he thought it would be kinder that way.'

'But you saw a photo of her when he accepted her as a friend? Do you remember what she looks like?'

Siena closed her eyes. 'Sort of. She had long dark hair, but the wind was blowing it across her face, so I couldn't really see what she looked like. I could tell from her arms that she was quite tanned. Maybe she'd been on holiday, or she might even have been foreign, although Izzy doesn't sound like a very foreign name. She looked quite slim, from what I could see of her in her shapeless nurse's uniform.'

'She's a nurse?'

'Yes. Didn't I say?'

Rachel's palms felt clammy. The description Siena had given of Turnbull's new girlfriend sounded familiar, and not just because it was similar to the accounts given by Dave Cox's neighbours; it also matched the woman seen sketching at the graveyard and the botanical gardens. Rachel pulled her phone out of her bag and selected her DI's name.

'Guv? I thought we agreed just to have the quick progress report call this morning.'

'Something's come up,' Rachel said, urgency evident in her voice. 'I need to know if PC Leverette had confirmation of the name of the surviving baby, Rosa Viegas's baby.'

'I'm pretty sure it was on the email,' Graham said, 'I'm checking now. Yes, here it is. The surviving baby was Isabella Viegas.'

The pieces in an extremely complex jigsaw puzzle were finally falling into place. Izzy was a shortened version of Isabella, as was Bella. *Oh my God!* Rachel thought, scraping her chair along the floor as she jumped to her feet. As an agency nurse, Bella could pick and choose which hospitals she worked in. *Was it just a coincidence that she had nursed Siena at Mountview, and had been on shift the day Simon had been brought in to Charing Cross, or had she planned it?* She would have known which hospital he would be brought to, should he survive, because of the location of the accident, and she would have known the location of the accident in advance if she had caused it. *This must have all been about revenge,* Rachel thought. The Porto police had let her mother and Beatriz down at the time of the rape, so Isabella was seeking justice for them by taking matters into her own hands. 'Graham, I need you to check if Bella Viegas is on shift at Charing Cross Hospital today. Ring me the minute you've got that information,' she said, terminating the call.

'What's going on, Rachel? Is that my Bella you're talking about?'

'I want you to stay here and look after my bag, Siena. I mean it,' Rachel said as Siena made a move to get up. 'I've got to get back to your dad.'

Rachel found herself running along the hospital corridors towards Simon Shaw's room for the second time that afternoon, only this time with even more urgency. She'd been searching for a link between Turnbull and the ex-footballers, and now she had found it in Isabella Viegas. Cox, Edison and Kiernan were all dead. Dawson was missing, possibly dead. The only murder that hadn't gone to plan was Simon Shaw's. *What if she's planning another attempt on his life?* Rachel thought as her phone began to ring.

'Talk to me, Graham.'

'Bella Viegas is on the late shift at Charing Cross today. Apparently, she's already signed in for her shift starting at 2 p.m. Is there anything you need me to do, Guv?'

'Not at the moment. This is just a hunch, I'll call if I need you,' she said, putting her phone on silent and slipping it back in her pocket.

CHAPTER FORTY-SIX

12.50 p.m. – Sunday

Although there was an armed guard on Simon Shaw's door, Rachel knew the guard wouldn't prevent a nurse from entering, particularly one he'd seen before. She rounded the corner and ran towards him shouting, 'Is anyone in there?'

'Only the nurse,' he replied.

Shit! Shit! Shit! Rachel thought, *I hope I'm in time.* Taking a moment to compose herself, she explained to the police officer what she wanted him to do.

'When I open the door, whatever appears to be happening, I want you to just stand visibly in the doorway behind me, but don't say or do anything. Is that clear?'

'Yes, Guv.'

Rachel reached for the handle and depressed it gently, easing the door open in an effort not to disturb Bella. The nurse was at Simon's bedside, her back was to the door and she was holding his arm with her left hand. At first it looked as though she was taking his pulse, but then Rachel saw the syringe in her right hand.

'You don't need to do that, Bella.'

The nurse didn't move.

'We know what happened in Porto, and we're going to try and reopen the case to get justice for Beatriz and her baby.'

'It's too late.' The nurse's voice sounded flat and unemotional. 'The Porto police department laughed at me when I went to them with new evidence. I had a recording on my phone of that disgusting Cox man showing off about what he and the priest did, but they wouldn't even listen to it. They said it wasn't worth spending the money to reopen the case because she was dead anyway. They left me no choice. Those perverts had to be punished. They had to pay for what they did.'

The phrase sounded familiar. *The threatening letters must have been sent by Bella, not Dave Cox,* Rachel realised. Her eyes were on the syringe. It was millimetres away from the prominent vein in the bend of Simon Shaw's elbow. *Could she grab it before Bella plunged it into his arm and delivered what she presumed would be a fatal dose of poison?* Probably not; she had to try and make her give it up voluntarily.

'You've already got all the guilty ones, Bella,' she said, easing slowly forward into the room. 'The footballers lied about who was in which room because they didn't want to get into trouble with their club. Simon Shaw wasn't there when Beatriz was assaulted, he was in James Dawson's room with your mother.'

'You think I don't know that they lied? You think just because he wasn't actually in the room he's innocent in all this? He's not. He could have spoken out, any of them could, but they were all too busy protecting themselves and their precious careers. They didn't care about Beatriz. They didn't see her as a young, frightened girl, just as some kind of whore to pleasure themselves with. They're disgusting, all of them.'

Rachel could see the needle edging closer to Simon's skin. 'But he could be your father, Bella.'

'And he is mine,' Siena said from the doorway, where she was standing next to the armed officer. 'Please don't kill him. Haven't you punished him enough?'

'You shouldn't be here, Siena,' Rachel said, without taking her eyes off the precariously positioned syringe. 'I told you to stay in the cafe.'

'I'm glad she's here to witness this. If it hadn't been for her, I may never have got to Simon Shaw. It was easy with the others, but he was trickier. There was security at the training ground and the stadium, and then he always drove straight home, like a good little husband to his perfect family. And then I found you on Facebook, Siena, always showing off about your wonderful soldier. He wasn't so wonderful cheating on you with me before dumping you, was he? It's a shame your suicide attempt didn't work, that would really have made your dad suffer. But it gave me a reason to suggest to Rob that he should ring your dad to see if you were okay. He'd told me your dad had never liked him, and I gambled that the call would end up with them having a go at each other. Your dad played straight into my hands by threatening Rob, who was telling the truth, by the way. He knew nothing of your failed suicide attempt and was genuinely upset when I told him about it. Maybe he'd started to realise what a mistake it was choosing me over you. I pretended to be all concerned, so he would think I'm a nice person. But I'm not nice,' she said, a sneer in her voice. 'When Rob said he was going to report me to the police because I'd taken a shot at your dad instead of just scaring him with the motorbike, I had to shoot him to shut him up.'

Siena began to cry again, huge, racking sobs, but Rachel couldn't risk going over to comfort her. The slightest movement from any of them could spook Bella, with devastating consequences.

'I loved Rob so much, and you didn't care about him at all,' Siena sobbed.

'Do you even know what love is?' she hissed in reply.

'Do you?'

'It's very close to hate, and I've known that all my life, in fact before I was even born. My mother didn't want me, but her religion forbade her to get rid of me. She probably died with a smile on her face knowing she would never have to set eyes on me.'

'But Bella, your mother isn't dead,' Rachel said.

'You're right about one thing,' the nurse said, turning to face Rachel and Siena for the first time. 'Bella's mother isn't dead, but she might as well be. She's an alcoholic, steadily drinking herself to an early grave, and all because of what those disgusting pigs did.'

Rachel didn't recognise the woman in front of her even though she had Bella's name badge pinned to her uniform. 'Who are you?'

'I'm Rebeca, also known to Rob Turnbull as Izzy, and Neil Edison as Rose. But Dave Cox knew me by my real name when I served him in a bar in Tavira. He was shouting his drunken mouth off about some tart from the town that he'd banged in Porto twenty-four years earlier. It was only weeks after Rosa had divulged the whole tragic story, thinking I was Bella. What a state to be in, so drunk that you can't even recognise your own daughter, but I knew it wasn't Rosa's fault. Cox and his teammates destroyed her life, too. I think my mum brought him to me in that bar so that I could clear her name.'

'Are you claiming to be Beatriz's daughter? You can't be – she was stillborn.'

'That's what everyone was supposed to think. My very existence was denied because of the shameful way I was conceived. Can you imagine how I felt when I found out? At first I wanted to die, but then I wanted to kill. You have no idea of the guilt I feel knowing how much suffering my mother endured because of me.'

'You're wrong,' Rachel said, feeling the palms of her hands turn moist, 'I know exactly how it feels when someone you love is subjected to unspeakably terrible things and you're powerless to help them. It happened to me when I was a child. My sister still blames me,' she said, her eyes never moving from the syringe.

'Bravo,' Rebeca said, mockingly bringing her hands together in applause. 'Very clever, pretending you understand.'

It was only a split second, but it was the chance Rachel had been waiting for. Without any thought for her own safety, she lunged across the room, knocking Rebeca off the chair and jolting the syringe out of her hand onto the floor. Rachel pinned her down as she reached for it, but Rebeca was too quick and grabbed it first. For a split second the two locked eyes. It was as though Rachel could see into her tortured soul.

'I'm telling the truth, Rebeca. I do understand.'

'Nobody does. When Bella wakes up, tell her I'm sorry I lied about not being Beatriz's daughter. There's no happy family in Albufeira, I made it all up after I found out that she knew about the rape. If I'd got away with the murders, I couldn't have lived the rest of my life with the look of pity in Bella's eyes. Everything I did was to get justice for our mothers.'

'Please, Rebeca, don't do anything stupid,' Rachel said, feeling her heart thumping against her ribcage. 'We can get you the best legal defence team. They'll be able to make a case for a crime of passion or diminished responsibility, I'm sure. I'm just so sorry you and your mother were so badly let down by the authorities.'

'It's too late. I don't regret killing those vile pigs, and I wouldn't be able to stand in court and pretend that I did. They got what they deserved,' Rebeca said, stabbing the syringe into her own arm.

'No! Stop! We can help.'

'No one can help me now,' she replied, closing her eyes as she depressed the plunger.

'What's in the syringe, Rebeca?' Rachel asked, urgently shaking the young woman. 'Tell me, and we can get the antidote. We're in a hospital, for God's sake.'

Rachel scrambled to her feet, suddenly aware that someone had pressed the alarm button. She could hear footsteps running along the corridor. 'Tell me,' she shrieked, but Rebeca shook her head slightly before starting to convulse.

'Get Siena out of here,' Rachel ordered as the crash team rushed into the room, assuming Simon Shaw had gone into cardiac arrest before realising they had an altogether different emergency on their hands.

Rachel felt helpless as she watched the doctors and nurses work frantically to try and save Rebeca's life, but it was to no avail. Less than ten minutes from the moment the needle had pierced her skin, Rebeca was pronounced dead. Her lifeless body was lifted gently onto a gurney and covered with a hospital blanket before being wheeled from the room.

Rachel sank down onto the chair at Simon Shaw's bedside, feeling shocked and saddened by what she had just witnessed. 'Why couldn't you just have told the truth, Simon?' she asked the prone figure on the bed. 'If you'd been honest from the start, Cox and Kiernan would have been punished, and Neil Edison and Rebeca would still be alive. What a bloody waste,' she muttered, burying her face in her hands and breathing deeply to bring her emotions back under control.

'Rachel? Is that you? What's going on? Has something happened to Simon?'

Rachel lifted her head to see Maddy standing in the doorway, an anxious look on her face. 'No, he's fine. I thought you were working?'

'I'm supposed to be, but halfway through the news bulletin about Rob I realised that my daughter's feelings are more important to me than my stupid job. I've put my work ahead of Siena once before, and we nearly lost her as a result of it. When we got to the first commercial break, I unclipped my mic and left them to it. Where is Siena?' Maddy said, her eyes scanning the room as she registered that her daughter wasn't there. 'Is she all right? Did you tell her about Rob?'

'Yes, I did.'

'How did she take it?'

'She was pretty upset, as you can imagine, but it was something she said while we were talking things through that made me worry for Simon's safety. I told her to stay in the cafeteria while I rushed back here, but she didn't listen.'

'What's happened?'

'A nurse, who I initially thought was Bella, was about to poison him.'

'What? I don't understand. Why would Bella want to kill Simon?'

'It turned out not to be Bella, but it was her best friend from back home in Portugal. Their mothers were the two girls who accused the Kings Park Rovers players of rape.'

Realisation started to dawn on Maddy. 'Oh my God. She was paying them all back for what they did to her mother. Poor girl. Where is she now?'

'She… she killed herself,' Rachel said, still struggling to come to terms with her inability to prevent Beca from turning the lethal injection on herself. 'I tried to tell her we would do everything in our power to help her, and that her actions were clearly as a result of diminished responsibility, but it was as though she had achieved what she set out to and there was no point in carrying on living.'

'Are you all right?' Maddy asked, clearly shocked to see her normally composed friend so visibly shaken.

'I will be,' Rachel replied. 'Look, now that you're here, we should go and find Siena. She overheard some stuff about the rape and her dad. You two have got a lot to talk about.'

CHAPTER FORTY-SEVEN

3.15 p.m. – Monday

'Are you sure you don't want to head off early, Guv?' DI Graham Wilson said from the doorway of his DCI's office. 'That was a pretty traumatic experience for you yesterday, watching Rebeca die in front of your eyes with nobody able to help her. Do they know what poison she used?'

'I'm still waiting for the full toxicology report, but early findings suggest it was batrachotoxin, one of the most poisonous substances on the planet. There's no antidote, which Rebeca would have known because she studied pharmacology at university,' Rachel said, gesturing for him to come into the room. 'According to Bella, she was a borderline genius academically and was a brilliant artist, too. She was only working in the bar in Tavira to help finance her further studies. Talk about the wrong place at the wrong time.'

'Well, she certainly wasn't taking any chances on Simon Shaw surviving the second attempt on his life,' Graham said, sitting down opposite her. 'He's got a lot to thank you for. You took a hell of a risk, though, Guv, she could just as easily have stuck the syringe in your arm when you jumped her.'

'I guess we never think about the danger we put ourselves in. I'm just so sad I couldn't talk her out of taking her own life. Bella was devastated when I told her what had happened, and she was so upset when she learnt that Rebeca had lied to her about having found her birth parents.'

'Why did she lie to her best friend? I'd have thought she would be the one person Rebeca could talk to.'

'Sometimes those closest to us are the ones we are least able to talk to in a crisis,' Rachel said, thinking of the many times she'd tried to persuade Ruth to talk about her experience at the hands of their depraved neighbour. 'It's almost like they're embarrassed by being a victim, as though they feel they should have been able to prevent what happened to them.'

'But nothing happened to her, Guv. It was her mother who was raped. How could that possibly be her fault?'

'It may seem irrational to us, but finding out her true identity must have hit a raw nerve with Rebeca and all she wanted after that was revenge.'

'You can't really blame her, Guv. What Cox and Kiernan did to her mother was despicable.'

'I don't blame her, I just wish we could have helped her. But once she knew how she had been conceived, she couldn't unknow it, if you see what I mean. I don't think she could ever have been happy again, even after killing the guilty parties. There was a tortured look in her eyes just before she stuck the syringe in her arm which was heartbreaking,' Rachel said, her voice cracking slightly. She had also seen that look in Ruth's eyes after the first time she'd tried to kill herself.

'Is Bella all right now?'

'It depends what you mean. Physically, yes. The sleeping potion Rebeca added to her hot milk was harmless apart from ensuring she slept for eighteen hours. That's how she was able to dress in Bella's uniform, name badge and all, and pass herself off as Bella at Charing Cross Hospital. Obviously it's going to take a lot longer for the psychological wounds to heal. She only lost her grandmother three days ago, and now her best friend. That's two funerals to arrange, and an alcoholic mother to keep an eye on. She'll need to be made of stern stuff.'

'A bit like you, Guv. Let me at least help you with the paperwork, and maybe front the wrap-up meeting? You've earned an early finish.'

'Actually, it's been good to keep busy, otherwise I'd have spent the whole day dwelling on what a pointless waste of life this whole affair has been. You know, you have to hand it to Rebeca. Once she'd had no response from the Porto police after recording Cox's confession, or should I say boast, on her mobile phone, she worked it all out with the precision of a military operation.'

'I still don't quite understand how she made the connection between the drunken ramblings of Dave Cox and the historic rape accusation.'

'It was probably down to the timing of him turning up at the bar in Tavira,' Rachel explained. 'Bella told me that Rosa had blurted out the story of Beatriz's rape to Rebeca when she was drunk, thinking she was telling her daughter. That must still have been fresh in her mind when he showed up a few weeks later, shouting his drunken mouth off. It probably started off as just a suspicion, but when she was rebuffed by the Porto police she must have decided to investigate and avenge her mother herself. I suspect she deliberately became Cox's girlfriend so that she could get information from him about the other men involved. Once she had all their names, he was of no use to her any more, so she killed him but still used his flat in Windsor as her base in England. What a shame that a talent like hers was put to such poor use. She'd have made a good police officer.'

'I feel embarrassed on behalf of our Portuguese counterparts that they didn't take her more seriously.'

'Her mistake was going back to the same officer who investigated the case in the first place. She thought he'd remember it and that would be helpful, but chances are he took a backhander from the club to make it all go away, so the last thing he wanted was for the case to be reopened.'

'Is there anything we can do about it?' Graham asked. 'I hate the thought of a corrupt police officer getting away with it.'

'Probably not, unfortunately,' Rachel replied. 'There was virtually no evidence originally, apart from Beatriz's account of events, and if there was a payment it would most likely have been in cash. Not only that, but of the four men who actually took part in or witnessed the rape, three of them are dead and James Dawson's whereabouts are unknown.'

'Are you convinced he wasn't involved in the killings?'

'The killings, yes. Rebeca made it clear in her dying declaration that she was responsible for all the deaths,' Rachel said, closing her eyes momentarily. The haunted expression on Rebeca's face flooded her mind. It was an image she knew would live with her for a long time. 'On the sexual assault matter, Dawson was a material witness and deliberately withheld information. We could probably make a charge stick of perverting the course of justice, but I suppose the question is, what would it achieve? If Dawson is to be believed, Rebeca has already got justice for her mum against the two rapists.'

'He was a no-show at Muscles again today. Do we keep looking for him?'

'I think we probably should. He clearly wanted to lay low for a while because he was scared, but there's a possibility that Rebeca has already got to him and we just haven't found the body yet.'

'That would be quite some body count, Guv,' Graham said, shaking his head.

'Yes, it's been quite a case,' Rachel replied, massaging her temples with her fingertips. 'How have you found working with Eleanor Drake? I was thinking she deserves a commendation for her work on this one. What do you reckon?'

'I agree. The sooner she's a detective, the better. She has sound instincts and a great work ethic. She'd be a great addition to the team,' Graham replied with conviction.

'I'm glad you said that, Graham. Some of the others fear her drive, but you don't, you just recognise her talent, and that's why I like working with you as my number two. Honesty, trust and loyalty, the three characteristics I admire the most.'

'We make a good team, Guv,' Graham said, a hint of gruffness to his voice.

'And you know what? I've changed my mind about knocking off a bit early because I know everything here is in safe hands. There are just a few things I want to finish off, and then I think I'll call in to see Ruth on my way home since our visit got cut short yesterday.'

'Good for you,' Graham said, getting up from his chair and heading towards the office door. 'See you in the morning, Guv.'

CHAPTER FORTY-EIGHT

3.30 p.m. – Monday

To Maddy, the hospital room seemed eerily quiet without the rhythmic sucking and blowing of the ventilator. Simon was still lying on the bed with his eyes closed exactly as he had done for almost a week, his head swathed in bandages and the bruise to his left cheekbone beginning to turn yellow around the edges. A tear formed in the corner of Maddy's eye, rolled down her nose and dropped off the end of it onto the back of her hand, which was holding his. She shook her head impatiently. *Why am I crying?* she thought. *I've got nothing to cry about. I've got my husband back from the jaws of death – I should be grateful.*

True to his word, Mr Carraway had prioritised Simon, making him his first patient of the day. The ventilator was turned off and the medication that had been administered to keep him in an induced coma was withdrawn at 8 a.m. that morning. He hadn't woken up instantly, as Maddy had imagined he would, but gradually he'd begun to stir, his eyelids flickering before slowly opening. It had been like watching a newborn baby. Simon looked straight at his wife, but seemed not to see her at first, as though he was unable to focus. When a slow smile spread across his face, she knew he had recognised her.

'Hi,' she had said, 'how are you doing?'

He had looked puzzled.

'You're in hospital,' Maddy had explained, answering his unspoken question. 'You had a bit of a bump on the head, so you've been sleeping it off.'

Simon had raised his hand to touch his bandages. 'How?' was all he could manage at first.

'Let's not talk about that now,' Maddy had said, steering away from the subject of his accident as she'd been advised to do, 'let's just concentrate on getting you well again. Would you like a drink?'

Simon had nodded. 'My mouth is as dry as the Sahara Desert.'

Maddy gently lifted his head and held the glass to his lips. Some water escaped and dribbled down his chin.

'I'm worse than when Siena was a baby,' Simon said. 'Is she here?'

Maddy lowered his head back onto the pillow, avoiding his gaze. Siena hadn't accompanied her to the hospital that morning.

*

The previous afternoon, Maddy and Rachel had found Siena in the hospital cafeteria with the armed guard who had been assigned to protect Simon. He had bought her a cup of sweet tea to help with the shock, but she hadn't touched it.

'Thanks for taking care of her,' Rachel had said while Maddy pulled up a chair and put her arms around her daughter's shoulders.

Siena had shrugged her off. 'Did you know?' she had demanded.

'Know what?'

'About the girl who was raped?'

'It was before I met your dad, and he never told me about it, but yes, I did know. I found out a few days ago.'

'And you still came here to sit at his bedside, knowing what he did?'

'Rachel told me he was wrongly accused. He didn't do anything, darling,' Maddy said, putting her hand on her daughter's arm, but again, Siena shook it off.

'Precisely. I can't believe the loving, caring dad that I know wouldn't speak up if he knew what those disgusting animals did to that poor girl. How could he live with himself? I don't care if he never wakes up,' she had railed, 'I never want to set eyes on him again. I want to go home,' Siena had said, pushing her chair back with so much force that it fell over. 'Now!' she shrieked.

Siena hadn't said a word on the drive home. She had gone straight up to her room, slamming the door behind her. When Maddy had knocked at half past six that morning to say that she was leaving for the hospital, there had been no response.

*

'Siena's not here at the moment, but she has been here every day,' Maddy had told Simon, 'sitting at your bedside and reading to you.'

'Anything good?'

'John Grisham.'

'Is he good?'

The consultant had warned Maddy that she should be prepared for a certain amount of memory loss. Until they did extensive tests with Simon fully conscious, they wouldn't know how much damage had been done.

'He's not bad,' Maddy had replied.

'How long have I been here?' Simon asked, his words beginning to slur.

'Oh, a few days,' Maddy said, being deliberately vague. 'I think you should try and rest now, and we'll talk more later.'

Simon had nodded before closing his eyes and drifting back off to sleep.

There had been several similar periods of consciousness when Maddy had kept the conversation vague and simple. On the hour, every hour, a nurse would come to check his vital signs, and each time Maddy was reminded of Bella and the probability that she was Simon's daughter.

Rachel had relented and told Maddy the full story of what had actually happened in Porto when she had rung to check on Siena the previous evening, deciding that she was okay to share the information now that the murder case was solved, following Beca's confession. Initially Maddy had felt numb, knowing that not only had Simon gone along with a terrible lie to protect his teammates, but he had also been totally besotted with a girl just weeks before he had met her. It had made her question whether he had only got together with her because he was on the rebound from the love of his life. Maybe that was the reason it had taken him a full six months before he was able to say he loved her. The special word 'loke' that he had invented for her now didn't seem quite so endearing; he obviously hadn't felt able to commit while he still had feelings for the Portuguese girl.

'I wonder what would have happened if the girl had contacted Simon and told him she was pregnant?' she had asked Rachel.

'I'm not sure it's healthy to dwell on thoughts like that,' Rachel had replied. 'He married you because he loved you, or I'm pretty sure you wouldn't still be together after all these years.'

Maddy wasn't so sure. 'I think he would have done the right thing by her and we would never have got together,' she had said, her heart heavy. 'I wonder why she didn't tell him?'

'Pride, maybe? Anger, because he didn't stand up to his friends and tell the truth surrounding Beatriz? There could be any number of reasons, but it's all a long time in the past,' Rachel had replied.

'Do you think he'll want to get to know Bella?'

'That's something you'll have to ask him.'

That question had been running through Maddy's mind all day. *If his answer was yes, would she be okay with it?* His eyelids were flickering again, signalling that he would soon be awake.

'Mum.'

Maddy turned to see Siena in the doorway. Her eyes were red where she'd clearly been crying. 'Come here,' she said, holding her arms out to her daughter and pulling her into a hug.

'Is Dad okay?'

'Yes. He's been awake on and off throughout the day.'

'I'm glad. I'm sorry I behaved the way I did yesterday. I was so angry with him for not standing up for that poor girl after what his teammates did. She was younger than me, Mum. Imagine what Dad would have done to anyone who had treated me that way.'

'I know, but you have to remember he was young too, and he was bullied into keeping quiet. I just wish he had felt able to tell me about it, though. It's had me questioning whether I really know him at all.'

'Dad loves you, Mum, more than anything in the world. In fact, I'd go so far as to say you are his world, and he's yours.'

Maddy pulled Siena into another hug, holding her so tightly that eventually she had to pull away, claiming she couldn't breathe.

'Has Dad been talking?'

'A little bit, but I haven't told him anything about the accident or the cause of it.'

'That's probably for the best at the moment. It's hard to believe that girl committed those terrible murders and, but for Rachel, she would have killed Dad, too.'

'I know. We have a lot to thank her for.'

They both fell silent for a moment before Siena said, 'It was shocking to see Rebeca kill herself, Mum. What a horrible way to die. And poor Bella, she was her best friend. She must be devastated.' Siena paused. 'If she does turn out to be my half-sister, do you think she'll want to get to know us better?'

'I think it's something the three of us will have to discuss when your Dad is feeling up to it.'

'Would you be okay with it, Mum?'

Before Maddy could answer, there was a movement from the bed.

'Siena? Is that you?' Simon said, stirring.

'Yes Dad, it's me. You gave us all a bit of a fright.'

'I'm sorry about that. Your mum says you've been reading to me.'

'I hope you've been paying attention cos I'm going to test you later,' Siena said, leaning in to give her dad a gentle hug.

Maddy felt her heart somersault seeing the two people she loved most in the world embrace. Whatever lay ahead, whether or not it included Bella, she felt sure they could get through it as long as they stuck together.

CHAPTER FORTY-NINE

4 p.m. – Monday

Before leaving her office for the day, Rachel sent a quick text to Tim:

I'm sorry about last night. It was very upsetting watching the life ebb away from that young woman and then having to explain what had happened to her best friend. I wouldn't have been very good company, but I'm free tonight if you are? Thanks again for looking after Ruth for me – she seemed to like you and trust me, and that is HUGE for Ruth. I'm going to pop in and see her for a couple of hours now to make up for rushing off yesterday, but I should be home by 7.30. Pizza?? Xxx

He hadn't replied by the time she was getting into her car ten minutes later, so when her phone rang, Rachel fished it out of her handbag expecting it to be him. It wasn't. The caller ID was showing Mountview Hospital.

'How weird is that,' she said into the phone, 'I'm just leaving work early so that I can pop in and see Ruth before supper. I hope that's okay?'

'Miss Hart? It's Imelda Kingdom here.'

Rachel recognised the name of the hospital director from when she had first secured a place for Ruth in the residential wing. 'There's not a problem, is there? Ruth hasn't attacked one of the nursing staff again, has she?'

'No, nothing like that.'

'Well, that's a relief,' Rachel said, breathing out heavily. 'She had quite a day yesterday. I brought my boyfriend to the hospital to meet her for the first time, and then had to rush off to a case I was working on, and we all know Ruth doesn't react very well to changes in her routine. So, how can I help? Is it summer fete time again? Are you looking for raffle prizes?'

There was a pause before Imelda Kingdom replied, 'Actually, I was just ringing to see if Ruth is with you.'

'Of course not, why would she be? Hang on a minute, are you saying she's not at the hospital?' Rachel said, the grip on her phone tightening.

'I'm afraid we can't locate her at the moment. The catering assistant left the breakfast tray on the small table by the window because she thought Ruth was sleeping and she didn't want to disturb her. As you know, we often do that with residents. But when the nurse went in with her medication just before lunchtime, the room was still in darkness with the breakfast tray untouched. She opened the curtains and realised it wasn't Ruth in the bed, it was a rolled-up duvet. She immediately raised the alarm, and we've been searching the hospital and grounds for her, but without any success so far.'

Rachel's world began to spin. Her hands felt clammy, making it difficult to hold onto her phone. *How could the staff at Mountview have let this happen?* she thought, forcing herself to take long deep breaths, trying to calm the mounting panic. 'When was she last seen?' she asked.

'Apparently at around eight o'clock last night when the catering staff collected her supper things. She didn't go through to the day room to watch television with the others, but that's not unusual according to the staff who look after her. As you know, she tends to keep herself to herself most evenings, once she's had her medication.'

Rachel's heart was thumping against her ribcage. *Ruth hadn't been seen for twenty hours and the hospital were only contacting her now.* 'Is any of her stuff missing?' Rachel demanded, forcing herself into police mode. 'Clothes, toiletries, mobile phone?'

'It's difficult to say. You'd probably be better placed to notice if any of her clothes and toiletries are gone, but I did notice that the phone holder on her bedside table was empty.'

Rachel could picture the metal stand with big plastic feet and hands that held the phone upright. She had bought it for Ruth after she'd accidentally knocked her phone on the floor for the third time, smashing the screen. 'Has anyone tried to call her?'

'I don't think so,' Imelda Kingdom said, 'but I'll try when we've finished our call.'

'Don't bother, I'll do it,' Rachel said, aware that her tone was on the sharp side, but unable to temper it. 'What about your CCTV footage? Has anyone looked at it yet?'

'We're about to start going through it, but I wanted to check first that she wasn't with you.'

'Well she's not, so I suggest you make a start on it,' Rachel said, barely able to control her anger at the hospital's incompetence. 'I'll be there as soon as I can,' she added, abruptly ending the call. *Ruth lives at the hospital for a reason*, Rachel thought, ramming the Audi into gear and exiting the car park at speed. *She doesn't function well in the outside world. We have to find her, and quickly.*

Twenty minutes later, Rachel slammed her car door and raced up the front steps of Mountview Hospital two at a time. On the drive over she'd tried Ruth's number several times but it had gone straight to voicemail. Mindful of not upsetting her sister she had left a message saying, 'Hi Ruthie, I know we arranged to meet for coffee today, but I can't remember where we said. Give me a call when you get the message.' She had also tried to ring

Tim several times, but he hadn't answered his phone either. The voicemail she left him was very different. 'Tim, Ruthie's gone missing from the hospital. I'm worried sick. I'm on my way to Mountview now – can you meet me there?' As she pushed open the front door, she could see Imelda Kingdom waiting in the reception area and she rushed straight over to her, ignoring the signing-in protocol.

'Is there any sign of her?' Rachel asked hopefully.

'No, I'm afraid not, Miss Hart, but there is something I'd like you to see,' she said, ushering her towards the doors usually reserved for staff, opening them with her swipe card and then guiding Rachel through a door marked SECURITY.

The room was small and dimly lit, making the dozen or so television screens on the wall opposite the door appear brighter. In the centre of the monitors that were showing moving pictures from various locations around the hospital was a screen that was frozen, and Rachel recognised an image of herself and Tim signing in at the reception desk the previous morning.

'This is Jason, our head of security,' Imelda Kingdom said, introducing the man sat at the control desk.

Rachel nodded in acknowledgement.

'I started going through all our CCTV footage from yesterday the moment Miss Kingdom got off the phone from you,' Jason said. 'Can you confirm that is you signing in yesterday, Miss Hart?'

'Yes. Why would you bother looking at that part of the CCTV footage when you know Ruth was seen much later in the day?' she said, unable to keep the irritation from her voice.

'Please bear with me, Miss Hart. Everything will become clear in a moment.' He twiddled a knob and the image on the central screen changed to a picture of Rachel on her own. 'Is this also you, Miss Hart, leaving the hospital at around midday?'

Rachel had to swallow down her annoyance. *What was the point of showing her images of herself?* She was fully aware of her own movements the previous day; it was Ruth she was interested in. 'Why are you even asking me that? You can see it is.'

The security guard retrieved a third image that showed a time code of 20.37.

'How about this one. Is this you, Miss Hart?'

Rachel stared at the screen, a chill running through her body. She shook her head.

'But I'm sure you can understand why the receptionist, Libby, thought it was,' Imelda Kingdom said. 'Libby's not in today, but I've just spoken to her on the phone and she confirmed that Rachel Hart signed out of the hospital last night, shortly after visiting hours.'

Rachel groaned and sank down onto a chair next to Jason. 'Why would you do that, Ruthie?' she murmured. 'Why would you want to leave your safe place?'

'Apparently, Ruth, as we now know it was, apologised that she'd forgotten to sign back in at reception after she'd been called away on a case earlier in the day, and Libby accepted that explanation. She's been working for us for five years and has seen you come and go after your Sunday visits hundreds of times, so she's very familiar with your face. The hairstyle must have fooled her. Ruth's hair is usually a bit wilder-looking than yours. I don't think Libby can be blamed for thinking that the person in this picture is you.'

'No, no, of course not,' Rachel said, still staring at the image on the screen. *Ruth must have been planning something when she asked me to dry her hair like mine*, she thought, *but why would she want to leave her safe place? I don't understand.* 'I wonder where she was going?' Rachel said, almost under her breath.

'That's something for you to ask your sister when you find her. Taking into account what she said to Libby, and the fact that she had deliberately rolled up a duvet to make it appear as though she was sleeping late this morning, it would appear that she planned this, so I can't really see how this is the hospital's responsibility.'

As Imelda Kingdom finished speaking, the text notification went off on Rachel's phone. She reached into her bag to retrieve it and gasped when she saw the sender. It was from Ruth.

Hi Rachel, I got your message, but it didn't make much sense. We didn't arrange to meet up, but I guess you know that and you were just trying to trick me into telling you where I went after leaving Mountview. You've always looked after me so well and I appreciate it, but at times it has felt as though I'm locked away in a prison when I haven't done anything wrong. I don't want to be a burden to you now that you have someone in your life that you obviously adore. Tim clearly feels the same way about you and I don't want to stand in the way of your happiness. Don't come looking for me, Rachel, because I don't want to be found. For the first time in my life I feel free. Have a happy life with Tim. Ruthie xx

Tears were spilling down Rachel's cheeks, blurring the words as she read them. When she got to the end of the message she quickly tapped on Ruth's number, hoping to catch her while her phone was still turned on, but it went straight to voicemail.

'Ruthie,' she implored, 'please pick up and speak to me. You've got this all wrong. I should never have brought Tim to see you yesterday. I'm so sorry, I should have asked you first. He doesn't mean anything to me, Ruthie. You're the most important person in my life, the only person I truly care about. If you don't want to stay at Mountview any more, then you don't have to. You always told me you liked it here. You said you felt safe, but if you've changed your mind you can come and live with me and we'll sort out a live-in carer. Please, Ruthie, please pick up the phone… please…' The long beep sounded, signifying the end of the recording. Frantically, she tapped on Ruth's number again, but it still went straight to voicemail.

'Rachel? I came as soon as I got your message.'

Rachel spun round to see Tim standing in the doorway with a security guard.

'Ruth's run away, and it's all my fault. She sent me a text message a couple of minutes ago but now she's not answering her phone. I've got to find her, Tim. She can't survive out there on her own. Oh God, I'll never forgive myself if anything happens to her.'

Tim took a step into the room and pulled Rachel to her feet before wrapping his arms around her. Despite her trying to push him away, he held her firmly until she'd stopped struggling and collapsed into his chest.

'Okay, now take a few deep breaths,' he said. 'That's it, that's better. You'll find her, Rachel, you're a top detective. All you need to do is focus.'

Rachel looked up into Tim's green eyes. They were filled with concern, but also encouragement. 'She said she doesn't want to be found. She said she felt like a prisoner living here and now she's free. I always thought I was doing the best thing for her, but what if I was wrong? Did she say anything to you over lunch about being unhappy here?'

'No, but to be honest she didn't really say much at all. I think the first thing you need to do is get on to your DI, Graham, isn't it, and have him put a trace on Ruth's phone. If she only sent that message a few minutes ago she can't be very far from that location.'

'You're right. I'll ring him now, and we'll soon have her back, and if she wants to live with me from now on then I'll just have to make it happen. Thanks, Tim.'

'For what?'

'For helping me to think straight, but most of all for being here when I needed you,' Rachel said, resting her head against his chest.

He held her close for a moment before gently easing her away from his body and looking deep into her eyes. 'I've already told you, Rachel. It took me a long time to find you and there's no way I'm ever letting you go.'

A LETTER FROM J.G. ROBERTS

I want to say a huge thank you for choosing to read *What He Did*. If you did enjoy it, and want to keep up to date with all my latest releases, just sign up at the following link. Your email address will never be shared and you can unsubscribe at any time.

www.bookouture.com/jg-roberts

As with *Little Girl Missing*, the bulk of the plot for this book was scribbled in a notebook while on holiday earlier in the year, but I have to confess and say that the idea for it wasn't entirely mine. I had submitted an idea for a second book in the Detective Rachel Hart series to Bookouture, which they must have liked because they asked me for a third. Mild panic ensued while I racked my brain for inspiration, but it was something my son said which produced the light bulb moment.

Book two became book three, and *What He Did* was born. I must also give credit to my other half here for the historic rape suggestion, which, as you now know, forms the backbone of the story. My son was also responsible for the name of the football team Simon Shaw and the others played for... 'Kings Park Rovers' sounds so much better than 'Hapstone Rovers', wouldn't you agree? It's been a joy revealing more of Rachel Hart's backstory, and building her relationship with both her work colleagues and her love interest, Tim, which will continue in book three.

I'm not going to lie; this was quite a complicated storyline, which at times had me tearing my hair out, but I hope you'll agree that my perseverance has paid off.

I hope you loved *What He Did*, and if you did I would be very grateful if you could write a review. I'd love to hear what you think, and it makes such a difference helping new readers to discover one of my books for the first time.

I love hearing from my readers – you can get in touch on my Facebook page, through Twitter, Goodreads or my website.

Thanks,
Julia Roberts

JuliaRobertsTV

@JuliaRobertsTV

www.juliarobertsauthor.com

ACKNOWLEDGEMENTS

Topping the list of people I would like to thank for bringing Maddy and Simon's story to print is my editor at Bookouture, Ruth Tross, although I must also thank Maisie Lawrence for her interim work on *What He Did* before Ruth joined the company. Ruth has been a pleasure to work with and has provided a focused guiding hand throughout the various stages of editing. She is also tremendously supportive and enthusiastic – I feel very fortunate to have her on 'Team Julia'. And it is teamwork – thanks go to everyone at Bookouture, from the cover designer, Lisa Brewster (don't you just love the cover? so atmospheric), to the copy editor, Lucie Cowie. Once again I'd like to thank my publicist, Kim Nash, whose energy and knowledge in promoting my books has been first class.

I always thank my family for the part they play in each new book. They are the ones who see the hours spent at the computer throughout each stage of the process, and have to put up with me vaguely nodding my head during conversations at the dinner table when my mind is clearly elsewhere working out a new twist in the plot – especially 'him indoors', who I can now refer to as my husband following our marriage in the summer after over forty-one years together.

I'd also like to thank my mum, Josie, who turned ninety-three a couple of months ago, for her unwavering support and belief in my writing, and also my brand new mother-in-law, Audrey, who always goes into her local bookshop in Spalding, Lincolnshire to order an extra couple of copies even though I always send her one.

But most of all, I want to thank you, my readers. I had a wonderful response to *Little Girl Missing*, the first in the Detective Rachel Hart series, and I hope you'll think that *What He Did* has been a worthy successor. I truly appreciate the time you spend reading my books, and love to receive your feedback in the form of reviews. Hopefully 'see' you all again in a few months for the third book in the Rachel Hart series.